12/94

Novels by Jane Yolen from Tor Books

BRIAR ROSE

SISTER LIGHT, SISTER DARK

WHITE JENNA

XANADU

Selected and Edited by JANE YOLEN

TOR fantasy ®

A TOM DOHERTY ASSOCIATES BOOK • NEW YORK

XANADU

A Tor Book
Published by Tom Doherty Associates, Inc.
175 Fifth Avenue
New York, N.Y. 10010

Tor® is a registered trademark of Tom Doherty Associates, Inc.

Library of Congress Cataloging-in-Publication Data

Xanadu / edited by Jane Yolen.
    p. cm.
    ''A Tom Doherty Associates book.''
    ISBN 0-312-85367-X (hardcover)
    1. American literature—20th century. I. Yolen, Jane.
PS507.X36 1993
810.8'015—dc20   92-36938
                                                       CIP

First edition: January 1993

Printed in the United States of America

0 9 8 7 6 5 4 3 2 1

To Isak Dinesen,

whose motto was

"Be bold, be bold,

but not too bold . . ."

Contents

Xanadu—
Wouldn't You?

When Samuel Taylor Coleridge penned an odd poem in the aftermath of an opium dream, he hardly expected it to become one of his three best-known works. The poem, "Kubla Khan," when compared to his "Rime of the Ancient Mariner," seems but an incomplete fragment in rather strange and bumpy rhyme. But critics noted early on that the poem was replete with dream symbology, hazy dream archetypes, and an aura of mystery. After all, it was Coleridge himself who wrote: "Dreams with me are no Shadows, but the very Existences and foot-thick Calamities of my life."

But, then, the Romantics tended to talk that way, as if uppercase letters crowded their sentences like daffodils upon the oft-lauded hills.

However, when searching for the right title for a collection of fantasy stories and poems, the idea occurred to us that we were—in effect—decreeing a stately pleasure dome. It would be complete with deep romantic chasms, women wailing for demon lovers, damsels with dulcimers, and men with floating hair of whom we should all beware. For the illiterate amongst us (or in modern P.C. parlance, the poetically and literarily challenged), these are all images from the Coleridge poem.

Over the years since the publication of "Kubla Khan," the word *Xanadu* has come to be a generic name for any magical realm. So it was with easy conscience we co-opted it. Though the poem is essentially euphoric—no doubt a result of the opium Coleridge had smoked—there are also hints of the sinister in it. And so this collection of new work by writers both in and out of the fantasy genre has pieces that are both euphoric and sinister. And, because Kubla Khan's magical kingdom seems, in the nonromantic, nondrugged-out light of a sensible 1990s day, rather silly, some humorous stories are included as well. Some are even miracles of rare device.

Footnotes available upon request.

—JANE YOLEN, P.J.F.
PHOENIX FARM

The Poacher

Ursula K. Le Guin

. . . And must one kiss
Revoke the silent house, the birdsong wilderness?

—SYLVIA TOWNSEND WARNER

I was a child when I came to the great hedge for the first time. I was hunting mushrooms, not for sport, as I have read ladies and gentlemen do, but in earnest. To hunt without need is the privilege, they say, of noblemen. I should say that it is one of the acts that make a man a nobleman, that constitute privilege itself. To hunt because one is hungry is the lot of the commoner. All it generally makes of him is a poacher. I was poaching mushrooms, then, in the King's Forest.

My father had sent me out that morning with a basket and the command, "Don't come sneaking back here till it's full!" I knew he would beat me if I didn't come back with the basket full of something to eat—mushrooms at best, at this time of year, or the fiddleheads of ferns that were just beginning to poke through the cold ground in a few places. He would hit me across the shoulders with the hoe handle or a switch, and send me to bed supperless, because he was hungry and disappointed. He could feel that he was at least better off than somebody if he made me hungrier than himself, and sore and ashamed as well. After a while my step mother would pass silently by my corner of the hut and leave on my pallet or in my hand some scrap she had contrived or saved from her own scant supper—half a crust, a lump of pease pudding. Her eyes told me eloquently, Don't say anything! I said nothing. I never thanked her. I ate the food in darkness.

Often my father would beat her. It was my fate, fortunate or misfortunate, not to feel better off than her when I saw her beaten. Instead I felt more ashamed than ever, worse off even than the weeping, wretched woman. She could do nothing, and I could do nothing for her. Once I tried to sweep out the hut when she was working in our field, so that things would be in order when she came back, but my sweeping only stirred the dirt around. When she came in from hoeing, filthy and weary, she noticed nothing, but set straight to building up the fire, fetching water, and so on, while my father, as filthy and weary as she, sat down in the one chair we had with a great sigh. And I was angry because I had, after all, done nothing at all.

I remembered that when my father first married her, when I was quite small, she had played with me like another child. She knew knife-toss games, and taught me them. She taught me the ABC from a book she had. The nuns had brought her up, and she knew her letters, poor thing. My father had a notion that I might be let into the friary if I learned to read, and make the family rich. That came to nothing, of course. She was little and weak and not the help to him at work my mother had been, and things did not prosper for us. My lessons in reading ended soon.

It was she who found I was a clever hunter and taught me what to look for—the golden and brown mushrooms, woodmasters and morels and other fungi, the wild shoots, roots, berries, and hips in their seasons, the cresses in the streams; she taught me to make fish traps; my father showed me how to set snares for rabbits. They soon came to count on me for a good portion of our food, for everything we grew on our field went to the Baron who owned it, and we were allowed to cultivate only a mere patch of kitchen garden, lest our labors there detract from our work for the Baron. I took pride in my foraging, and went willingly into the forest, and fearlessly. Did we not live on the very edge of the forest, almost in it? Did I not know every path and glade and grove within a mile of our hut? I thought of it as my own domain. But my father still ordered me to go, every morning, as if I needed his command, and he laced it with distrust—"Don't come sneaking back until the basket's full!"

That was no easy matter sometimes—in early spring, when nothing was up yet—like the day I first saw the great hedge. Old snow still lay greyish in the shadows of the oaks. I went on, finding not a mushroom nor a fiddlehead. Mummied berries hung on the brambles, tasting of decay. There had been no fish in the trap, no rabbit in the snares, and the crayfish were still hiding in the mud. I went on farther than I had yet gone, hoping to discover a new fernbrake, or trace a squirrel's nut hoard by her tracks on the glazed and porous snow. I was trudging along easily enough, having found a path almost as good as a road, like the avenue that led to the Baron's hall. Cold sunlight lay between the tall beech trees that stood along it. At the end of it was something like a hedgerow, but high, so high I had taken it at first for clouds. Was it the end of the forest? the end of the world?

I stared as I walked, but never stopped walking. The nearer I came the more amazing it was—a hedge taller than the ancient beeches, and stretching as far as I could see to left and right. Like any hedgerow, it was made of shrubs and trees that laced and wove themselves together as they grew, but they were immensely tall, and thick, and thorny. At this time of the year the branches were black and bare, but nowhere could I find the least gap or hole to let me peer through to the other side. From the huge roots up, the thorns were impenetrably tangled. I pressed my face up close, and got well scratched for my pains, but saw nothing but an endless dark tangle of gnarled stems and fierce branches.

Well, I thought, if they're brambles, at least I've found a

lot of berries, come summer!—for I didn't think about much
but food when I was a child. It was my whole business and
chief interest.

All the same, a child's mind will wander. Sometimes
when I'd had enough to eat for supper, I'd lie watching our
tiny hearth fire dying down, and wonder what was on the
other side of the great hedge of thorns.

The hedge was indeed a treasury of berries and haws, so
that I was often there all summer and autumn. It took me
half the morning to get there, but when the great hedge was
bearing, I could fill my basket and sack with berries or haws
in no time at all, and then I had all the middle of the day to
spend as I pleased, alone. Oftenest what pleased me was to
wander along beside the hedge, eating a particularly fine
blackberry here and there, dreaming formless dreams. I
knew no tales then, except the terribly simple one of my
father, my stepmother, and myself, and so my daydreams
had no shape or story to them. But all the time I walked, I
had half an eye for any kind of gap or opening that might
be a way through the hedge. If I had a story to tell myself,
that was it: There is a way through the great hedge, and I
discover it.

Climbing it was out of the question. It was the tallest
thing I had ever seen, and all up that great height the thorns
of the branches were as long as my fingers and sharp as
sewing needles. If I was careless picking berries from it, my
clothes got caught and ripped, and my arms were a net of
red and black scratches every summer.

Yet I liked to go there, and to walk beside it. One day of
early summer, some years after I first found the hedge, I
went there. It was too soon for berries, but when the thorns
blossomed, the flowered sprays rose up and up one above
the other like clouds into the sky, and I liked to see that, and
to smell their scent, as heavy as the smell of meat or bread,
but sweet. I set off to the right. The walking was easy, all
along the hedge, as if there might have been a road there
once. The sun-dappling arms of the old beeches of the forest

did not quite reach to the thorny wall that bore its highest sprays of blossom high above their crowns. It was shady under the wall, smelling heavily of blackberry flowers, and windlessly hot. It was always very silent there, a silence that came through the hedge.

I had noticed long ago that I never heard a bird sing on the other side, though their spring songs might be ringing down every aisle of the forest. Sometimes I saw birds fly over the hedge, but I never was sure I saw the same one fly back.

So I wandered on in the silence, on the springy grass, keeping an eye out for the little russet-brown mushrooms that were my favorites, when I began to feel something queer about the grass and the woods and the flowering hedge. I thought I had never walked this far before, and yet it all looked as if I had seen it many times. Surely I knew that clump of young birches, one bent down by last winter's long snow? Then I saw, not far from the birches, under a currant bush beside the grassy way, a basket and a knotted sack. Someone else was here, where I had never met another soul. Someone was poaching in my domain.

People in the village feared the forest. Because our hut was almost under the trees of the forest, people feared us. I never understood what they were afraid of. They talked about wolves. I had seen a wolf's track once, and sometimes heard the lonely voices, winter nights, but no wolf came near the houses or fields. People talked about bears. Nobody in our village had ever seen a bear or a bear's track. People talked about dangers in the forest, perils and enchantments, and rolled their eyes and whispered, and I thought them all great fools. I knew nothing of enchantments. I went to and fro in the forest and up and down in it as if it were my kitchen garden, and never yet had I found anything to fear.

So, whenever I had to go the half mile from our hut and enter the village, people looked askance at me, and called me the wild boy. And I took pride in being called wild. I might have been happier if they had smiled at me and called me by my name, but as it was, I had my pride, my domain, my wilderness, where no one but I dared go.

So it was with fear and pain that I gazed at the signs of an intruder, an interloper, a rival—until I recognised the bag and basket as my own. I had walked right round the great hedge. It was a circle. My forest was all outside it. The other side of it was—whatever it was—inside.

From that afternoon, my lazy curiosity about the great hedge grew to a desire and resolve to penetrate it and see for myself that hidden place within, that secret. Lying watching the dying embers at night, I thought now about the tools I would need to cut through the hedge, and how I could get such tools. The poor little hoes and mattocks we worked our field with would scarcely scratch those great stems and branches. I needed a real blade, and a good stone to whet it on.

So began my career as a thief.

An old woodcutter down in the village died; I heard of his death at market that day. I knew he had lived alone, and was called a miser. He might have what I needed. That night when my father and stepmother slept, I crept out of the hut and went back by moonlight to the village. The door of the cottage was open. A fire smouldered in the hearth under the smoke hole. In the sleeping end of the house, to the left of the fire, a couple of women had laid out the corpse. They were sitting up by it, chatting, now and then putting up a howl or two of keening when they thought about it. I went softly in to the stall end of the cottage; the fire was between us, and they did not see or hear me. The cow chewed her cud, the cat watched me, the women across the fire mumbled and laughed, and the old man lay stark on his pallet in his winding-sheet. I looked through his tools, quietly, but without hurrying. He had a fine hatchet, a crude saw, and a mounted, circular grindstone—a treasure to me. I could not take the mounting, but stuck the handle in my shirt, took the tools under my arm and the stone in both hands, and walked out again. "Who's there?" said one of the women, without interest, and sent up a perfunctory wail.

The stone all but pulled my arms out before I got it up the road to our hut, where I hid it and the tools and the handle a little way inside the forest under a bit of brushwood. I crept back into the windowless blackness of the hut and felt my way over to my pallet, for the fire was dead. I lay a long time, my heart beating hard, telling my story: I had stolen my weapons, now I would lay my siege on the great thorn-hedge. But I did not use those words. I knew nothing of sieges, wars, victories, all such matters of great history. I knew no story but my own.

It would be a very dull one to read in a book. I cannot tell much of it. All that summer and autumn, winter and spring, and the next summer, and the next autumn, and the next winter, I fought my war, I laid my siege: I chopped and hewed and hacked at the thicket of bramble and thorn. I cut through a thick, tough trunk, but could not pull it free till I had cut through fifty branches tangled in its branches. When it was free I dragged it out and then I began to cut at the next thick trunk. My hatchet grew dull a thousand times. I had made a mount for the grindstone, and on it I sharpened the hatchet a thousand times, till the blade was worn down into the thickness of the metal and would not hold an edge. In the first winter, the saw shivered against a rootstock hard as flint. In the second summer, I stole an ax and a handsaw from a party of travelling woodcutters camped a little way inside the forest near the road to the Baron's hall. They were poaching wood from my domain, the forest. In return, I poached tools from them. I felt it was a fair trade.

My father grumbled at my long absences, but I kept up my foraging, and had so many snares out that we had rabbit as often as we wanted it. In any case, he no longer dared strike me. I was sixteen or seventeen years old, I suppose, and though I was by no means well grown, or tall, or very strong, I was stronger than he, a worn-out old man, forty years old or more. He struck my stepmother as often as he liked. She was a little, toothless, red-eyed old woman now. She spoke, very seldom. When she spoke, my father would cuff her, railing at women's chatter, women's nagging. "Will you never be quiet?" he would shout, and she would shrink away, drawing her head down in her hunched shoulders like a turtle. And yet sometimes when she washed herself at night with a rag and a basin of water warmed in the ashes, her blanket would slip down, and I saw her body was fine-skinned, with soft breasts and rounded hips shadowy in the firelight. I would turn away, for she was frightened and ashamed when she saw me looking at her. She called me "son," though I was not her son. Long ago she had called me by my name.

Once I saw her watching me as I ate. It had been a good harvest, that first autumn, and we had turnips right through the winter. She watched me with a look on her face, and I knew she wanted to ask me then, while my father was out of the house, what it was I did all day in the forest, why my shirt and vest and trousers were forever ripped and shredded, why my hands were callused on the palms and crosshatched with a thousand scratches on the backs. If she had asked I would have told her. But she did not ask. She turned her face down into the shadows, silent.

Shadows and silence filled the passage I had hacked into the great hedge. The thorn trees stood so tall and thickly branched above it that no light at all made its way down through them.

As the first year came round, I had hacked and sawn and chopped a passage of about my height and twice my length into the hedge. It was as impenetrable as ever before me, not allowing a glimpse of what might be on the other side nor a hint that the tangle of branches might be any thinner. Many a time at night I lay hearing my father snore and said to myself that when I was an old man like him, I would cut through the last branch and come out into the forest—having spent my life tunnelling through nothing but a great, round bramble patch, with nothing inside it but itself. I told that end to my story, but did not believe it. I tried to tell other ends. I said, I will find a green lawn inside the hedge . . . A village . . . A friary . . . A hall . . . A stony field. . . . I knew nothing else that one might find. But these endings did not hold my mind for long; soon I was thinking again of how I should cut the next thick trunk that stood in my way. My story was the story of cutting a way through an endless thicket of thorny branches, and nothing more. And to tell it would take as long as it took to do it.

On a day near the end of winter, such a day as makes it seem there will never be an end to winter, a chill, damp, dark, dreary, hungry day, I was sawing away with the woodcutter's saw at a gnarled, knotted whitethorn as thick as my thigh and hard as iron. I crouched in the small space I had and sawed away with nothing in my mind but sawing.

The hedge grew unnaturally fast, in season and out; even in midwinter thick, pale shoots would grow across my passageway, and in summer I had to spend some time every day clearing out new growth, thorny green sprays full of stinging sap. My passage or tunnel was now more than five yards long, but only a foot and a half high except at the very end; I had learned to wriggle in, and keep the passage man-high only at the end, where I must have room enough to get a purchase on my ax or saw. I crouched at my work, glad to give up the comfort of standing for a gain in going forward.

The whitethorn trunk split suddenly, in the contrary, evil way the trees of that thicket had. It sent the saw blade almost across my thigh, and as the tree fell against others interlaced with it, a long branch whipped across my face. Thorns raked my eyelids and forehead. Blinded with blood, I thought it had struck my eyes. I knelt, wiping away the blood with hands that trembled from strain and the suddenness of the accident. I got one eye clear at last, and then the other, and blinking and peering, saw light before me.

The whitethorn in falling had left a gap, and in the maze and crisscross of dark branches beyond it was a small clear space, through which one could see, as through a chink in a wall: and in that small bright space I saw the castle.

I know now what to call it. What I saw then I had no name for. I saw sunlight on a yellow stone wall. Looking closer, I saw a door in the wall. Beside the door stood figures, men perhaps, in shadow, unmoving; after a time I thought they were figures carved in stone, such as I had seen at the doors of the friary church. I could see nothing else: sunlight, bright stone, the door, the shadowy figures. Everywhere else the branches and trunks and dead leaves of the hedge massed before me as they had for two years, impenetrably dark.

I thought, if I was a snake I could crawl through that hole! But being no snake, I set to work to enlarge it. My hands still shook, but I took the ax and struck and struck at the massed and crossing branches. Now I knew which branch to cut, which stem to chop: whichever lay between my eyes and that golden wall, that door. I cared nothing for the height or width of my passage, so long as I could force and tear my way forward, indifferent to the laceration of my arms and face and clothing. I swung my dull ax with such violence that the branches flew before me; and as I pushed forward, the branches and stems of the hedge grew thinner, weaker. Light shone through them. From winter-black and hard they became green and soft, as I hacked and forced on forward, until I could put them aside with my hand. I parted the last screen and crawled on hands and knees out onto a lawn of bright grass.

Overhead the sky was the soft blue of early summer. Before me, a little downhill from the hedge, stood the house of yellow stone, the castle, in its moat. Flags hung motionless from its pointed towers. The air was still and warm. Nothing moved.

I crouched there, as motionless as everything else, except for my breath, which came loud and hard for a long time.

Beside my sweaty, blood-streaked hand a little bee sat on a clover blossom, not stirring, honey-drunk.

I raised myself to my knees and looked all round me, cautious. I knew that this must be a hall, like the Baron's hall above the village, and therefore dangerous to anyone who did not live there or have work there. It was much larger and finer than the Baron's hall, and infinitely fairer; larger and fairer even than the friary church. With its yellow walls and red roofs it looked, I thought, like a flower. I had not seen much else I could compare it to. The Baron's hall was a squat keep with a scumble of huts and barns about it; the church was grey and grim, the carved figures by its door faceless with age. This house, whatever it was, was delicate and fine and fresh. The sunlight on it made me think of the firelight on my stepmother's breasts.

Halfway down the wide, grassy slope to the moat, a few cows lay in midday torpor, heads up, eyes closed; they were not even chewing the cud. On the farther slope, a flock of sheep lay scattered out, and an apple orchard was just losing its last blossoms.

The air was very warm. In my torn, ragged shirt and coat, I would have been shivering as the sweat cooled on me, on the other side of the hedge, where winter was. Here I shrugged off the coat. The blood from all my scratches, drying, made my skin draw and itch, so that I began to look with longing at the water in the moat. Blue and glassy it lay, very tempting. I was thirsty, too. My water bottle lay back in the passage, nearly empty. I thought of it, but never turned my head to look back.

No one had moved, on the lawns or in the gardens around the house or on the bridge across the moat, all the time I had been kneeling here in the shadow of the great hedge, gazing my fill. The cows lay like stones, though now and again I saw a brown flank shudder off a fly, or the very tip of a tail twitch lazily. When I looked down I saw the little bee still on the clover blossom. I touched its wing curiously, wondering if it was dead. Its feelers shivered a little, but it did not stir. I looked back at the house, at the windows, and at the door—a side door—which I had first seen through the branches. I saw, without for some while knowing that I saw, that the two carved figures by the door were living men. They stood one on each side of the door as if in readiness for someone entering from the garden or the stables; one held a staff, the other a pike; and they were both leaning right back against the wall, sound asleep.

It did not surprise me. They're asleep, I thought. It seemed natural enough, here. I think I knew even then where I had come.

I do not mean that I knew the story, as you may know it. I did not know why they were asleep, how it had come about that they were asleep. I did not know the beginning of their story, nor the end. I did not know who was in the castle. But I knew already that they were all asleep. It was very strange, and I thought I should be afraid; but I could not feel any fear.

So even then, as I stood up, and went slowly down the sunny sward to the willows by the moat, I walked, not as if I were in a dream, but as if I were a dream. I didn't know who was dreaming me, if not myself, but it didn't matter. I knelt in the shade of the willows and put my sore hands down into the cool water of the moat. Just beyond my reach a golden-speckled carp floated, sleeping. A waterskater poised motionless on four tiny dimples in the skin of the water. Under the bridge, a swallow and her nestlings slept in their mud nest. A window was open, up in the castle wall; I saw a silky dark head pillowed on a pudgy arm on the window ledge.

I stripped, slow and quiet in my dream-movements, and slid into the water. Though I could not swim, I had often bathed in shallow streams in the forest. The moat was deep, but I clung to the stone coping; presently I found a willow root that reached out from the stones, where I could sit with only my head out, and watch the golden-speckled carp hang in the clear, shadowed water.

I climbed out at last, refreshed and clean. I rinsed out my sweaty, winter-foul shirt and trousers, scrubbing them with stones, and spread them to dry in the hot sun on the grass above the willows. I had left my coat and my thick, straw-stuffed clogs up under the hedge. When my shirt and trousers were half dry, I put them on—deliciously cool and wet-smelling—and combed my hair with my fingers. Then I stood up and walked to the end of the drawbridge.

I crossed it, always going slowly and quietly, without fear or hurry.

The old porter sat by the great door of the castle, his chin right down on his chest. He snored long, soft snores.

I pushed at the tall, iron-studded, oaken door. It opened with a little groan. Two boarhounds sprawled on the flagstone floor just inside, huge dogs, sound asleep. One of them "hunted" in his sleep, scrabbling his big legs, and then lay still again. The air inside the castle was still and shadowy, as the air outside was still and bright. There was no sound, inside or out. No bird sang, or woman; no voice spoke, or foot stirred, or bell struck the hour. The cooks slept over their cauldrons in the kitchen, the maids slept at their dusting and their mending, the king and his grooms slept by the sleeping horses in the stableyard, and the queen at her embroidery frame slept among her women. The cat slept by the mousehole, and the mice between the walls. The moth slept on the woollens, and the music slept in the strings of the minstrel's harp. There were no hours. The sun slept in the blue sky, and the shadows of the willows on the water never moved.

I know, I know it was not my enchantment. I had broken, hacked, chopped, forced my way into it. I know I am a poacher. I never learned how to be anything else. Even my forest, my domain as I had thought it, was never mine. It was the King's Forest, and the king slept here in his castle in the heart of his forest. But it had been a long time since anyone talked of the king. Petty barons held sway all round the forest; woodcutters stole wood from it, peasant boys snared rabbits in it; stray princes rode through it now and then, perhaps, hunting the red deer, not even knowing they were trespassing.

I knew I trespassed, but I could not see the harm. I did, of course, eat their food. The venison pastry that the chief cook had just taken out of the oven smelled so delicious that hungry flesh could not endure it. I arranged the chief cook in a more comfortable position on the slate floor of the kitchen, with his hat crumpled up for a pillow; and then I attacked the great pie, breaking off a corner with my hands and cramming it in my mouth. It was still warm, savoury, succulent. I ate my fill. Next time I came through the kitchen, the pastry was whole, unbroken. The enchantment held. Was it that as a dream, I could change nothing of this deep reality of sleep? I ate as I pleased, and always the cauldron of soup was full again and the loaves waited in the pantry, their brown crusts unbroken. The red wine brimmed the crystal goblet by the seneschal's hand, however many times I raised it, saluted him in thanks, and drank.

As I explored the castle and its grounds and outbuild ings—always unhurriedly, wandering from room to room, pausing often, often lingering over some painted scene or fantastic tapestry or piece of fine workmanship in tool or fitting or furniture, often settling down on a soft, curtained bed or a sunny, grassy garden nook to sleep (for there was no night here, and I slept when I was tired and woke when I was refreshed)—as I wandered through all the rooms and offices and cellars and halls and barns and servants' quarters, I came to know, almost as if they were furniture too, the people who slept here and there, leaning or sitting or lying down, however they had chanced to be when the enchantment stole upon them and their eyes grew heavy, their breathing quiet, their limbs lax and still. A shepherd up on the hill had been pissing into a gopher's hole; he had settled down in a heap and slept contentedly, as no doubt the gopher was doing down in the dirt. The chief cook, as

I have said, lay as if struck down unwilling in the heat of his art, and though I tried many times to pillow his head and arrange his limbs more comfortably, he always frowned, as if to say, "Don't bother me now, I'm busy!" Up at the top of the old apple orchard lay a couple of lovers, peasants like me. He, his rough trousers pulled down, lay as he had slid off her, face buried in the blossom-littered grass, drowned in sleep and satisfaction. She, a short, buxom young woman with apple-red cheeks and nipples, lay sprawled right out, skirts hiked to her waist, legs parted and arms wide, smiling in her sleep. It was again more than hungry flesh could endure. I laid myself down softly on her, kissing those red nipples, and came into her honey sweetness. She smiled in her sleep again, whenever I did so, and sometimes made a little groaning grunt of pleasure. Afterwards I would lie beside her, a partner to her friend on the other side, and drowse, and wake to see the unfalling late blossoms on the apple boughs. When I slept, there inside the great hedge, I never dreamed.

What had I to dream of? Surely I had all I could desire. Still, while the time passed that did not pass, used as I was to solitude, I grew lonely; the company of the sleepers grew wearisome to me. Mild and harmless as they were, and dear as many of them became to me as I lived among them, they were no better companions to me than a child's wooden toys, to which he must lend his own voice and soul. I sought work, not only to repay them for their food and beds but because I was, after all, used to working. I polished the silver, I swept and reswept the floors where the dust lay so still, I groomed all the sleeping horses, I arranged the books on the shelves. And that led me to open a book, in mere idleness, and puzzle at the words in it.

I had not had a book in my hands since that primer of my stepmother's, nor seen any other but the priest's book in the church when we went to Mass at Yuletime. At first I looked only at the pictures, which were marvelous, and entertained me much. But I began to want to know what the words said about the pictures. When I came to study the shapes of the letters, they began to come back to me: *a* like a cat sitting, and the fat-bellied *b* and *d*, and *t* the carpenter's square, and so on. And *a-t* was *at*, and *c-a-t* was *cat*, and so on. And time enough to learn to read, time enough and more than enough, slow as I might be. So I came to read, first the romances and histories in the queen's rooms, where I first had begun to read, and then the king's library of books about wars and kingdoms and travels and famous men, and finally the princess's books of fairy tales. So it is that I know now what a castle is, and a king, and a seneschal, and a story, and so can write my own.

But I was never happy going into the tower room, where the fairy tales were. I went there the first time; after the first time, I went there only for the books in the shelf beside the door. I would take a book, looking only at the shelf, and go away again at once, down the winding stair. I never looked at her but once, the first time, the one time.

She was alone in her room. She sat near the window, in a little straight chair. The thread she had been spinning lay across her lap and trailed to the floor. The thread was white; her dress was white and green. The spindle lay in her open hand. It had pricked her thumb, and the point of it still stuck just above the little thumb joint. Her hands were small and delicate. She was younger even than I when I came there, hardly more than a child, and had never done any hard work at all. You could see that. She slept more sweetly than any of them, even the maid with the pudgy arm and the silky hair, even the rosy baby in the cradle in the gate-keeper's house, even the grandmother in the little south room, whom I loved best of all. I used to talk to the grandmother when I was lonely. She sat so quietly as if looking out the window, and it was easy to believe that she was listening to me and only thinking before she answered.

But the princess's sleep was sweeter even than that. It was like a butterfly's sleep.

I knew, I knew as soon as I entered her room, that first

time, that one time, as soon as I saw her I knew that she, she alone in all the castle, might wake at any moment. I knew that she, alone of all of them, all of us, was dreaming. I knew that if I spoke in that tower room she would hear me: maybe not waken, but hear me in her sleep, and her dreams would change. I knew that if I touched her or even came close to her I would trouble her dreams. If I so much as touched that spindle, moved it so that it did not pierce her thumb—and I longed to do that, for it was painful to see— but if I did that, if I moved the spindle, a drop of red blood would well up slowly on the delicate little cushion of flesh above the joint. And her eyes would open. Her eyes would open slowly; she would look at me. And the enchantment would be broken, the dream at an end.

I have lived here within the great hedge till I am older than my father ever was. I am as old as the grandmother in the south room, grey-haired. I have not climbed the winding stair for many years. I do not read the books of fairy tales any longer, nor visit the sweet orchard. I sit in the garden in the sunshine. When the prince comes riding, and strikes his way clear through the hedge of thorns—my two years' toil— with one blow of his privileged, bright sword, when he strides up the winding stair to the tower room, when he stoops to kiss her, and the spindle falls from her hand, and the drop of blood wells like a tiny ruby on the white skin, when she opens her eyes slowly and yawns, she will look up at him. As the castle begins to stir, the petals to fall, the little bee to move and buzz on the clover blossom, she will look up at him through the mists and tag ends of dream, a hundred years of dreams; and I wonder if, for a moment, she will think, "Is that the face I dreamed of seeing?" But by then I will be out by the midden heap, sleeping sounder than they ever did.

Lucy Maria
Lisa Tuttle

It is a serious business when a child falls in love. When people talk about love, as they often do, as "sexual attraction," I think of those kissing dolls sold in novelty shops, papier-mâché heads bobbing on springs, drawn towards each other inevitably, inexorably made to connect by hidden magnets. You could imagine, from the language, that sex was a set of magnets buried in human flesh. But isn't there something else involved, an attraction of souls, which is regardless of sex, regardless of age?

I think so. When Janet, my six-year-old, wept in my arms for James, the seven-year-old next door, my own heart ached.

I have not, these past eight years, brooded much on the past. Being married with two small children and a house to look after keeps me anchored in the present, with no time for vain regrets. I married Robert on the rebound, as they say, but he is a good man, and we have made a satisfactory life together.

Satisfactory, until now. Now I sit in the kitchen in the middle of the night, unable to sleep, trapped in the past.

Can it be only coincidence that this afternoon my daughter's unhappiness reminded me of my own past hurt, and that this evening, looking for distraction, I picked up *The Times* and saw an obituary for Mrs. Edward Templeton?

Edward, I thought. Edward, who should have been my husband, is free at last. As a man he had wanted to marry me. But as a child he had given his heart to a funny little old-fashioned girl named Lucy Maria. He promised himself to her when he was a child, and sealed his fate. For what are the desires of adults when weighed in the balance with those of children?

When we were children, living in a leafy London suburb, Edward and I were playmates. It wasn't Edward I loved in those days, but his older brother, Julian. Seven years older than I, away at public school for most of the year, Julian seemed unattainable, but I was determined. I laid plans. Edward, a year younger than I, became my favoured friend.

In love with my fantasy of Julian, I was then incapable of appreciating Edward, whom I thought too young. I was the leader in all our games; I was older, and bolder, and sometimes, I am sorry to say, I bullied him. But he was willing to be led by me, even when I proposed we should explore the haunted house.

We had no idea by whom or what it might be haunted, only that it had an evil reputation. It was let to a different family every year, unusual in those more settled days before the war. The house, in its own grounds at the end of a private drive, was also one of the larger ones in our neighbourhood. For a few months, in the summer of 1939, the house was empty of tenants, apparently abandoned except for the regular attentions of a hired gardener.

It was a disinclination for naughtiness, not a fear of ghosts, that made Edward unwilling to trespass, yet I taunted him with cowardice, until he gave in. We set off, in broad daylight, with candles and matches to explore the darker recesses of the house, but I didn't really think we would get inside. We would wander around in the shrubbery and peer through windows and I would make us both shiver by claiming to see something moving in the shadows, but the house was sure to be locked.

It was Edward who noticed the open window at the back.

I stared up at the dark space between white sash and white sill and thought it was like a partly opened mouth.

"It's too high," I objected. "And anyway, it's probably fixed so it won't open any wider, the way our kitchen window is."

"You fit in through your kitchen window. I can give you a leg up here just like I do there."

To me that half-opened window looked like a trap. Set by whom? The house was empty, so who could have left it open?

As if he read my thoughts Edward said, "Probably the gardener makes his tea in the scullery there. He must have a key to the house. He probably forgot he'd opened the window. Give us a leg up, and I'll go through and let you in by the door."

His sudden keenness worried me more than the open window. The balance of power was shifting between us. Not wanting to let him see me afraid, I braced myself and offered him my clasped hands for a step up. He vanished headfirst into the house.

Would it have made any difference in the end if I had gone first? Would she have shown herself to me, or kept hidden?

I'll never know. Edward went into the house, leaving me alone for . . . two minutes? Five? It wasn't very long, but a great deal can happen in a minute, the shifting of a fate, one's whole future life altered because of a look, a few whispered words.

He was looking livelier than his usual rather serious self when he opened the back door. "Here, you'll never guess: there's someone already in the house—a little girl."

I looked around the bare, empty back hall, cross that some other child had beaten us out. "Who is she?"

"Miss Lucy Maria Toseland, she says. She's a funny little thing—but you'll see." He raised his voice, calling. "Lucy?"

I pushed past him into a room full of heavily shrouded furniture and felt that uneasy prickle which accompanies the game of hide-and-seek.

"Come out," I said, rather sharply.

"Don't frighten her," said Edward, behind me. Then, coaxing, "You needn't be afraid, Lucy. She's a friend."

There was no response. I moved further into the room and began to look behind the furniture, not touching anything.

"I don't think she's in here now," said Edward. "She must be in another room."

"Why is she hiding?"

"She might be frightened. She's very young."

"What's she doing here, then, all by herself?"

"She says she lives here. Her parents went away and left her."

"People don't do that, just leave their children. She's lying."

"No."

A hint of steel in that one word; something I'd never heard from Edward. I looked at him in amazement. "Did she say *when* they went away?"

"She doesn't know . . . she's only little. She said a long time, but it can't have been, she can't have been on her own for long—she's too tidy, her hair's been brushed, and someone's tied a ribbon in it—she could never do that herself. She's wearing ever such a funny old-fashioned dress with petticoats, a bit like that one in Granny's picture, remember?"

The flesh on my arms tried to crawl up to my shoulders, and for a moment I knew the truth.

At that moment, Edward ran off, calling: "Lucy, Lucy Maria, please come out!"

Although I wanted to leave, I was more afraid of being

alone, so I ran after him, hearing, just ahead of me, his glad shout: "There you are!"

I found him in the front parlour. The curtains were drawn against the ruinous effects of sunlight, and the atmosphere was dim and vaguely subaqueous, but I could see well enough that he was alone.

"Here she is, you see, she's shy of strangers."

"Where?"

"Just here." He gestured, then frowned. "Lucy? Now don't be silly, Lucy, I told you she's a friend—you said you'd come out; you mustn't hide any more."

I watched him wandering around the ghostly shapes in the dim room, bending and turning as if searching for a hidden child. The doorway I blocked was the only way—apart from the windows, which had not been opened—in or out of the room. No one had passed us in the hall, and there was no one here now. Which meant there never had been.

"Well done, Edward," I said. "Points to you. You had me fooled, all right."

He turned, frowning slightly.

"It was a good one, but I've rumbled you."

"What do you mean?"

"Your little ghostly girl in the old-fashioned dress. You made her up. And I believed you. My word, you *have* learned how to tell them, and no mistake!"

His hand came up in an oath. "It's no story. She was here. Honestly, I was talking to her just a minute ago. And of course she's not a ghost—she's a little girl."

Edward wasn't joking. He really had seen and spoken to a little girl who wasn't there. My back prickled and I whirled around, terrified something might be creeping up on me from behind, and although there was no one there, once I had started moving I did not seem able to stop, but went running pell-mell for the back door, letting out a low, wailing moan as I ran.

He called to me to stop, but I couldn't stop. My role as leader, the need to save face, these things didn't weigh with me at all in my panic. I didn't even slow down until I had reached the gates at the end of the drive, out of sight of the house. There I paused, panting, feeling guilty for having abandoned him. But I could not, to save my soul or his, make myself go back. It was pushing my courage to its limits simply to stay where I was and wait as the minutes dragged themselves past.

At last—it might have been half an hour or more—he came into view, walking slowly, looking bemused by my obvious fear. "She wouldn't have hurt you, you know. She couldn't hurt anyone."

"But she's dead, isn't she? She's a ghost?"

"Ye-es," he said uncertainly. "I suppose. I tried to touch her and my hand passed right through her. There was nothing there. I could see her, but I couldn't feel her at all."

"Oh!"

He looked at me. "Yes, it frightened her, too. She doesn't know she's a ghost. She knows something is wrong, but not what. She has no idea about being dead, no idea at all."

"What does she think has happened to her?"

"She says her family went away without her; she doesn't know why she didn't go with them, or how long ago it happened. Before they left, there was something, something about her parents, something someone did to her which frightened her a great deal, which I couldn't understand, and then she said they all went away, taking another little girl who looked just like her, and they didn't hear her when she cried."

It was Edward now who wanted to go back to the haunted house and I who kept finding excuses. I had another reason for preferring adventures closer to home, as long as it was Edward's home, and that was his brother, Julian, back for the summer. I liked rainy days the best, days when Edward and I had to play indoors, days Julian often stayed in, too, reading books or listening to the wireless. I was happy just to have him near, to look at him, and when he spoke to me,

I was in heaven. One day, I remember, he taught us card tricks.

As I was drawn to Julian, Edward was drawn to his ghost. He argued with me in vain, and finally, one morning when I turned up as usual on his doorstep, his mother told me that Edward had already left—for my house, she assumed.

Of course I knew where he had really gone. I held out for as long as I could, but, as the summer passed and Edward seemed quite happy to play without me, pride, curiosity, boredom and jealousy all worked in me to overwhelm my fading memory of fear, and finally I told Edward I would go with him.

He had stopped asking by then, but he seemed pleased. His love for Lucy Maria was not exclusive; he wanted her to have friends, for others to know and love her as he did.

The day we went turned out to be the gardener's day; we caught sight of a stocky, overalled figure as we rounded the curve in the drive and beat a hasty retreat. I wasn't sorry to put off the visit to another day, but Edward fretted all through the afternoon, and insisted on going back after tea instead of waiting until morning. He said that Lucy Maria was expecting us and he couldn't let her down.

But the scullery window was locked. Not merely shut, as he had learned to shut it so a passing glance would see nothing wrong, but latched shut from the inside. The back door was locked, the front door, too. I was relieved, but Edward was frantic as he ran around the house, trying every window on the ground floor.

"Can't your Lucy Maria let us in?"

"Don't be silly! If she could do that, she could let herself out, couldn't she? She's a soul without a body, she's helpless, she's trapped—you don't understand at all, do you?"

"How should I understand? I've never even seen this creature. For all I know, you made her up, to tease me."

He stared at me in disbelief and, I think, dislike; made a tortured sound, and turned his attention back to the problem of the locked house.

His agony was so obvious I felt ashamed of myself. I had also noticed how low the sun was. I grabbed his arm. "Ned, I'm sorry. I know she's real, and I'm sorry about the window, but, look, it's getting late. Let's go. We can come back in the morning. I'll come with you, and we'll have the whole day to find a way in. But we have to go now. If we're late, they may not let us out tomorrow. It's not your fault. She'll understand."

"Grown-ups," he growled, like a curse. "It's *their* fault." But I knew from the slump of his shoulders that he had given in.

As we walked away from the house he kept looking back and suddenly he stopped. "There she is, she's watching—see?"

My eyes followed his pointing finger to a first-floor window and I saw: a little dark-haired girl in a white dress, ruffled pantaloons below, standing very still and looking out.

"You see? That's Lucy Maria."

I saw. And then she was gone, and I was looking at an empty window, blank as a sightless eye.

A primitive, unthinking terror possessed me. For the second and not the last time in my life, I ran away from that house, and from Lucy Maria.

Did Edward go back? Did he manage to get inside? Did he see Lucy Maria again?

I don't know. Before I saw him again, before anything could be resolved, it was wartime, and the summer was over. I was packed off, with Mother and the babies, to relatives in Wales. Edward, too, was evacuated—but I only learned that later. I was not to see him again for many years.

Edward alone of his family survived the war. His parents were killed in an air raid, and Julian died in action in 1943. I had the news in a letter from my father, who had no idea of my feelings for Julian, referring to him as "the brother of your old chum Edward." It was curious; I hadn't seen

Julian for four years, and might never have seen him again even if he had lived, but the news hit me very hard; in some ways, I feel as if I never really got over it.

My formal education came to an end at about the same time as the war. There had been talk about teacher training, but I knew I didn't want to teach. I lived at home—this was our new home, in Berkshire—and commuted to London to do a secretarial course until I got tired of it, then drifted about between coffee bars and house parties, occasionally working at some undemanding job.

In 1949 I still spent my weekends at home in Berkshire, but during the week I worked in a bookshop in the Charing Cross Road, and shared a flat in Holborn with three other girls. It was in the bookshop, ten years after I'd last seen him, that Edward Templeton came back into my life.

I looked up as I always did at the sound of the bell that rang whenever the door opened, and thought he was an unlikely customer. A broad, open, very English face, fair hair, clear blue eyes untroubled by the clouds of intellect—I not only knew the type, I knew *him*.

"Julian." Maybe the news of his death had been a mistake, and all the years I'd lived since no more than a dream.

I don't know if he heard me. I'm not even sure I spoke aloud. He came further into the shop, to where he could see me. I was staring at him, as unselfconsciously as a child and as unable to stop. I was afraid he would vanish.

"It *is* you," he said, and the sound of his voice broke the dream. "Remember me?"

"Edward," I said. "Of course."

"I saw you last week, in a Soho coffee bar, and I thought I knew you, but I couldn't think how. Then I remembered . . . but by then you'd gone. Somebody said he thought you worked in a bookshop, so I've been searching ever since."

"I can't think how you recognized me. It's been ten years."

He looked me up and down, and I felt myself responding

to his gaze. "Mmmm. You're bigger now, of course, but otherwise you're just the same, only prettier. How could anybody forget those eyes? Anyway, you recognized me too—don't deny it."

I didn't feel like explaining who I had seen in his face. "Well, now that you've found me, what are you going to do with me?"

"Take you out to dinner—for a start."

There were a couple of other boys I was dating at the time, but Edward was soon the only one. Within a few months he had proposed marriage, and I accepted. We did talk about the past, in the way that lovers always do, marvelling at the twists and turns of fate which have brought them together, but I never told him of my love for his late brother, and he never mentioned Lucy Maria. It seems strange now, but I had put the whole haunted house episode completely out of my mind.

It was as part of our search for a home to share that Edward suggested we take a look at the suburb where we had first met as children. I objected that it was inconvenient, unattractive, too expensive, too far from our friends . . . Laughing, he stopped me.

"All right, all right, we can't live there. But let's go and have a look at the place for old times' sake . . . a romantic walk together along the paths where we used to play. I haven't been there since before the war, and I wonder how it survived. What do you say?"

I said yes, because it was obviously what he wanted. It seemed a small concession.

"Remember the haunted house?" he asked, after we had looked, from a distance, at his old house and mine—both of them, we agreed, much smaller than we remembered.

Haunted house. The words gave me a queer little shock and I shook my head in automatic denial, before I'd had time to think.

"Don't you? That's funny. I thought you'd never forget it. I thought you might never get over being so frightened. The things that children think will last forever . . . So you don't mind if we go there now?"

I began to remember. "Not inside."

"I'm not proposing we trespass, no."

At the sight of the posts which marked the end of the private drive I felt a premonition, or a memory, of fear.

"You were such a brave girl, much braver than I was. I could never understand how you could be afraid of her."

"You mean the dead can't hurt us? Maybe not, but people have always been afraid of ghosts. They don't belong in this world, they're intrusions. They can't be trusted. Isn't that reason to be afraid?"

"She wouldn't have harmed you, or anyone," he said. "She couldn't." And he walked faster as we came in sight of the house, so that I had almost to run to keep up, and when he stopped, suddenly, I almost ran into him.

He didn't notice, transfixed by something he had seen. I followed his gaze, knowing already, so that when I saw it, too, I didn't know if it was with my present eyes or in memory.

"Lucy Maria," I said.

Then she was gone.

He turned to me. "You saw her too?"

I was shaking, but he didn't notice. I managed to nod, unable to speak.

"Poor Lucy—still trapped here, still alone—"

He ran to the house, but the curtains were drawn at the front so he ran around to the back. I noticed, as I followed, that the lawn was overgrown and the shrubberies looked a little wild. It wasn't a wilderness; it was still being tended, but obviously not as carefully as ten years ago. It was hard to be sure, with the curtains all drawn, but it seemed likely that the house was unoccupied, and that the pattern of temporary rentals continued, with occasional gaps.

"Maybe we could rent it," he said.

"Us? Live here?" The idea was nightmarish.

"Then she wouldn't be alone. We could take care of her."

His eyes glowed. "I made a promise when I was a boy that I would come back and save her. And if I couldn't help her escape I would stay with her, and look after her, and make sure she was never lonely again. God, how could I have forgotten?" He shook his head, looking rueful. "I thought it was a dream, or a kid's game. But it really happened. She's real. You know she is; you saw her, too, in the window. She's still waiting."

He looked at me hopefully. "Oh, do say yes, darling! You're not afraid, are you?"

I was afraid, but, as always with him, ashamed to admit it.

"She can't hurt you and—don't you see?—we can help her. We were helpless when we were children, but not now!" He grasped my icy fingers and held them in his warm hands, willing me to feel what he felt.

I looked into his pleading, eager, loving eyes. Loving someone is wanting what they want. I said, rather feebly, "But what if she doesn't like me? She didn't, you know."

"Nonsense! She'll love you when she gets to know you, just as I do! She'll be like our own child."

I knew I would not have refused if Edward had been pleading on behalf of some living, displaced child. For we had talked about adopting war orphans, about sharing our home, our love and our good fortune with those who had none, creating a family around us immediately, without waiting for the children who would be born. It might have seemed odd to anyone else that the first child we adopted was a ghost, but this ghost was real to us, a part of our shared childhood. I couldn't pretend not to believe, and I had no justification for my fear of her. Really, if I examined it, wasn't my chief emotion jealousy? He had loved her. Something in his passion stirred the memory of Julian, and the long nights I had wept and prayed and wished to have been allowed to save him, or at least to do something for him before he died. Like mine, Edward's childhood sweetheart was dead. We both had our dead . . . and we had each other. It wasn't fair of me to be jealous. Why not be generous?

"If it's not too expensive," I said.

"Darling!"

He embraced me. Over his shoulder, I looked at the house, wondering if Lucy was watching. I shut my eyes and kissed Edward back.

The owner of the house was a Miss Toseland. I wondered if she was a sister or a cousin, or perhaps a posthumous niece, of Lucy Maria. She employed an agent, of course, to deal with property affairs, but Edward wanted to see her personally. I wasn't sure why. She agreed, reluctantly, to receive us at her home in Hampstead the following Friday morning.

She was an intimidating figure. Not tall, but rigidly upright, a woman in her seventies with snow-white hair and eyes so dark they seemed as black as her old-fashioned dress. Like birds' eyes, I thought: there seemed no human feeling behind them at all.

To my astonishment, Edward was not intimidated by her coldness, and we had scarcely been seated in her grey and lavender sitting room before he'd told her the house was haunted.

"I don't believe in that spiritualist nonsense," she said. "So if you've come to try and convert me, or to try and get money out of me for some scheme, you may as well leave now."

"I'm not a spiritualist, but I've seen something, and I am curious to know if the phenomenon has been reported before."

"Certainly not."

"Did you ever live in the house?"

"I did. As a small child. Our family left to live abroad in 1879 and we never returned. I have not set foot in that house since the day my parents carried me out of it, seventy years ago. So you see, Mr. Templeton, it is quite useless to ask me about any so-called spiritualist phenomena in that house.''

"You had no experiences yourself, as a child, living there?''

"I have no memories of that time. I was, of course, very young when we left.''

"Did you have any sisters?''

"Several,'' she said dryly, and glanced at the clock on the mantelpiece.

"Lucy Maria?''

"I beg your pardon?'' She looked startled; it was the first emotion she had shown.

"Was one of your sisters called Lucy Maria?''

She stared at him. "*I* am Lucy Maria.''

I looked at him, looking at her.

Softly he said, "You lost something in that house, long ago. Something very valuable got left behind.''

For a long moment they sat with gazes locked. Then, stiffly, with great determination, she stood up and reached for the little silver bell on the mantelpiece beside the clock. "I don't know what your game is, Mr. Templeton, but it isn't going to work. I am neither so foolish nor so rich as you seem to think.'' She picked up the bell and rang it.

Confused and humiliated, I stood up beside Edward, unnoticed by either of them.

"This isn't a con game, and I'm not asking you for anything. I'm telling you this for your own sake. There is something in that house you can ill afford to live without.''

She laughed a little, not sounding amused. "I have done without it for seventy years.''

The maid came in. Miss Toseland said, "My visitors are leaving.''

"You have lived without it, of course, but perhaps you wouldn't like to learn later that it had been destroyed through carelessness, or that someone else, not you, had profited by it . . .''

"Someone like you?''

Edward gave her his steadiest gaze. He was the very picture of the honest Englishman, the man everyone instinctively trusts. When I read Conrad's *Lord Jim*, I pictured Edward's face. He said, "I thought it only fair to tell you. Before you rent the house again, to me or anyone else, go there yourself, first. Go through every room. Satisfy yourself that you know what is there. Don't leave it to someone else, no matter how much you trust him." He turned to me then, putting his hand lightly at my waist. "We'll go now. I've said what I had to say."

"Wait."

We were at the door. Edward turned back.

"You won't tell me what it is, this valuable thing?"

He shook his head. "It would be better if you saw yourself."

"And if I ignore your advice?"

"I shall do as I planned and rent it through your agent."

"The honest thief?" There was a pause. Then, to the maid she said, "Tell Bayley to bring the car around. My visitors will be travelling with me." When the maid had gone she said to Edward, "I should tell you that my chauffeur is also a skilled pugilist. I always feel quite, quite safe with him."

"I'm sure you should." Edward was smiling and relaxed.

"Would you point out this valuable object to me personally, once we're in the house?"

"I think you'll find it yourself without any difficulty. But of course if you need my help, it's yours."

She left us alone in the sitting room while she prepared to go out, and I pounced on Edward at once.

He seemed surprised. "I thought you understood. Miss Toseland is Lucy Maria."

"But she's not dead!"

"Not physically, no. But the ghost in the house is her soul. Something must have happened to her when she was a child, just before the family moved. I wish I could remember what she told me. Perhaps an illness or some violence from which she almost died . . . or maybe it was a spiritual death, some shock which split her. Miss Toseland lived, but she grew up without a soul."

I found it remarkably easy to believe her a woman without a soul. "But what was all that about a treasure? She'll never rent it to us now. And why on earth should you want her to go to the house?"

"To bring them together again. She can rescue Lucy Maria; she's her only hope. If they can be reunited."

"And if they can't?"

"We won't have lost anything by trying. A rich old woman will think I'm mad, or a failed confidence trickster. If she asks again I might pretend to believe some painting there is by an old master." He smiled and stroked my cheek. "It will work. I feel certain this is the right thing to do."

We had never approached the house in a car before, but it made no difference. I felt the fear as we passed the gates at the end of the drive, and I clutched Edward's fingers, seeking reassurance.

"How strange to return," murmured Miss Toseland.

"Why did you never come back before now?" asked Edward.

"There was never any reason. The house belonged to my father, until his death, and then to my brother. When it came to me in due course I had no personal use for it; as a rental property it was better left in the hands of a competent agent."

The chauffeur stopped the car in front of the house and got out.

"Is it as you remember?" asked Edward.

The old woman was staring up at the house. "I don't remember."

The chauffeur opened the door for her but she did not move. I could see that she didn't want to get out, didn't want to go in.

"Does it frighten you?"

That made her move. "The impertinence!" Resting on

her servant's arm, she got out and we scrambled after. She marched up to the house and unlocked the front door with hands that scarcely trembled.

In the front hall she looked at him challengingly. "Where will I find this treasure?"

He cocked his head as if listening. "Upstairs. In the nursery, maybe."

She snorted. "Nursery, indeed!" She turned towards the stairs and, swifter than the chauffeur, he sprang to her side, offering his arm.

I felt a pang, the register of a betrayal, and I looked at the chauffeur as if we shared it. His face was unreadable, and he didn't look at me, but at his mistress, who allowed Edward to help her mount.

At the top of the first flight she had to rest. She was breathing heavily, and with the hand not clutching Edward's arm she reached towards her throat uncertainly. "I feel . . . I . . . is it not dark in here? Is it not cold? Bayley, get my—I feel . . . I . . ."

We were all looking at her. We all saw it happen. The taut parchment of her face seemed to crumple and shred, and the black ice of her eyes melted into something warmer and brighter. Then she laughed: the clear, high, sweet trill of a happy child. She laughed, and she jumped up and down and clapped her hands for joy.

"Oh, Ned," she cried, in a child's voice, not Miss Toseland's cold, refined tones, "you've done it—I always knew you would! I'm free!"

And she flung herself at him, hanging on his neck like someone much smaller, and covered his face with kisses.

Bayley must have thought she'd gone mad. His mouth hung open slightly as he stared.

I knew better. And, as I watched my fiancé holding another woman close to him, allowing her kisses, welcoming them, smiling with a foolish, fond delight, I also knew worse.

This was what he wanted. This, more or less, was what he had planned, or at least hoped for.

My eyes met his. His smile was tempered a little—he must have seen my anguish—as he said softly, "I have to take care of her. You do see that? I promised her. She doesn't have anyone else to love her. You understand?"

I did understand. That added to the horror of it. I couldn't even blame him. He had loved her as a child and he loved her still. I understood, and I loved him, but I couldn't live with him. I turned around and ran for my life.

It was my mistake to believe that all ghosts are of the dead. The living, too, leave ghosts behind them. If it is true the dead can't harm us, the same can certainly not be said of the living.

Sitting in my kitchen all alone as the night wore away and morning came on, I thought about the living and the dead in my life, eight years after Edward had gone, as I thought, out of my life forever. I wondered where he was now, what he was thinking, how he was feeling with Lucy Maria dead. It had been another mistake, I realized, to think that I was "over" him, or that he was out of my life, or ever could be, until both of us were dead. I was so lost in my thoughts that I did not notice the sounds of movement from another part of the house until my husband appeared in the doorway, in his dressing gown, asking sleepily if something was wrong.

I stared at him. For a moment he looked like a ghost to me, and I thought that if I waited he would disappear.

Unnalash

Tanith Lee

Dark thought built the castle, and sprites. And so it was like that, shadowed and soaring. But no one saw it, except when He called up a demon. And perhaps the demon marvelled and admired. Or did not.

Beyond the castle the rocks, from which it had been raised, ran sheer into the ocean. There was nothing else in sight. No ship came near.

He liked to regard the sea, from His high windows, some of which had coloured glass and so altered its appearance. Now a crimson sea, and now a sea so green it was like the primal water of the world. From high places of the towers too, He would study the stars, divining from them the fates of Mankind, about which He cared not at all.

Of course, being a magician, introspection pleased Him. And being powerful, lacking for nothing—for He might have gone anywhere He wished at once, or had anything He desired brought to Him in a flash—He was generally abstemious, almost frugal. Stars and skulls interested Him, rare gems of great or little worth, peculiar objects from the ocean, ancient books, poisons, poetry.

There was one other in the castle.

Years before, the magician had married. That is, He had had brought to Him a young woman He had seen and selected by magical means. She was utterly terrified, and after He had bound her to His will, she was a sort of ghost.

She died in childbirth one year later, perhaps after all frightened to death by the supernatural agents that waited on her.

The child lived. It was brought up by elementals, and so thought them nothing unusual. It was a girl. She was beautiful.

The magician did not see her until her thirteenth birthday. Then she was conducted into His presence in a vast long room whose open arches gave on sky, and sea below.

She wore a dark red dress with a narrow band of gold at the waist. She was slender and pale, with long hair of the black that is really blue. And her eyes were a blue almost black.

"Do you know who you are?" the magician asked her.

"They say," she meant the elementals, "that I am your daughter."

"Yes. It is so. And what is your name?"

"They call me Unnalash."

The magician nodded. He concurred with the name.

And Unnalash looked and saw a tall slender man with black hair and beard and black eyes hollow from gazing on other planets and past centuries, words of love He had never felt and liquids which killed. All of which was clearly written on His face.

She knew she must please Him, for the elementals were deeply afraid of Him and had communicated their fear. She knew He had created her and so she should be grateful.

"I am glad to see you, Unnalash," said the magician, her father. "We will meet sometimes in a garden I will make for you, and at night we will dine together."

Afterwards the elementals petted her, saying she had done well, He had liked her. But they were so insubstantial their caresses were like chill breezes, more annoying than pleasant. They were also mostly invisible. Unnalash tried never to be unkind to them.

She was lonely, but she had no name for her condition, and no method whereby to judge it. And so she did not know.

In this way too she did not know that she was beautiful, or even, really, that she was a woman; at least not what being a woman might mean.

And to Him . . . she was a gem. She was one of the rarer pieces of His collection. And He had fashioned her. She was His.

Possibly it occurred to Him that prophetically He had had the castle built for this very reason, the reason of Unnalash, to contain her, like a casket of stone. No one could get near. There were no ships. The lands of the earth were miles off.

His treasure. Safe.

He had the garden made in a day and a night.

It had walls—the sides of the castle, topped by towers—which were fifteen or thirty feet high, but up these for a wide distance grew dark green climbing plants and hedges of roses palest pink as the skins of babies. In the garden were lawns of clipped green grass which never grew and never faded, and which were starred by tiny flowers like coins of gold and silver, amethysts, carnelians, and petals of white china. There were walks of marble paving, bordered by hedges cut into fantastic shapes, up which wild grapes festooned themselves, in drops of jade. At the ends of the walks were pools where lilies bloomed, nenuphars the pale hot blue of the sky.

In the garden were creatures, perhaps summoned, or perhaps made. Bees gathered in the flowers making sounds like tiny zithers. Grasshoppers buzzed in the bushes. Birds flew from the ornamental trees to the arches of filigreed stone, but never farther, never away. Frogs chirped by the pools. A large tortoise, like a carapaced pebble, lived in the shade of a marigold tree.

All these things would come to Unnalash and allow her to touch and talk to them. They did not, however, speak.

The elementals, too, ceased to say very much to Unnalash, beyond the basic politenesses. She realized quickly that her father, the magician, had restricted them. For now, her dialogues were to be with Him.

Sometimes in the garden, she became aware that He looked down on her from one of the towers. At first she had raised her hand in timid greeting. But He did not acknowledge the gesture, and so she ceased to offer it.

Now and then He would enter the garden, in the cool of the day, and walk about with her, instructing her in the nature of the plants and the animals. Or occasionally He arrived in the earliest morning, and she must hurry down to be with Him.

Aside from His lessons to her on the flora and fauna of the enclosed garden, the magician told His daughter of the lands of the world, which He spoke of as if they had passed away. To begin with, she thought that they had, and once she asked Him what had become of them—for she found them interesting and varied and unremittingly strange. The magician informed Unnalash that the world still existed, but she would never see it. She did not question why not, for obviously it was His will.

In the evenings frequently they dined together, and after they had dined, usually on very ordinary, simple food, and water in long golden goblets set with crystals, He would read to her from His books. He had a sonorous yet oddly flat voice. With this He hypnotized her, so that whatever He taught her or read to her, she could not help but afterwards remember.

Some of the teachings were very cruel, involving death.

The magician told His daughter she had no need to fear death. By His arts, and by skills He would teach her, she would always remain young and beautiful. And so she learned that she was both.

Now and then, for long periods, Unnalash did not see the

magician. He was closeted in His apartments engaged upon some experiment or study.

But when she was fifteen, He gave her a ring of gold and quicksilver—which by sorcery He was able to fix—and in the ring was a large ruby.

"You will always be mine," said the magician. "I fathered you and made you."

Unnalash of course consented to His words and His premise. What else did she know?

He had never touched her, but now He placed His dry thin hand upon her head. Unnalash understood that she was honoured by being the possession of her father.

And still she had found no word for loneliness.

One day, when she was seventeen, Unnalash sat reading in an arbour of roses. Her father had taught her to read by means of a smooth stone which, placed under her pillow, whispered to her as she slept. The book was in six alternating chapters. Three described fair, chaste, virtuous women, whose lives were redolent of sweetness. And the other three, wicked women, who practiced evilly and perished horribly. Unnalash was repelled by these latter chapters and paused continually, to rest her mind by looking about the garden.

The magician had locked Himself away to become involved in some great occult conjunction of planets. She had not seen Him for three days and nights. But she did not miss her father.

Although she had called to the tortoise, and it had come, and let her caress its shining shield, it had then gone away again. The feathered things and insects busied themselves singing. The elementals never ventured in the garden.

Unnalash sighed. She was—but there was no word. And anyway, by now, it had become herself.

Then a shadow fell across the lawns. It was not the perpetual psychic shadow of the castle, which was always there, to one side or the other.

No, it was the reflection, cast upon the ground, of a huge bird.

Unnalash stared up into the orb, or rather the rectangle of blue sky.

And the bird passed again.

Was it a gull? Surely, too vast, its wings enormous—an eagle. It must be that. For her reading and her father's lessons had given her many answers to many questions, and not all of them correct.

But Unnalash, because she was accustomed to the birds of the garden which came to her when she called, called now to this one. And sure enough, the bird circled once more over the garden, and then moved floating down, with only two or three gigantic beats of its wings to guide it.

It settled lightly and perfectly before the arbour.

How curious a bird it was.

Unnalash gazed. And firstly from her reading, and then from the form of her father the magician, she came to see that this too was a man, but a man with wings.

It seems, although He had been so careful to lock her up, within high, unbreachable walls, out on the ocean, miles from land, the wise magician had not known or learned or thought of such a thing.

"You called to me," said the winged man, "and so I came down into this place. Flying is my joy. I hunt the sea for fish. I see their glitter and I dive and catch them, and then I eat them on the wing. Or I return to an island, and there I rest. I alight nowhere without a reason. Why am I here?" And then, having looked at Unnalash a long while, he said, "You are the reason I am here."

Unnalash had not ever been lessoned to be bashful. But now she lowered her eyes, for the winged man astonished her.

He was tall, like her father, but otherwise quite unlike. The wings were white, but the skin of the winged man was dark gold in colour and stretched on tablets of musculature, so that he resembled a statue in a book. And this, feather and muscle and skin, was all he wore, for he was naked. The hair on his head was like the gold in the castle and the gold in the ring of Unnalash. And at his groin it was the same shade. And there was too a portion of anatomy which, in books, Unnalash had glimpsed before. She did not understand it.

"Are you a demon?" asked Unnalash. For—again in books—she had been shown man-like beings with wings.

The winged man shook his head and laughed pitilessly.

"I? I am Ravire. I am myself."

"Ravire," said Unnalash.

"How new my name sounds when you say it. Say it again."

So Unnalash said his name a second time.

"Never," said the winged man, Ravire, "have I seen a woman like you. You are most beautiful. You are too beautiful, and yet, one does not want to change you."

"My father made me," said Unnalash, sadly. Perhaps she did not know she sounded sad.

"No, no," said Ravire, in any case. "You made yourself. In the egg—or in the womb, for you wingless ones are different. Probably you are like your mother."

"My . . . mother?" inquired Unnalash.

But Ravire did not enlighten her further. He stepped close, and a warm wild scent came from him, and the tip of his right wing brushed her. Unnalash trembled, and did not know why.

"You cannot bewitch me," she said. "I am my father's."

"No," said Ravire. "Now you are mine."

Unnalash was confused, and for the first time in her life two tears fell from her eyes.

Ravire caught them with the edges of his fingers. He drank them.

Then he drew her aside, into the arbour, where the roses curved deeply over their heads and they could not be seen even by one looking from a tower.

* * *

Ravire taught Unnalash different matters. He taught her how he was. A prince of an isle in the sea, far off. Of a palace of caves and green fern, and the garden of the ocean. How he pursued the fish like silver and the fish like emeralds, and ate them up, and they became himself, and how, when he excreted, he buried these faeces honourably, for they were the dead.

He told her too how he had made love to women, of his kind, and of hers. He showed her.

He did not disrobe her. He was decorous, and touched her through her clothes, but his hands were fires, feathers, waters, and inner sounds. She did not know that this was sin, for though the chapters in the books had spoken of chastity and carnal knowledge, she had never grasped what either state must be. He made love to her, he possessed her. Such terrible pain, such bliss.

Everything passed in an afternoon, as perhaps elsewhere in other gardens.

When the sun began to light upon the western walls, Unnalash urged Ravire to be gone.

"My father has told me, I must never see or know anyone save Himself, and the creatures of the castle."

"Will you obey him now?" asked Ravire.

"I am powerless," said Unnalash.

"Tell him nothing, do not confess. I will visit you tomorrow."

"Come at midday," she said. "Fly to that tower there. My chamber is there and I will send my attendants away. He will not see, for He avoids the heat of noon."

So duplicitous she had become at once. But she was swift at learning. She had had two excellent teachers.

For seven days, Ravire came to Unnalash, from behind the noonday sun.

Perhaps he would have tired of her. He had the world, and she was fixed, as if chained down. But for seven days, he did not tire. And as he arrived, he took the fish from the water

and ate them, so he bore into her room the perfume of the
sea. He lay on her, and fanned with his wings as he
achieved ecstasy. They seemed both to fly then, there in the
chamber in the rock.

They were naked together now. Gold and quicksilver.
Like the ring with the ruby heart.

And for those seven days, the magician was at His stud-
ies, the great conjunction holding Him in His apartment of
skulls and poisons and paper love.

"Tonight we will dine together, Unnalash," said the magician, crossing the shades of the evening garden.

Unnalash sat before an arch of pierced stone, reading a
book on the Beasts of the Zodiac.

She looked up meekly, and He saw her face. It was
masked as if with a pod of beaten bronze, such an altered
face, so new.

He guessed at once, as if trumpets had resounded from
the walls, she was no longer His.

"How have you passed the time?" He asked therefore,
almost playfully. She did not recognize any warning,
though He was never playful before in her life.

"I have read, Father."

"You must have learned very much. When we have eaten
our meal, you shall come up to my apartment and tell me of
it."

Unnalash looked at Him now covertly, for never previously had He taken her into His rooms of magic. But she
was only obedient, always, until now, and now only in one
way had she failed.

While they dined, a serpent thought came to Unnalash,
and queried of her if she might not tell the magician, despite
everything, that a winged man had ventured into the garden, that he was beautiful—now she had fathomed the
term—and pure, unusual as some great fish-eagle, of interest, then. But Unnalash knew to reply to the serpent: No. It

was this intermittent conflict in her, maybe, which produced the effect of a mask.

When the elementals had served them the last of the meat and fruit, and the last trickle of water, they were alone, the father and His daughter.

"We will go up now."

And so they left the meal unfinished, and this too had never happened before.

They ascended into the magician's topmost towers.

On the stairways were three heads with flaming eyes which watched them come, and before the tall door was a sword with a dripping point which, as the magician approached, turned aside.

Unnalash was not terrified. No one had ever taught her that she should be. Yet she felt—unease.

The door opened. He spoke a word, and lamps sprung alight with a cool clear gleam.

A tree grew through one wall, but it was a tree of bones. From it hung the skin of an enormous snake, and that of a lion.

Darkness filled the coloured windows, but the lamps found glints in them like jewels in a mine, rose red and indigo and umbrous green.

On a stand of brass was the skull of a creature which had walked the world before men, and in its forehead was set a large yellow pearl. Elsewhere were other skeleton items and heads of all types, of bone and stone, wood and alabaster and agate. Shells and corals rested passively, while in phials and bottles bubbled liquors of appalling death. And on the walls, past which the lamps continually floated up and down, were scrolls in jars and books with clasps of gold.

On a huge table of granite balanced a giant scales made of ebony and silver. In one side lay a white feather.

Unnalash started when she saw it.

Below the scales, held open by four rat skulls encased in orichalc, was a paper with a poem written on it.

"These poets," said the magician, "when they speak of

love, it is always in vain. They write from the glorious agony of denial. For fulfillment in anything is disastrous. Search must be eternal, refusal constant. Yet," He added, "I have loved you, Unnalash. And out of your proper love for me, grant me one thing."

Unnalash murmured that she would.

"One hair of your head," He told her. "Pluck it yourself."

Unnalash reached up and plucked a hair of her black-blue tresses. It hurt her sharply, as if a red-hot pin had been run into her scalp.

The magician took the hair and dropped it into the empty dish of the scales.

At once, this dish went crashing down onto the table and the feather danced up in the air.

Unnalash gave a savage, involuntary cry.

"Did you suppose," He said, "that you could swindle me? I have mirrors by means of which I can see inside the sinews of your heart. Do you think I cannot delve into your mind? You have betrayed me. You have consorted with a *gull*."

Unnalash saw a light had come into the coloured windows. It was the moon rising on the sea.

It seemed to her this light was her judge, that it shone on her and she had no recourse.

"Come to the window," He said, "my faithless daughter."

And at His words the middle casement flew open wide, and there was space with the white moon lying on it, and the black sea glittering beneath.

Unnalash knew terror, at last, although it had never been taught to her. Then her father picked her up in His arms, and she knew shame, for He had only touched her once before, and Ravire had touched her in all ways that are possible.

But then every emotion blended and ended in a searing conflagration of animal fear. For it came to her what He was about to do.

"No—" she cried.

"You are not mine," said the magician, and He cast her from the window, threw her out into the great hole of air and sky.

Unnalash fell, spinning and screaming in a flail of hair, against the rising of the moon.

Until, from the wide window, He stretched forth His hand, and a brazen ray shot from His fingers and caught her as she spun. And she was gone. Unnalash had vanished.

Through the air, and into the black wet embers of the sea, tumbled a golden fish. This now was Unnalash. And this broke the surface of the water like a talisman flung from heaven.

And as the waves closed on her and she breathed in them, she thought: *What has become of me?*

Other fish swam through the sea, great fish, and small, like stars. They did not communicate with Unnalash, for even though she had their form, she was not one of their tribe. She was still herself, caged in a fish's shape, breathing and seeing as a fish does, thinking in a dim lost way that was neither fish-like nor human.

All night she drifted about, sometimes turning herself in a circle, for instinctively she kept to the places where the rocks of the castle went down into the water. All night she asked herself, *What has become of me?* Over and over.

The night had no end. But then it ended. The sun rose. The water changed to a thin bright green, and Unnalash darted up towards the sun, and broke the weave of the ocean. But she could not breathe in the air now, so she went down again, two or three slim layers of water down, and floated there, and drifted, and turned herself about, though she had almost forgotten now what the rocks meant.

And she thought once, *He will forgive me.* But she was not certain who this was.

*   *   *

The sun ascended to the top of the sky. And from out of the sun came arrowing a golden shape on broad white wings.

As he drove across the sea, Ravire dived and dipped and gathered up a silver fish and ate it alive in the air.

Then he flew near the castle, towards the special window. But as he swept close, he saw the castle was no longer that at all. It was only a cliff, faceless, without towers, without even a cave or channel to enter by. And when he dared it and pressed against the rock, there was a lion standing on a ledge above. It had a skull for a face and a mane of snakes. It snarled, and from its mouth burst flames.

Ravire leapt away. Unnalash had told him her father was a magician, and obviously their idyl was done.

More than pain, Ravire experienced great anger, jealous rage, for he now was as powerless as she.

And as he soared down the shuttered cliff, he saw something burn in the ocean below.

It was a fish of gold, which had come up to the very surface, as if seeking him. Surely, the magician's prize, perhaps some pet he fed by his own fingers from the high windows that were no more.

Ravire stooped on sailing wings and seized the golden fish in both his hands. He bore it to his lips as if to kiss, and swallowed it whole.

Full of rage and frustration—and of love, although he did not know it, or how—Ravire flew away across the sea.

Sometimes he felt a peculiar fluttering under his heart. But finally this stilled. Then there was a sort of deadness there, as if he had received a blow.

At sunset, he came to the island where most often he rested. Flat plains rose into woods, and above these was a cone, a mountain whose top was stippled with white ice. All the island now was gold, and it reminded him of how he had devoured the magician's fish. At least he had had that.

As he flew inland, men and women came out of their

little villages in the honey light, to point to him and make gestures of homage. For here, he was venerated as a demon, or perhaps a god.

Ravire went up to his eyrie under the mountain, to the palace of caves hung with green ivy and ferns. He drank from the fountain which glimmered sunlit from the rock.

The sun sank slowly behind the mountain cone. Melancholy sank upon Ravire.

No one could come up to him here, save his own kind, who generally lived elsewhere. It was a fastness beyond assault. Hawks circled the sky and dropped after the sun, but there was no one else.

The winged man slept in the highest cave, and when he woke it was the twilight before dawn, with the last star like a candle on the plain beneath.

The numbness was still under his heart. He did not want anything, not to eat or drink, not even to urinate or defecate. The healthy functions of his body were frozen to stone.

Ravire rose angrily into the air, and soared down the length of the mountain.

He skimmed the woods of cedar and pine and cinnamon, and brushed the high corn of the plain with his wings.

As the light began to return, three girls moved out of a village with jars for a well. One of these girls was paleskinned with hair like coal.

Ravire sailed towards them, a spear in flight, and the girls wailed and let go their water jars. Two ran away, but the dark girl, she only fell to her knees and covered her face. Ravire grasped her. He lifted her up in the air and flew with her back to his cave-castle, and there he held her whimpering, in his arms, staring at her with his eyes and kissing her, until she was in a trance. Then he lay over her mercilessly. She screamed again, with hurt, and he fanned with his wings in ecstasy.

Afterwards he was better. The numbness had left him. He ate and drank from the larder of the mountain and performed the other natural functions in his normal ritualistic way.

The girl lay like one dead.

She lay like this for months, although he brought her berries to eat and foods he stole from the villages or which they left out for him as offerings. He did not again make love to her. She was not like Unnalash. Nor did he return her to her home, for she had become inert and curiously heavy.

Presently he saw why. Her belly swelled.

Ravire touched her quite gently and she turned her head away.

When her labour began, then he did take her, with great awkwardness, down the mountain, and she shrieked yet again in his arms.

He left her at a village where there were midwives, and from the air, he watched the child brought out alive, but the girl had died.

Then an enormous disgust came over him.

He rose up high and flew away, away to other places where his own kind lived.

Among the villages, the girl was reared with care. They knew precisely who she was. They waited on her like servants, slaves, and talked to her in low voices. They did not touch her past the age of four.

"She is not like him," they said.

But this they took as a mark of his sagacity, their demon-god, a test he had set them.

They became aware, as the years went by without a sighting, that he was gone, and then they were afraid they had displeased him. And on the girl, his daughter, they lavished everything they might, for his sake. They did not presume to give her a name.

Then at last, when she was thirteen, they saw their error.

They dressed her in a white dress with a garland of roses for her hair red as the flood of her mother's blood. They conducted her up from the plains in a procession in the dusk, with lighted torches and coloured lamps, scattering incense and singing. They took her as high up the cone as they were able, which was actually not very far, just clear of the woods of cinnamon and pine and cedar. They put her on a bare rock like a throne, and laid the skins of leopards over her lap to keep her warm. And then they went away.

The girl sat there quietly for a few hours, and then she heard the noise of huge wings, and she looked up, and got to her feet.

Ravire had come back, perhaps scenting the villagers' mystery, perhaps only because now he had been long enough with his own kind that they had come to bore him once more. And so it was the other way about; the villagers had scented his return, like burning on the wind.

He alighted close to where she stood.

She saw a tall and golden man like bronze in the after-light, his white wings wide, and written in his face a life of fishing waters, flying skies, preying and rapine, this world and its future.

"Do you know who you are?" Ravire asked her.

"They say," she meant the villagers, "I am your daughter."

"Yes, it is so."

Her skin was pale, and her hair the black that is blue and her eyes the blue that is black. She was exact in all details. "What is your name?" he said.

"They said that you would name me."

"I do. You are Unnalash."

The winged man nodded.

And Unnalash bowed her head.

She knew she must please him, for the villagers were deeply afraid of him and had communicated their fear. She knew he had created her and so she should be grateful.

"I am glad to see you, Unnalash," said Ravire, her father.

And He spread His wings, and took her up to His castle of green caves.

Return

Patrick Nielsen Hayden

True Thomas, the Rhymer, was kidnapped by the Queen of Elfland and held there for years uncounted, never aging. Then one day, suddenly and quite without ceremony, he finds himself thrown back into the real world to live and die like a normal human being. He lands, of course, on his harp.

Poor Thomas sits there in the middle of a meadow, nursing his broken instrument, when up walks a young woman previously unknown to him.

"I know you," she tells him. "You're Thomas the Rhymer. See, I even know your ballad."

"My ballad?" he says.

She sings a verse. "Got it off a Steeleye Span record," she explains. "I'm not surprised you haven't heard it—you were gone long enough. I've been looking for you longer than a twelvemonth and a day."

"Record?" murmurs Thomas. He feels stupid. Who is this woman who knows all about him from a song? He's the one who writes the songs.

"Oh, you know, folk rock," she says. "Milkmaids and

battle laments. Not great stuff but it's about all we had after you cut out. Do you know how tired we got of looking for you? One minute it's Thomas this and Thomas that and the next minute, poof, you're gone. I guess Elfland must have been pretty good, hey?"

"Beautiful and terrible," says Thomas. "You can't possibly know."

"Oh, horseshit," she says. Thomas nearly drops his harp. Young ladies don't talk like that in the ballads he comes from. "Horseshit," she repeats. "Guys your age all talk that way. Like we can't possibly know what you've been through. I thought you'd be different."

"I'm sorry," says Thomas. "I'm just a minstrel."

"Yeah, sure," she says. "That's why you have your own ballad, because you're just a minstrel. You're the Rhymer. Stardust, golden."

Thomas looks miserable. "I'm not what I was," he says lamely. "I can't lie to you."

"Oh, that's right, she ran that number on you," she says. "They're good at that, it's what they do." She looks away for a long moment, withdrawing into her down jacket and shaking her head, then turns back. "Hey, look, do you need a cup of coffee or something? There's a mall we can eat in right down the road. We could talk."

True Thomas looks directly up at her at last. She's eager, she really wants to know, and she knows he's connected somehow. Slowly, dark eyes never leaving hers, he stands up.

"You think you want magic, but you don't," he says. "Enchantment is a kind of curse. You never get over it. Not to the end of your days." As he lurches to his full height his hair and cloak snap back in the sudden wind and the sun flashes off the remaining strings of his harp and his hair and the cloak and the strings all shimmer and tremble, like some greater and more awful thing trying to enter the world. His voice rises, breaks. "Do you want to be like me?" He staggers forward and for a brief moment it appears his billowing cloak will engulf her whole in its folds.

"Of course I don't want to be like you," she says. "But it would have been nice to have a choice. You say enchantment is a curse? Of course it is. So are life and work and being in love, at the wrong time and in the wrong measure." She takes a breath. "You took all the magic that wasn't nailed down and had grand adventures and left the rest of us here in the boring everyday world to talk about you and try to figure it all out, and now you want us to drop the subject? You think you *invented* being the lifelong victim of a faerie curse? You go to hell, True Thomas."

Thomas appears to deflate, like a collapsing balloon. The billows of his cloak fall, drooping around him like beagle ears.

"Or come along with me. The coffee shop's right over that way. Up to you."

Far away, Thomas hears on the wind high, silvery laughter.

Arm in arm with the Queen of Elfland's daughter, True Thomas, the Rhymer, trudges down the road to the mall. And reflects, not for the first time, on the strange revenge of elves.

Gravity

Pat Schneider

Falling into gravity
allows us to know weight.

—BETH GOREN

A dream uninterpreted
is a letter unopened.

—TALMUD

I am a small man without a head
standing in the rain. I laugh
at the woman in the doorway
who worries that I will get rain
in my face. She doesn't understand.

I am a young woman walking
with a man who has no head.
He is pleasant enough,
but it is raining. I take
the cuff of his collar in my hand
and pull him away. I want to go.
I do not want to stand in the rain
any longer under the eyes
of the woman in the doorway
who will not shut her mouth.

I am a woman in a doorway.
There is a little man outside.
He has no head. His neck

is open, and hollow. It receives
rain. The woman beside him
is young. She grabs him
by his collar and pulls him along,
but she is not angry.
Nor does she seem unkind.
They both laugh at me when I say
to her, you are letting rain
fall on his face. I guess
it was a stupid thing to say,
but how do you say rain
is getting into his chest cavity?
They are leaving. I should have
asked them in, out of the weather.
I'm sorry they are going,
but I'm glad when they are gone.

I am a dreamer dreaming
myself standing in a doorway,
dreaming a dwarf with no head,
a young woman taking him away.

I am a woman remembering
a dream, trying to read
the letter. It is no use.
The language is foreign.
It comes from the place
where one falls into gravity
and knows weight.
I am a woman remembering a dream
and wanting to go back there
into that rain again.

To Scale

Nancy Kress

When you get home on Saturday night, your father is drunk
again. He's a polite drunk; nothing in the living room is
broken. There's only the spreading stain of his last whiskey
on the worn carpet beside the overturned glass. You gaze
down at the small, wispy man lying there unconscious, the
hems of his polyester suit pants twisted up over white sweat
socks to reveal the skinny, hairy ankles underneath. One
shoe off, one shoe on, diddle-diddle-dumpling my dad
John. Everyone says you are the spitting image of him at
your age—everybody, that is, who ever notices either of
you. Usually you try to avoid mirrors. You are seventeen.

After you get him into bed—he's very light—you scrub
hard at the whiskey spill on the roses-on-black carpet. It
was your mother's. The smell disappears, replaced by pine-
scented ammonia like hospitalized trees, but the petals of
one rose stay discolored no matter what you do. Finally you
give up and turn out the living room lamp.

It's 11:00 P.M. Not very late; you didn't stay long in town.
Just went to the hardware store, had a hamburger, drove
around awhile in the battered pickup, watching couples

whose names you know from school walking and laughing
on the summer streets. Then home again, because where
else was there to go?

There isn't anywhere else now, either. But you're restless.
You can't sleep this early. You go through the kitchen out
onto the porch, banging the screen door behind you.

A little wind murmurs in the trees. You put your hands on
the splintery porch railing and lean out into the night. It
smells of wild thyme, hemlock, mysteries. But through the
open bedroom window comes the sound of your father's
snoring, arrhythmic and faltering. You go down the steps
and start across the weedy lawn.

Here, the stars are magnificent: sharp and clean in a
moonless sky. You tip your head back to study them as you
walk. Halfway to the road, a huge black shape hurls out of
the darkness straight at your throat.

You scream and throw up one arm. The shape hits and
you both go down. You scream again, a high-pitched shriek
that echoes off something, and try to roll away from the
beast's jaws. Someone shouts, "King! King! Here, boy!
Yo!"

The dog hesitates, then opens its mouth and snarls at you.
From over your own upflung arm you see its eyes glow.
Starlight reflects off its teeth. Frantically you keep rolling,
but then the dog turns and trots across the road, where the
voice is still yelling, "Yo! King, yo!"

Shakily you get to your feet. Mr. Dazuki strolls up, flicking cigarette ashes. "He get you?"

Your jeans are torn at the knee. Your arm is bloody, but
that's from scraping the ground. "No," you say. And then,
"Yes!"

"He break the skin?"

"No."

"Then you're all right," Dazuki says casually, and turns
to leave. On the other side of the road he half turns. You can
hear his grin in the darkness. "Don't be such a wimp, boy.
Dogs're only afraid of you if you're afraid of them."

You are shaking too bad to risk an answer. You force

yourself to walk slowly. Back inside your house, you lock the door and then stand for a long time against the refrigerator, your cheek pressed to its smooth coolness.

When your breathing has slowed, you go through the basement door down to the cellar.

Forty years ago the cellar had been subdivided into a maze of small rooms. Some have concrete or plywood walls; a few are walled in hard, bare dirt. You go past the discarded furniture, the broken washer/dryer set, the chamber with the sad piles of frayed rope and rusted fishing poles and paint cans whose contents have congealed into lumps of Slate Blue or Western Sky. Nobody but you ever goes down here.

At the far end of the house, in a cool windowless room that once was your mother's fruit cellar, you turn on bright 200-watt bulbs wired into overhead sockets. The room springs into light. It is about twelve feet square, but less than half of the floor space is left. The rest is occupied by the dollhouse.

It started with the fruit shelves. After your mother died, you ate one jar of her preserves every day, until they were all gone. Strawberry jam, apple butter, peach jelly, stewed rhubarb. Sometimes you got queasy from so much sweetness. Your stomach felt like a hard taut drum, and that made you a little less empty. But then the fruit ran out. The shelves were bare.

You covered them with her collection of miniature glass animals: swans and rabbits and horses of cheap colored glass, bought at state fairs or school carnivals. They looked awful on the bare, splintery shelves, so you brought in weeds and rocks and made a miniature forest. On the central shelf you put some dollhouse furniture you'd found in a box at the back of her closet. It looked old. You wanted to make it look better, so you found a scrap of carpet for a miniature rug. You found a doll's tea set at the Wal-Mart. You built a little table.

When the fruit shelves were full, you had no more reason to stay down here.

You built another row of shelves in front of the first. You've always been good with your hands, even at twelve. The shelves had a professional look. Making tiny furniture for each shelf wasn't hard. The scale was easy to work with, easier than real furniture would have been. You found you could make it look exactly how you saw it in your mind.

When you were fourteen, you read about a craft fair in the next town. You took your father's truck and drove there, even though fourteen is too young to drive legally in this state. Already your father didn't notice.

Miniature dishes for sale. Pillows, mailboxes, tea towels, cat bowls, weather vanes, scythes, doorknobs, toothpaste tubes, televisions, Tiffany glass, carpenter's chests. You couldn't believe it. You had seven dollars in your jeans. You bought a package of Fimo dough, a pamphlet on electrifying dollhouses, and a set of three tiny blue canning jars filled with miniature jelly.

By now the dollhouse is eleven or twelve layers deep. You built each one out in front of the next, with no way through except unseen doorways seven inches high. Official miniature scale is one inch to one foot. Each layer reaches to the ceiling and has twelve floors, with several rooms on each floor. Some rooms are furnished with cheap plastic dollhouse furniture you found in bulk at a factory closeout, dozens of pieces to the two-dollar pound. Some are furnished with simple, straight-lined beds and tables of balsa which you can turn out three to the afternoon. Some are elaborate period rooms over which you worked for months, with furnishings as authentic as you could devise or could buy mail-order. You work twenty hours a week at Corey Lumber for twice minimum wage, forty hours a week in the summer; Mr. Corey feels sorry for you. Your father never asks what you do with your money.

Somewhere in the impenetrable maze of tiny rooms is a Georgian drawing room with silver chandelier and grand piano from Think Small. Somewhere is a Shaker dining room with spare, clean lines in satiny cherry. Somewhere is a Tidewater Virginia bedroom, copied from a picture in

Nutshell News, with blue velvet hangings, inlaid table, and blue delftware on the polished highboy. You will never see these rooms again; they've been covered over by newer layers. You don't have to see them again. You know they're there, hidden and unreachable. Untouched. Safe.

You pick up a piece of 32-gauge, two-conductor stranded wire and a 25-watt pencil-tip soldering iron from your workbench. You are wiring a room for a pair of matching coach lights. They go well with a six-inch teak table you found cheap at a garage sale. Some kid had thoughtlessly carved HD across its top, but you can sand and restain that. The three matching side chairs are also restorable. You have learned to reupholster seats one and a quarter inches wide.

School lets out in mid-June. You work full-time at the lumberyard. Your father gets up after you've left the house for his drive into the city, where he works as a data-entry clerk. You get home before he does, fix something to eat, leave his food in a covered dish in the oven, and go to the basement. By the time you come up, he is sitting in the living room, lights off in the summer dusk, drinking. His speech is very careful.

"Hello, son."

"Hi, Dad."

"How was work?"

"Good," you say, on your way out.

"Going out?"

"Gotta meet some friends," you say, which is a laugh. But he nods eagerly, pleased you have such a social life. When you come home at ten or eleven, he's passed out.

This is the only way, you think, that either of you can bear it. Any of it. Most of the time, you don't think about it.

In July a girl comes into the lumberyard—not a woman looking for newel posts or bathroom tiles, but a girl your own age, with high teased bangs and long earrings and Lycra shorts. This is so rare in the lumberyard that you stare at her. She catches you.

"What're you staring at?"

"Nothing," you say. You feel yourself blush.

"Yeah? You saying I'm nothing?"

"No, I . . . no, you . . ." You wait to see if more words will emerge, but no more do. Now she stares at you, challenging and sulky. You remember that you don't like this kind of girl. She is the kind who combs her hair all class period, gives teachers the finger, sneers at you if you answer in history, the only class you like. You start to turn away, but she speaks to you again.

"You got a car? Want to drive me home after this dump closes?"

You hear yourself say, "Sure."

It turns out she is Mr. Corey's niece, sent to live with him for the summer. She works the register afternoons. You suspect she's been sent away from her own town because her family can't cope with her, and that Mr. Corey's taken her in out of the same sympathy that made him pay you more than he had to. You've never known how to think about that extra money, and you don't know how to think about Sally Corey, either. You still don't like her. But she tosses her head at the register and rolls her eyes at customers behind their backs and sticks out her ass when she dances in place between sales, and you feel a warm sweet hardness when you look at her. By the end of the week you have driven her to a roadside bar where neither of you got served, out to the lake, and to a drive-through ice cream place.

"Hey, let me see where you live," she says, for the third or fourth time. "What are you, too poor or something?"

"No," you say. At that moment, as in several others, you hate her. But she turns on the pickup's front seat and looks at you sideways over the lipstick she's smearing on her mouth, and maybe it's not hatred after all.

"Then what?" she demands. "What is it with you? You a fag?"

"No!"

"Then take me home with you. You said no one's there but your old man."

"He'll hear us."

"Not if he's *asleep*," she says with exaggerated patience. "We'll go downcellar or something. Don't you have a cellar?"

"No."

"Well, then, the backyard." She lays a hand on your thigh, very high, and something explodes inside your chest. You start the truck. Sally grins.

At home, your father's silhouette is visible through the living room window. The television is on; sharp barks of canned laughter drift into the night like gunfire. You lead Sally in through the kitchen door, finger on your lips, and down the basement stairs. You lock the basement door behind you with a wooden bar you installed yourself.

In the first of the tiny cellar rooms, across from the broken Westinghouse washer, is an old sofa. You and Sally fall on it as if gravity had just been invented.

She tastes of wild thyme, strawberries, mystery. After several minutes of kissing and wild grabbing, she pushes you away and unbuttons her blouse. You think you might faint. Her breasts are big, creamy-looking, with wide dark nipples. You touch them just as she reaches for the zipper on your jeans. You forget to listen for footsteps above. You forget everything.

But later, afterwards, something is wrong. She rolls lazily to her feet and looks down at you, splayed across the couch, gloriously empty.

"That's it?" she says. "*That?*"

You are apparently supposed to do something more. Shame grips you as you realize this. You can't think of anything more, can't imagine what else is supposed to happen. Her glare says this stupidity is your fault. You stare at her dumbly.

"What about *me*?" she demands. "Huh?"

What about her? She was there, wasn't she? Does that

mean she didn't like it? That you—oh, God—did it wrong somehow? How? Can she tell you were a virgin? You go on lying across the sofa, a broken spring pressing into the small of your back, helpless as an overturned beetle.

"*Christ,*" Sally says contemptuously. She drags her blouse across her chest and flounces off. You expect her to climb the steps, but instead she moves into the next room, idly flicking light switches and peering around.

In a second you are on your feet. But you're dizzy from getting up too fast, and your fallen jeans hobble your ankles. By the time you catch her, she has reached the fruit cellar and switched on the light.

"Jesus, Mary, and Joseph!" She stares at the looming density of the dollhouse. Only one shelf of the current outermost layer is still empty. "*You* do this?"

You can't answer. Sally fingers a miniature plastic chair, a stuffed cat, a tiny rolling pin from Thumbelina's. She walks to your workbench. You have been antiquing a pre-made Chippendale sofa: darkening the fabric with tea, wearing out the armrests with fine steel wool. Vaseline, you have discovered, makes wonderful grease stains on the sofa back.

Sally starts to laugh. She turns to you, holding the Chippendale, her face twisted under her smeared makeup. "Doll furniture! He plays with little dollies! So *that's* why your prick is so itty-bitty!"

You close your eyes. Her laughter goes on and on. You can't move. This is the end of your life. You will never be able to move again. It's all arrived here together, in this moment, under the 200-watt bulbs, in the sound of this girl's ugly laughter. The kids at school who don't know you're alive (but they will now, when Sally meets them and spreads this around), your father's distaste for you because you're not good enough, the wussy way you're terrified of King's teeth, the endless days where the only words anyone ever says to you are "Twenty-pound bag of peat moss." Or "Hello, son." And the two are the same words.

A howl escapes your lips. You don't know it's going to happen until it does, and at the sound of it your eyes fly open. Something has left you, gone out on the howl—you can feel it by its absence. Something palpable as the hiss of escaping gas under boiler pressure. You can feel it go.

Sally is gone.

At first you think she's gone back upstairs. But the wooden bar at the top of the steps is still in place. You grope your way back downstairs and stare at the dollhouse.

The plastic chair is tipped over, and the tiny rug askew, as if Sally had just dumped them contemptuously back into their miniature room. You look closer. There are tiny scuff marks on the floor beneath the far doorway, the one leading into the dollhouse's inner regions.

The next morning Mr. Corey meets you at the lumberyard gate. "Billy, what time did you bring Sally home last night?"

You are amazed how easily you lie. "About nine-thirty. She wanted me to drop her off at the corner, so I did."

Mr. Corey doesn't seem surprised by this. "Do you know who she was meeting there?"

"No," you say.

The corners of his mouth droop. "Well, she'll be home when she's ready, I guess. It's not as if it's the first time." After a moment he adds hopelessly, "I knew you'd be too good for her."

You have nothing to say to this.

When you get home from work there is blood on the porch steps. Heart hammering, you start through the kitchen towards the cellar stairs, but your father calls to you from the living room.

"It's okay, son. Just a flesh wound."

He is sitting in the rocker, his hand wrapped in a white pillowcase gone gray from washing. The whiskey bottle is a new one, its paper seal lying on the table beside his glass.

The glass is unbroken. Your father's face looks pale and unhealthy. "I didn't see the dog in time."

"King? King attacked you?" A part of your mind realizes that these are the first nonstandard sentences the two of you have exchanged in weeks.

"Is that the dog's name?" your father says blearily.

"Did he break the skin?"

He nods. You feel rage just begin to simmer, somewhere below your diaphragm. It feels good. "Then we can sue the bastard! I'll call the police!"

"Oh, no," your father says. He fumbles for his glass. "Oh, no, son . . . that's not necessary. No." He looks at you then, for the first time, a look of dumb beseeching undercut by stubbornness. He sips his whiskey.

"You won't sue," you say slowly. "Because then you'd have to go to court, have to stay sober—"

Your father looks frightened. Not the terror with which he must have met King's attack, but a muzzy, weary fear. That you will finish your sentence. That you will say something irrevocable. That you, his son, will actually talk to him.

You fall silent.

He says, "Going out, son?"

You say, your voice thick, "Gotta see some friends."

On the porch, you start for the truck. Something growls from the hedge. King barks and breaks cover, rushing at you. You jump back inside and slam the door. After a minute, when you can, you pound your fists against the refrigerator, which rattles and groans.

Your father, who must surely hear you, is silent in the living room.

You go down the cellar stairs. You don't even turn on any lights. In front of the dollhouse, you close your eyes and howl.

The suffocating anger leaves you, steam from a kettle. Coolness comes, a satiny enameled coolness like perfect lacquer.

From somewhere deep inside the dollhouse comes a faint, high-pitched bark.

You turn on the overhead bulbs and peer inside as far as you can. It appears that three layers in, a wing chair might be overturned, but it's hard to be sure. Two layers in, a hunting print from Mini Splendored Thing is askew on a wall.

At the foot of the cellar stairs you notice something white. It's Sally's cotton panties, kicked into a corner. You don't remember the kicking. The panties aren't what you expect from hasty scans of *Playboy* at the Convenient Mart, not black lace or red satin or anything. They're white cotton, printed with small blue flowers. The label says "Lollipops." You dangle them from your fingers for a long time.

You go back to the dollhouse. You think about King hurtling himself out of the darkness, the gleam of his teeth by starlight. Those teeth closing on your father's hand. The speck of blood already soaked through the gray pillowcase.

You close your eyes and concentrate as hard as you can. Afterwards, you peer into the mass of the dollhouse, trying to gaze through tiny doorways, past Federal highboys and plastic refrigerators. You see nothing. There is no sound. Eventually, you give it up.

You feel like a wimp.

The next day Sally is back at the cash register. She wears no makeup, and her hair is wrapped tightly in a French braid. When you catch her eye, she shudders and looks wildly away.

"Where's my dog?" Dazuki demands. "I know you did something to my dog!"

"I never touched your dog," you say truthfully.

"You got him in there and I'm coming in to get him!"

"Get a search warrant," you hear yourself say.

Dazuki glares at you. To your complete amazement, he turns away. "You damn well bet I will!" But even to your ears this sounds like bravado. Dazuki believes you. He doesn't think you'd imprison his dog, whether from cowardice or honesty or ineptitude. There will be no warrant.

You glance at the living room window, which was wide open. Your father must have heard how you told off Dazuki. Both you and the asshole were shouting. He must have heard. You go into the house.

Your father has passed out in his rocking chair.

Two days later, an upholstered Queen Anne chair on the fourth shelf of the first layer has been chewed. The bite marks look somehow desperate. But each one is only three twenty-fourths of an inch deep, to official scale. They are mere pinpricks, nothing anyone could actually fear.

The first day of school comes. By the end of third period, American Government, it is clear to you that Sally Corey has said something. When you walk into a room, certain girls snicker behind their hands. Certain boys make obscene gestures over their crotches. Very small obscene gestures.

You spend fourth period hiding out in the men's room. While you are there, hands bracing the stall closed while delinquent cigarette smoke comes and goes with the bang of the lavatory door, something happens to you. Fifth period you walk into Spanish III, coolly note the first boy to mock you, and listen for his name at roll call. Ben Robinson. You turn in your seat, look him straight in the eye long enough for him to start to wonder, then turn away. The rest of the period you conjugate Spanish verbs so the teacher can find out what useful information everybody already knows.

At home, in front of the dollhouse, you close your eyes. Ben Robinson. Ben Robinson. You howl.

There is a scuffling noise deep in the dollhouse.

For an hour you work at your bench. The Chippendale sofa is finished; you are building a miniature American Flyer sled of basswood. It will have a Barn Red finish and a rope of crochet cotton. You think of this sled, which you have never owned, as the heart of rural childhood.

After an hour, you close your eyes again and concentrate on Ben Robinson. When you're done, you inspect the doll-house. The second-layer furniture that has been knocked over ever since the night with Sally Corey is now standing upright. On the bottom shelf of the first layer, which is coincidentally where you plan to put the American Flyer, you find very small, dry pellets. When you carefully lift them to your nose on the blade of an X-acto knife, they smell like dog turds.

The second weekend in September there is a miniature show in the Dome Arena in the city. The pickup truck has some-thing wrong with the motor. You take the bus, and spend time talking with craftsmen. To your own ears your voice sounds rusty; sometimes days go by without your speaking two sentences to the same person. At school you talk to no one. No one meets your eyes, although sometimes you hear people whispering behind you as you walk away from your locker or the water fountain. You never turn around.

But here you are happy. An artisan describes to you the lost-wax method of casting silver. A miniature-shop owner discusses the uses of Fimo. You study room boxes from the eighteenth century and dollhouses extravagantly fitted for the twenty-first. You buy some miniature crown molding, wallpaper squares in a William Morris design, a kit to build a bay window, and a bronze bust of Beethoven seven eighths of an inch high.

At home, the fruit cellar is not completely dark. Tiny lights gleam deep inside the dollhouse, too deep for you to see more than their reflected glow through doorways and windows. You stand very still. Only the outer two layers of the pile have any electrified rooms. Only in the last year have you learned how to wire miniature lamps and fake fireplaces.

While you're standing there, the small lights go out.

* * *

You start skipping school one or two days a week. You aren't learning anything there anyway. What does it matter if the tangent of the sine doesn't equal the tangent of the cosine, or the verb *estar* doesn't apply to permanent states of being? You are tired of dealing in negatives. You can't imagine any permanent states of being.

"Going out, son?" he asks. His hand trembles.

"No," you say. "Leave me alone!"

Sometimes there are lights on deep in the dollhouse, sometimes not. Occasionally furniture has been moved from one room to another. The first time this happens, you move the wicker chair back from the Federal dining room to the Victorian sun porch, where it belongs. The next day it is back in the Federal dining room, pulled up to the table, which is set with tiny ceramic dishes. On some of the dishes are crumbs. You leave the wicker chair alone.

At the end of September you find a tiny shriveled corpse on the third shelf of the bottom floor, in a compartment fitted like a garden. It's King. The dried corpse has little smell. You cover it with a sheet of moss and carve a tombstone from a half-bar of hand soap your mother once brought from a hotel in New York.

Once or twice, sitting late at your workbench, you catch the faint sound of music, tinny and thin, from an old-fashioned Victrola.

"Listen," Mr. Corey says, "this can't go on."

You wipe your hands on your apron, which says COREY LUMBER in stitched blue lettering. In your opinion, the stitching is a very poor job. You're thinking of reinforcing it at home. "What can't go on?"

He looks you straight in the eye, a big man with shoulders like hams, fat veined through the muscle. "You. You talk short and mean to customers. Yesterday you told old Mrs. Dallway her windows weren't worth repairing, and your voice said she wasn't worth it, neither. You never used to talk to people like that."

You say, "I keep the stock better than it's ever been before."

"Yeah, and that's another thing. It's too good. Too neat."

You just look at him. He rubs a hand through his hair in frustration.

"That's not what I mean. Not too neat. Just too . . . it doesn't have to be that exact. Paint cans lined up on the shelf with a ruler. The same number of screwdrivers in each bin. You fuss over it like an old hen. All the small crappy details. And then you're rude to customers."

You turn slowly, very slowly, away.

"Just forget the small stuff and concentrate on the service that people deserve, all right?" Mr. Corey's tone is pleading now. He always liked you. You don't care.

"Yeah," you say. "What they deserve. I will."

"Good kid," Mr. Corey says, in tones that convince neither of you.

Dazuki has a new dog, a pit bull. It's chained in his front yard just short of the road. You stand by your mailbox and watch it stretch its chain, leaping and snarling. You go downcellar and give the dog two hours in the dollhouse, while you work on a nanny-bench kit from Little House on the Table. Banging and yelping, very faint, come from deep in the dollhouse. Once there is a grinding sound, like a dentist's drill. Glass breaks. For the last twenty minutes, you add Dazuki himself.

When you go back outside, about 7:30 P.M., the pit bull is lying across its chain. Its neck is bloody; one ear is torn. It catches sight of you and cowers. You go back inside.

The nanny bench turns out perfectly.

On Saturday afternoon Mr. Corey fires you. "Not for good, Billy," he says, and somehow he is the supplicant, pleading with you. "Just take a few weeks off to think about things.

We're slow now anyway. In a few weeks you come back all rested, snap bang up to snuff again. Like you were.''

"Sure,'' you say. The syllable tastes hot, like coals. You take off your apron—you reinforced the stitching last night—and hand it to him. You seem to be seeing him from the small end of a telescope. He is tiny, distant, with few details.

"Billy . . .'' he says, but you don't wait.

The house is silent. In the mailbox is the new catalogue from Wee Three. Holding it, you go in through the kitchen, down the stairs, and jab the light switch in the fruit cellar. Nothing happens.

You reach to the ceiling, remove one of the bulbs, and shake it. It doesn't rattle. The disc-belt sander on your workbench won't turn on. But inside the dollhouse are the reflections of lights. In the windowless dark of the fruit cellar they gleam like swamp gas.

Upstairs, the refrigerator doesn't hum. The kitchen lights won't turn on. In the living room your father lies in a pool of his own vomit on your mother's rug.

You yank open the drawer in the scarred rolltop where bills are kept. It's all there: Three monthly warnings from the electric company, followed by two announcements of service cutoff. Threatening letters from collection agencies. Politer ones from the bank that holds the mortgage. Your father's pay stubs. The last one is dated four months ago.

Your father is shrinking. He looks like Corey did: a speck viewed from the wrong end of a telescope. The speck dances randomly, a miniature turd in Brownian movement on the end of an X-acto blade. You realize you are shaking. You kick him, and he grows again in size, until he and his pool of vomit fill the living room and you have to get out.

You go downcellar.

More lights gleam inside the dollhouse, some of them a lurid red. The dentist-drill grinding is back. There are other noises, fitful and rasping but faint. Small. Very small.

You close your eyes and the howl builds, against your

father, against Corey, against the world. It builds and builds.

Before the howl can escape, your mind is flooded with objects, all miniaturized, all familiar, whirling in the fireball path of some tiny meltdown. Your work apron is here— COREY LUMBER—and your mother's rug, with all its stains. Sally's Lollipop panties and the rolltop desk. The set of baseball cards you had when you were ten, and the set of Wedgwood china inexplicably left to you in your grandmother's will. Your mother's hairbrush, the old cookie jar with the faded green giraffes, even the pickup truck, littered with McDonald's wrappers. Everything rushes at you: small, petty, and in shreds. The rug has been chewed. The desk legs, broken off, lie among shredded books. Splinters that were once nursery toys catch at the inside of your eyelids. Shards of Wedgwood are razor-sharp. Everything whirls together in a space of your soul that is shrinking still more, contracting like a postnova star, collapsing in on itself to the howl of a frightened dog.

Your yell comes out. "Noooooooooo . . ."

You open your eyes. The fruit cellar is completely dark.

You grope your way upstairs, outside, gulping huge draughts of air. It is later than it could possibly be. Orion hangs over the eastern horizon. It is past midnight.

You lean against the mailbox for support, and look up at the vast immensities of the stars.

In a few more minutes you will go back inside. You'll clean up your father and get him to bed. You'll start to sort through the bills and notices and make a list of phone numbers to call. In the morning you'll call Mr. Corey, set up an appointment to talk to him. You'll use ammonia on the rug.

And then you'll bring the dollhouse upstairs, layer by layer, piece by piece. Even though there's no place to put it all. Even though the miniatures that you made won't look nearly as realistic by sunlight, and some of the tiny pieces will surely end up lost among the large-scale furniture in the rest of the house.

The Stone Girl

Elise Matthesen

She wasn't a stone girl at first, of course. Even after she was, it wasn't something as you would notice right off. I came after it happened, so there wasn't any "befores" for me to be comparing, but her sister said there wasn't much change to look at. Just one day to the next her skin getting colder, a little more solid.

I came when her sister finally allowed that she needed help with the work around the place. The stone girl still moved then, though she was slow. Deliberate, like she had to think where her arm should be next. Wasn't much could be done by her in the way of chores. She had told her sister this, the words coming one by one, dropping like pebbles in a pond. The sister asked in town the next day for help. I came directly; there wasn't anything that greatly held me to the place I had been. Truth be told, I wasn't much the kind that could be held. So I came, and if I wasn't expecting anything fine, well, then, I wasn't likely to be disappointed. That was how I figured. But they had a welcome for me, and a place prepared. They treated me nice, too, the sisters: I had a feathertick fine as theirs, and we ate from the same kettle.

The feathertick I pulled into the sleeping porch after the first few nights, seeing as it was a warm spring. That way I could be up and about in the mornings without having to go through and wake them. I didn't know for sure if the stone girl slept or not, but her sister I expected could use any rest that was offered her.

I asked early what the cause for all this might have been. It's not something I had ever heard tell of before, even living on the edge of the Marshes. The sister told me that one day the stone girl had come back to the house shivering and shaken. She hadn't been able to tell her sister much, just that she had gotten tangled in some spellweb. Or maybe it was some bargain made by an old marsh wisewit that maybe didn't get paid off at the time and just sort of hung there until it caught the sleeve of the next person walking by. The stone girl didn't know, and her sister, though she studied on it, couldn't bring a better guess to it. Anywise, the sense and direction of it was clear: it was a Change Spell. What came was stone; what went was flesh. Or at least touch, warmth, receiving and reaching out. Those were flesh things.

That was why the lover left, the sister told me. He wept some and raged against the Marshes and against spellpowers in general and wisewits in particular, and he came and sat with the stone girl on the front stairs. After a while he came to realize that she couldn't feel it when he clasped her hand and complained over the unkindness of fate. Not too long after that he was walking out with another young woman. I saw them once when I was pulling Annie-go-courting for the dyepot. They were careful not to walk out toward the Marshes, though, so I hadn't seen them after that. The sister was with me that one time, and I saw her turn her head until they were past.

"Maybe she don't feel it," she said, "but I do." I didn't ask her what she meant.

The once that I asked, the sister told me that the stone girl knew what was going to happen to her. Said she felt it somewhere inside, all wrote out like a book, only she didn't know the words for the whole of it. Maybe she did, and her sister was just chary of relating it; it's not something I can know. Anywise, they're entitled to some secrets between them, if that's the way of it. What she did tell me was this: The stone girl would change, stone for flesh, until all of her was gone except the heart. Then when she died, her heart would turn into a beautiful bird and rise up singing. When the sister told me that, I tried to imagine such a bird. Maybe all of jewel colors, or red like the sun through the morning clouds.

"It might not be too long," she told me, "but even if it is, I'm bound to stay. She was proud, wouldn't beg me for it, but I know she wanted it. Wanted me to promise I'd stay and wait for that bird." She was silent for a stretch. "Ought to be some rare sight, that bird." We both of us sat awhile, looking at the clouds leaking color from the sun behind them. She made a little sound like the way the wind moves the rushgrass, and then we sat some more.

I was kind as I knew how to be with the stone girl, but it wasn't a thing that was easy. One day I felt a breeze coming up from the pond, and I went to put a big soft shawl around her. It was a thick patterned thing all in colors like the hues of marshflowers. The sister had made it. I had it mostly tucked in before it came to me that the stone girl probably couldn't feel it anyway. Neither shawl nor breeze, come to that. I stood there like a post for a bit, thinking, until the sister came into the room and caught me at it. Might be that my thoughts were writ large on my face, or maybe the sister had the advantage of having gone over the same ground herself. Anywise, she knew what I was coming to under-stand, and how I felt about it. I let her draw me away and back onto the porch, and I let her tell me.

She said she expected I was right about the stone girl not being able to feel much any more, but she had thought this out and come to a resting place with it. "Maybe she's in there, feeling everything, and just can't speak of it to us. I'd rather we took the chance and offered comfort to her. I think she knows; she can still see and hear us some, I expect. And even if she can't feel it, it makes me no matter. It's still comfort to me." And after thinking on it I came to decide that she was right.

I was out on the steps of an evening counting stars when I heard the sister's loom stop. Her footsteps moved across to the stone girl's chair and then fell quiet. There was a moan like November wind, and a thump. I looked in to see the sister kneeling against the stone girl's chair, hugging her and weeping.

She looked up at me when I poked my head in. "I felt her Change," she said.

I looked at the stone girl. Her mouth was a little open, like she had been trying to say something.

"Is she dead?" I asked, coming into the circle of firelight.

"No," her sister said, continuing to stroke the unresponsive arm. "No. She's not quite to the other bank of the water yet." And she sat there, keeping vigil, with her eyes clear and the tears falling like spring rain.

I went out on the steps again. The stars were still there. I sat and thought about birds with wings all of jewels and fire.

It ought to be a rare sight. I expect I'll stay and be witness to it.

Attention Shoppers

Steven K. Z. Brust

Attention shoppers:
Find all of your picnic needs in aisle five
For today only, all paper plates and napkins
Are half price
Charcoal and lighter fluid,
Forty percent off
Plastic cups and utensils
One-third off
Thank you for shopping.

Attention shoppers:
Find all of your panic needs in aisle five
For today only, all purple plates and napkins
Are half price
Charcoal and liar fluid,
Forty person trough
Plastic cups as usual
One firm cough
Thank you for shopping
In my house.

Attention stoppers:
File all of your manic seeds in island jive
For pay only, all pauper states and napalm
Are half the prize
Gargoyle and litter floods,
For perverts, all
Plaintive cuts and cruel
Done for nought
Thank you for shopping
In my head.

Attention poppers:
Vile calls varied needs in Iceland drive
Foreplay only, call ropers stale and native
Art has the size
Gargle with little food,
For penance, y'all
Blatant ruts are cool
Done been caught
Thank you for chopping
Off my head.

The store will be closing in ten minutes.
Please bring final purchases to the checkout lanes.

The store will be cosy in fine minces.
Please bring filed birches to the checkmate lames.

The whore is now dosed.
Please sing flying birds to checkered flames.

The whore is now dosed.
The whore is now dosed.
The whore is now dosed.
Attention shoppers.

Jaguar Lord

Anna Kirwan-Vogel

This is how it was when Chan Bahlum took his first jaguar.

The morning star was rising around dawn at that time, in the latitudes of the red cat. A runner came in from the head men of Blue Rock to inform Pacal, Lord of Palenque, the Shield of his People, that a jaguar had come down from upriver and killed a deer hunter by his canoe early one evening. The villagers had come out running at the howling of the frantic dogs, to discover that the hunter had startled the cat while it investigated a buck hung up to be smoked. The jaguar's tugging at the deer had partly pulled down the smoking-stage of saplings, but hadn't loosened the wet maguey ropes knotted around the hunks of carcass. And so, when the deer's owner had arrived, the beast had tried to drag the hunter himself off into the trees. The man's fresh blood had spattered the browning slabs of venison.

The horror of the sight buzzed in the Blue Rock farmers' outcry. This death bore awful portent for the village. The disemboweled hunter had been the best spearman in Blue Rock, and Chac the Drinker of Blood had taken him: had caught him in an unarmed moment. The man's only brother had already died, of lung fever two years before. Now who in the village could go forth? The men's knees were like cedar roots, unmovable. Their hearts cried out in terror, for who could face a jaguar save another jaguar? Thus, the head men sent to Pacal to ask for help.

Lord Pacal was in the fifth day of his fasting after the birth of a daughter. He was heard to remark that a band of peccary might harry a jaguar to its end. The men of the village all together ought to track the man-eater and snare it with nets and dispatch it with boar spears, without delay. But the cat had eaten a man who'd shared their dinners with them: everyone knew such a fight was the most unpredictable kind of contest.

Now, Chan Bahlum was fourteen years old, first son of Lord Pacal and his chief wife, Lady Hela, and he yearned to cut his hair and wear the spotted skin of manhood. He was standing in the eastern courtyard of the palace by the cage of songbirds when he saw the huge form of his father's great friend, Etzmoan, old Flint Hawk, hastening along the portico toward the reception house. Etzmoan was the captain of the Jaguar Guard, second only to Pacal himself in the councils and in courage.

Chan Bahlum thrust the green jay he had been hand-feeding back into the wickerwork cage. "I thrice salute you, Wise Cousin!" he called out quickly, hoping to slow down the courteous Etzmoan for some conversation.

"Thrice greetings, Sun's Cub. My Lord your father has summoned me outside council hours."

These were the words Etzmoan spoke, and Chan Bahlum heard all their meaning of honor and guarded urgency. He ran up the nine steps to the shaded porch and followed in an undignified manner until he caught up with the long-legged warrior.

In the reception house, Lord Pacal sat concealed behind a blue-green quetzal-plumed screen marked with two great red circles of macaw feathers, circles which stared out like eyes at the exhausted Blue Rock runner. The courier himself lay prostrate on the floor, not once raising his face. Chan Bahlum and Etzmoan hurried forward from the doorway, flinging about their shoulders the Presence garments of dull weave which the wise Pacal required all visitors alike to wear in that room where justice was done, sentences and bargains enacted, wishes granted or denied. They strode forward to greet Pacal, but they dropped to their knees when they passed the screen (as was their privilege, the Lord's kinsmen) and came into sight of the shining reflection of the sun which was his visage.

Lord Pacal's visage, let it be said, was sad that morning. To Chan Bahlum, indeed, his father always looked grave; even behind his laughing remarks his son saw spare philosophy, because Pacal's face was slender as a maize cob compared to Hela's lush, tender features. It was not hunger that straitened Lord Pacal's features now, for he fasted often; nor the birth of a daughter rather than a son, for Lord Pacal had many children, sons and daughters, and he named them all himself. But he had watched the Blue Rock runner through the pierced screen while he waited upon Etzmoan's appearance. And Pacal mourned the death of that hunter, and he mourned the death which must surely follow, the death of the jaguar.

Many times he had gone to hunt the ferocious ones, the Lord himself. He had taken his long spear into the misty zone of death, and spilled the blood of those dark, hungry suns of the night forest, and taken their skins to wear, and he was their Lord in his heart. And men are relieved when the black-flowered cats are killed, but no one who has caused them to die is happy of their death.

Now the Lord's contemplative expression did not break when he waved his counselor and his heir to the fringe of his mat. They stooped, touched the mat next to his sandal, and sat before him.

"When Chilam told me the almanac yesterday, he told me there would be a jaguar in the southern marches. Now our cousins in Blue Rock have sent us their brave courier to say this jaguar has eaten man's flesh."

"We are the corn of the Jaguar," Etzmoan replied in the luck-ritual that must parry such tidings. Pacal himself had said the same words when he'd heard the grim report.

"Who of my Guard will offer himself?" Pacal inquired formally.

Chan Bahlum knew Etzmoan had not been called at random, and would thus volunteer his own steady spear rather than advance a less distinguished warrior to lead the foray. And Chan Bahlum knew his father would never entrust a first hunt, his own princely trial of nerve, to anyone less reliable than cousin Etzmoan; and that Etzmoan would not go out again to hunt jaguar for the ritual hundred and eighty days after killing this one. So this was his chance, and the only chance Chan Bahlum would have for a very long time.

"Lord, my Lord, my Great Lord, head of my father's lineage," Etzmoan declared, "I offer my own spear to the service of Blue Rock, her head men and her people. I will pursue the raiding jaguar and make him thy chamber ornament."

Pacal had spoken loudly enough to be heard by the man beyond the screen, and so, now, did Etzmoan. Chan Bahlum knew no ritual for what he must do next, but he saw he must also speak up like a man, and he knew with sudden certainty that his father must regard any offer the prince made to Blue Rock as a decision he could not deny.

"Lord Father, my Lord, my Great Lord, Sower of the seed of my life," he began, striving to sound as though he were not making up on the spot the noble phrases that must snare his future. "I offer myself to the service of Blue Rock, under the guidance and tutelage of my lord cousin, for the continual glory of our lineage—please, please, let me go too," he finished in a rush, unable to sustain the rhetoric any longer.

Pacal regarded his oldest son with piercing tenderness, but he spoke first to Etzmoan. "So be it, Lord Etzmoan, You Who Speak With the Night Sun, Captain of the Jaguar

Guard. I send my best servant to Blue Rock. Find the murderous jaguar and tell him with your spear that Blue Rock is as my own house to me and that the people there are as my children." Then, finally, he turned to Chan Bahlum and said, "So be it, First Son, Sunshine of my First Wife My Sister, Precious New Leaves of Corn. I send my own flesh to Blue Rock. Find the murderous jaguar and tell him with your spear that Blue Rock is as your own house and that the people there are as your brothers. Bid them promise fealty to the Lords of the Mats of Otolum, we who are their shield."

Now, hidden behind the quetzal screen from the curious eyes of the grateful, sweaty supplicant at the other end of the room, Pacal scratched at an insect bite on his divinely twisted right foot. He whispered, "Your mother said you would be after me one day soon to give you something tough to chew. It's time. You will do exactly as Etzmoan says; that is my command and my advice. He knows all there is to know of valor and of honor; he will give you no foolish work. Obey him with patience, Cub, for thus he obeys me. So; you think you are ready?"

The water lily bud knotted into Pacal's forehead band glowed like the sun's heart in the yellow torchlight. Chan Bahlum loved his father. "I am frightened," he whispered back, "but I am ready."

"You have always been solid as a tree. Go now, tell your mother you're going, and order your gear."

Pacal had given them his own best team to bear the litter, eight giants with massive shoulders and forearms big as Chan Bahlum's calves. Their sandals scudded so quietly on the forest track, it was as if the vibrations rather than the sound sent the monkeys and macaws shrieking off into the green canopy. So strong were the king's bearers, too, that Etzmoan sat cross-legged swaying from side to side as though at rest in a hammock, with hardly a lurch. Chan Bahlum was less poised; but then, he was tense with excitement, although the jaguar at Blue Rock was still hours away.

"Sun's Cub," Etzmoan began formally, inclining his head toward his cousin, "Jade Bead of the King's Most Precious Ornament, my Young Lord—the time is at hand when I must humbly instruct you in the secrets of the Jaguar Guard, which are our power and our protection. When time allows, this is the custom. Shall I proceed?"

Chan Bahlum looked at his kinsman's tattooed face. Would he be told how to heel the spear to bear the big cat's weight? Or how to track the trackless tree branches where the Night Sun dragged its prey? Thrilled, he nodded; then, seeing Etzmoan waiting as if for some ritual, he said, "I bid you proceed."

"This is the true story of the Jaguar Men. This is how they came by mastery. This is how it was in the time of the beginning," Etzmoan explained.

"In the days before the rubber trees gave milk, a black jaguar came down from the mountain to the village of Bent Reeds, and he killed a man and ate him. Then the man's spirit was in the jaguar, and said to the jaguar, 'Well, you ate me, now you must do what I tell you. There's a man back in my village who stole a sack of pheasants I had snared. Since you killed me it's up to you to take my vengeance on him. Let's go down to the field and eat him up.'

"The jaguar was still a little bit hungry, because this fellow he'd killed was thin as a stick. So he agreed. And the jaguar with two spirits went to the second man's field and killed again.

"The first man's spirit and the second man's spirit found themselves together somewhere behind the bloody jaws of the black jaguar. No one had said it would be pleasant, but once you're dead, you're dead, and no going back to the way it was before. They were both angry, and the jaguar was, after all, not a rabbit. He was getting used to human flesh. Men are the corn of the jaguar. Men are easy to harvest. 'What about that bastard that lives down by the papaya grove?' said the second man's spirit. 'He cheats whenever he plays ball. He's cheated both of us. If we've got to give up the open sky, then we'll take him with us.' So the black jaguar killed another man.

"And it went on like that. All the dead men's spirits became more and more hateful, crowded in like that with their worst enemies. And the jaguar's breath stank from blood, and the blood matted on his fur. They kept him so busy getting even with everyone, he didn't even have time to clean himself.

"After a while there was no man left in the village that all the spirits could agree to murder. But there was a beautiful woman who lived in the forest by a dark pool, and they discovered they all wanted to fuck her; so all these dead men's spirits, these nine wicked ghosts behind the black jaguar's teeth, compelled the jaguar to do a very bad thing. The jaguar hunted the woman by the pool and leapt on her and raped her.

"With that much spirit in the fuck, of course she got pregnant, and when her baby was born he was half human and half cat. So he was called Ah Ek Xix. Every day his mother took him out at dawn to show him how the mist rises in the jungle, and how to watch for it where it starts to rise first. Then she would take him there, because that's where the jade is. Ah Ek Xix could find jade wherever it was under the earth or under the stream. His eyes could find jade in the white glare of noon or in the darkest shadows.

"Finally, when Ah Ek Xix was fourteen years old, his mother said, 'Now you must act like a man. You must go and kill your first jaguar. If you take a lantern, you will find a great red-gold cat, and everyone will honor you.'

"But Ah Ek Xix took no lantern. He went out at night, nine nights in a row he went out into the jungle and stood under the trees in the darkness. He heard all the trees said at night. He heard how the rubber trees make milk, and that's how we know about rubber. He heard how the copal tree weeps perfume, and that's how men know about copal incense which the Gods love. Finally, on the ninth night, he saw two beads of jade off in the darkness. He threw his spear with all his strength.

"*Ai-i-i!* That was the scream of nine wicked men's spirits! They were going to the land of Death for good this time, to be tortured forever by the Lords of Death!

"But the Black Jaguar looked at Ah Ek Xix before it closed its jade-green eyes, and its own spirit spoke to him. 'Thank you, my son, for freeing me from those impure souls. Now I am clean. Now I go to the green pools of the Rainy Mountain, where it is always the season of water lilies and the butterflies will rest at my paws. Now you are no longer Ah Ek Xix—you are Ah Bahlum, the Jaguar Lord.' "

Etzmoan cleared his throat and pulled the stopper out of the neck of his gourd water flask; after he'd offered it to Chan Bahlum, who refused, he took a deep swallow. "That story tells you how not to kill a jaguar. It just goes to show how different men are now from the Old Ones. If you did things that way, you would probably be the jaguar's next bowl of hominy."

Now Chan Bahlum reached for the water bottle and sipped thoughtfully. "He went without light."

"Yes."

"And he threw his spear."

"Yes." Etzmoan nodded approval. "Where was his next spear? Against a tree? Which tree? What if it fell? A thrown spear can kill only if the cat is willing. And you have only your own throwing strength behind it. But if you set the butt of your spear against the earth—" He pulled a long dart from the quiver that lay alongside the litter cushions and demonstrated by butting it firmly against the muscle of his thigh. "That way, the strength of the Earth vanquishes the jaguar. We pray for this in the prayer before hunting. We pray that the jaguar will charge, and we keep the spear aimed at his chest. When all the prayers have been said properly, the jaguar rushes straight to his death. It is a good sacrifice."

But Etzmoan looked troubled, and Chan Bahlum saw this. "Cousin, will this happen at Blue Rock?" he asked. Through the doorway of those words, he heard his own fear of the hunt enter for the first time, and the fear came and lay trembling along his backbone.

Etzmoan did not answer at once. He trailed his hand over the side of the litter and caught at a snaky spray of syrup-flower, snapping the branch and bringing the red-speckled blossoms close to his face. The tubular flowers bobbed with the measured gait of the bearers. "This jaguar has eaten man's flesh. The man he ate may have been unclean—he had been carousing. That much of the story is real—the man-eater is the most unpredictable."

He shrugged. "Well, you must never expect you can predict any cat's moves. I have worn this pelt for the thirty years I've been Ah Bahlum, as you will wear one soon. Before each hunt, I go to my Lord your father's compound, where the drug-fed jaguars are, and I rub my hands in their fur until I am musky with their sweat. I make myself one of them, so that I dream their dreams and I can find them in the forest. But even I cannot tell for certain what they will do before they do it."

It was only the second week of the dry season, but the Snake Tail of the Traders' River was down. The bearers had to carry them all the way past the third landing to find deep enough water for the sleek mahogany shell that would take them the rest of the way to Blue Rock. But two turns farther down the river, and the languid green stream was even now sufficiently deep to carry them smoothly, faster than the bearers could have run when they were fresh.

Blue Rock was not a large village. Its one-room prayer house had the only stone roof in the clearing, and some of the outlying cottages sat on wooden platforms that were not even whitewashed. To Chan Bahlum's eye, accustomed only to the cultured permanence of the city and the lusty garden village of his own family's country house, Blue Rock seemed dank and rotting; almost as if it might itself slide like a turtle into the river, by and by, and disappear.

But the head man there was the head of the Owl family, one of the hereditary border lineages which were supposed to hold the southeastern frontier in raiding season. He had posted a lookout to tell him when someone came from the Lord's palace, and late that afternoon he was at the silty scallop of mud where boats nudged into the bank, to greet them and demonstrate his courtesy and relief and admiration of their reputations.

In this regard, Chan Bahlum watched Etzmoan's statesmanship. His own comportment was a trifle too stolid to be elegant, for he was caught between the thought of how he must set his spear to earth and the evident discomposure of the old Owl, who saw only one man come to hunt jaguar— one man, one stripling, two slaves, and one lidded basket of hounds, when the village had hoped for a gang of veterans who would make short work of the menace. They all thought they had heard the jaguar in their sleep the night before around the fringes of their own bare cornfields. The canny guard captain Etzmoan made short work of their compliments, pleading as his excuse the restless dogs, who must be taken immediately to the dead hunter's hut and the one certain trail of the murderous jaguar.

The smoking-stage hovered over the little clearing like a broken stick puppet, hunched and awry as the Buzzard Lord clown in the Death Day dances. Flies clotted on the slack rods and cords. The hunter's widow had been taken away to her neighbors' hearth, where she was praying to the Hanged Goddess. She had not slept since the scraps of her husband's body had been found.

The dogs were pacing and jumping against their leashes, whimpering at the smells of blood and jaguar urine and strangers. Three arm lengths from the water's edge the undergrowth was tamped into a rude, almost invisible path, and there Etzmoan found an enormous paw print. "Look," he said tersely to Chan Bahlum. "One toe is crushed, a new injury he still favors. He will not have gone so far we'll have a long hunt. Dart! Sow! Tanager!'' At the sound of his voice on their names, the hounds dropped to their haunches and sat trembling, their eyes fixed on their master's face. They wanted off their lines. He would give them what they wanted.

So they went out into the blue-green darkness. The two bearers went with them, one toting the extra spears and the string bag of provisions and the water bottles, and one going ahead swinging a long-bladed knife side to side, slashing a way for them to follow the dogs.

Dart was the leader of the hunt. Time after time he would come up on the big cat's marks—a clawed tree trunk, a pile of droppings—whimper, bark his short, sharp comment, and bound off on the trail the men could scarcely see.

Sow was older, broader in the chest, her pelt and ears scarred from years of chases. Chan Bahlum remembered the afternoon when he had not been much bigger than a puppy, himself, when he had tried over and over to get Sow to let him ride her as a young monkey rides its elders. She had shrugged him off repeatedly, but never nipped or left the game. In any hunt, Etzmoan remarked, she could be counted on to back up any other dog that was under attack, coming in close to distract puma or jaguar or snorting peccary so the pack could regroup.

Tanager was Dart's son, still very young. His coat was a bright flag flickering between the trees when he ranged ahead or off to one side. This was his fifth hunt. Even he, thought Chan Bahlum, knows more about it than I do.

The trail was hardest to follow while they were still near Blue Rock. The midden and human smells attenuated, though, as the light path out to someone's burnt plot became a tunnel of dew-sodden week-old smoke overlaid with newer cat and blood traces. At one spot, where the jaguar had stopped and shredded the bark of a sapota across a patch as wide as a man's chest, Etzmoan found more paw prints. Chan Bahlum saw that the injured claw had begun to bleed again. Dust had settled on the blood, and it had blackened, but it was not dry: the track was several hours old, the cat still several hours ahead of them.

It was now quite late in the afternoon. "Our enemy ate the night before last," Etzmoan considered aloud. "He will hunt tonight. He will move away from the river at twilight, perhaps take a rabbit or agouti. But he will be on the move after midnight and not inclined to conceal himself. It is when he is strongest. We will find him then."

"Why should we not follow him now, when we are finally catching up?" Chan Bahlum's legs ached from the rapid hike without rest, but he did not wish to seem winded.

"He might climb a tree and clean his beard after the rabbit. If the dogs became confused, we'd have him between us and Blue Rock. He could begin to pursue us. Or head back there when he wanted his main course. We will watch for him all evening, but go after him only after the moon is up." He looked shrewdly at Chan Bahlum, then thumped the haft of his spear on a knobby root. "We need not fear spirits abroad at night. The worst is the one we are seeking—the others will bow to us as we pass."

They continued along the path for some distance farther until they came into a fallow field full of saplings, with no big trees hanging over the center. This had been a farmer's clearing four years before. The last red sun would warm them there, and they would eat, though they would not make a fire the Lord of Death Cimi Bahlum would smell at a distance as he licked his bloody paws.

They sat on the ground then, and drank sweet corn porridge from lacquered gourd flasks. Chan Bahlum and Etzmoan did not talk much with the bearers, because the bearers were slaves. They were from communities patronized by a bat god, though, good guards for moonless nights by virtue of their excellent hearing; and the gentlemen's conversation occasionally was directed toward their overhearing. They were hunting together, they must think together.

Etzmoan recounted stories of Pacal's hunts, how the jaguars behaved, how the dogs took commands, how such-and-such a cousin or noted ambassador had been sinew-ripped by cats in this neck of the woods or up north, how the jaguars, when their times came, were killed. The stories were long whispers, a soft, rasping noise like the chirr of insects.

The sun went down. Fireflies came out, flickering from visibility to invisibility among the spindly locusts midfield and the araceas at the edge of the spirit-filled forest. Around midnight, the hunting party stirred themselves out of the contemplative wait they'd sunk into, and roused the dogs by leading them in a circle around the abandoned corn patch. Tanager found the scent where they'd first entered the clearing, and he was off. Etzmoan now carried a burning pine torch. Chan Bahlum loped along behind him, entranced with the shadows fleeing from the path and spilling back into place as the grim party advanced.

So they went along, for the span it would take an old woman to spin a whole basket of cotton. The jaguar was close now. From time to time, the bearer with the spears tucked them under his elbow against his side and took up the jaguar-caller he had on a thong around his neck. It was made from a calabash open at both ends, a piece of deerskin stretched across it like a drumhead. A long fruit peel hardened with beeswax hung inside it, and the slave would gently stroke the fruit peel with his fingers to produce a low, gut-loosening grunt like a jaguar's own. Chan Bahlum moistened his lips on the eerie realization that any time now the cat would catch its first scent of its pursuers and wonder if they portended challenge.

If the jaguar sees I am the smallest, Chan Bahlum thought, he will rush toward me in his first attack. If I catch him then, that will be best. My spear will be in place, my heart will leap up. I will be a man. I will marry soon.

Cehmaninopal, my sister, will come to my room again as
when we were small. And I will have a wife from another
place, too, Tonina or Yaxchilan, a beautiful girl with a long
waist and good hips and flowers rouged on her cheeks and
inside the curve of her breasts.

The shadows leapt up and fled before the eye of torchlight. The rest of the jungle was black; black. Had the moon
been full, in that place it would still have been useless.

Etzmoan, holding the smoking torch, stepped over a
fallen ceiba trunk. Then suddenly he gasped and fell sideways, back onto an upturned knee of the ceiba. The torch
jerked, but he held it even as he clutched at his leg, and
Chan Bahlum saw on the ground a stride from the ceiba the
too-smooth branch that swayed gently—for only an instant.
A night-hunting viper, its forelength raised and ready to
strike again, watched him reach to seize a spear from the
bearer behind him.

The heart-shaped head of the snake was as big as the
boy's hand, but as it twisted forward again, fangs foremost,
the son of Pacal drove his spear through it. The massive
shudder of the animal pulled Chan Bahlum off balance toward the tree trunk. Later, he did not remember how it was
that his skin had been scraped raw along the ribs. But the
viper stayed spitted and then went limp.

Chan Bahlum climbed over the ceiba. He wedged the dead
thing against a root and pulled his spear loose, its obsidian
tip smeared with blood and blue-white slime. Etzmoan
hung painfully across the hammock of leaves and branches.
His face in the fire glare and black shadow was constricted
with the pain of the wound: the straight stripes of his warrior paint showed jagged as lightning. The viper had been a
yellowbite, the most poisonous kind. It had struck on the
side of the leg between shin and calf, and the fang marks
and the flesh around them were already turning grey.

Whining and shaking, Sow and Dart came running back
into the halted circle of light. Chan Bahlum took a leash one
of the bearers had been carrying and, laying his spear beside

him for the moment, he wrapped the leather cord tight below Etzmoan's knee, above the bite. "You must not walk home, Lord Cousin," he ordered. "I know you must not walk." It was the first time Chan Bahlum had ever commanded his older kinsman.

The dogs were crowding around, jumping and yammering at the dead snake and the buzzing blackness of the trees. The first bearer, who had passed the viper by a breath, now stood by nervously clutching his broad, chipped knife.

"My Lord, I put you at risk. Forgive me. There is *chacah* leaf medicine in my pouch. There. The little sack." Chan Bahlum was frightened at how softly Etzmoan's smoky voice came out. He worked at pulling free the toggle that held the pouch at the older man's belt.

In the woods off beside them, Tanager suddenly began to growl. Dart bristled, raised his nose in the almost still air. Sow dropped her whimpering and cocked a scarred ear. Chan Bahlum thought of the cat-boy hearing the sap calling to him in the black night, and he reached for his spear just as Tanager howled and fell into the torchlight, his bound crippled by a great gash of bloody haunch.

Then nothing. The bearers closed in behind Chan Bahlum with stone knife and hastily unbound spear bundle. Etzmoan got both hands on the torch, holding it low, and, with a grunt of pain, edged his back up against the bend of tree trunk. Chan Bahlum stood away from his wounded cousin and wondered how he could heel his spear when he didn't know where the cat was. The spear was upright, its leaf-shaped blade above Chan Bahlum's eye level, still daubed with the serpent's last moment. He slowly twisted the butt end in a niche of stone or root, feeling its way into the damp earth.

A ruddy dove called up high. Another answered.

Fireflies twinkled, green-white. Green. Two green fire-flies: jade beads. Chan Bahlum lowered the spearhead, pointing.

The black Lord Death broke cover, hurling himself down

like a game's last ball, a murderous headshot. His claws and teeth were halfway up the spear shaft before the point drove into his chest. *So, have my hand—just die,* Chan Bahlum thought. He could not keep his eyes fixed on the black jaguar's terrible, changing face, but he locked his wrists and fell to one knee and shoved the spear deeper into the Nine Worlds of Death and all their crumbling weight.

The jaguar never reached his hand; it rolled, its back legs desperately pulling, the spear slicing inside and loosening. The big cat's head thrashed awkwardly against the ceiba, against Dart, against Etzmoan's knees. Chan Bahlum arched his back, pushed himself sideways to heave the jaguar over. The cat flailed, trembled, slashed Etzmoan's thigh almost as a drowning man grasps what he sees last. Hot blood poured over Chan Bahlum's arms, and his hands slid on the spear shaft.

Then the screaming stopped. The spear bearer dropped the extra weapons and pulled Chan Bahlum away from the dead stare of the jaguar's enormous corpse, wiping the prince's face with a cloth sack, bending again and again to touch his forehead to Chan Bahlum's sandals. The other bearer took the torch from Etzmoan and jammed it into a forked limb, then moved the thong tourniquet above the three ribbons of blood across the guard captain's leg. The venomous swelling did not seem to be climbing above the place where the black cat's last act had let Etzmoan's blood.

"Your prayers were well said," Etzmoan said when Chan Bahlum took his hand.

Tanager lay panting, licking at his ripped hindquarter, and Sow hovered above him; one of her ears hung by a dripping red flap. Chan Bahlum vaguely remembered her beside him when the jaguar first showed.

Inside the fight, time had swallowed itself like water falling into water. Chan Bahlum looked around, hearing the sap calling to him in the green darkness, hearing the ruddy doves.

He had thought the Night Sun's glory was like his father's, a holy strength which would fill him when he stood before it, which he would behold with reverence. But now his heart was hollow as a gourd flask. He had seen life leap away from this animal's perfect muscle and bone as the shadows always leapt away from light.

The old man at Blue Rock would be surprised to hear whose spear had done the deed, he thought. But weariness had been tailing him for hours, and came now and lay along Chan Bahlum's backbone; and all the glory he had hoped for was wrapped in mats back at the Reception House of Otolum. That torn skin in which his spear was still buried— Chan Bahlum would be the next to wear it. An obsidian blade beside his face would cut a handful of his hair for manhood.

"Your prayers were well said," he heard his warrior cousin say again. Then Etzmoan touched Chan Bahlum's sandal.

Is this how it was in the Beginning? Chan Bahlum wondered.

And he thought, *Now I am truly a Jaguar Lord.*

Pale Moon

Frances Stokes Hoekstra

Each winter, when Miss Eleanor Drew came to Philadelphia to meet with present or prospective campers, she had Sunday lunch at Laura and Mattie's house. Although Mattie felt she belonged to Miss Drew very much the way she belonged to her sister and mother and father, to see Miss Drew in winter was not the same as being at camp in the summer. The intense anticipation which built within Mattie the morning of Miss Drew's visit, which flooded her so that her cheeks burned and her mother had to remind her to calm down and especially not to monopolize the conversation during lunch, was left unsatisfied when Miss Drew drove off again in her old Chevy. Each time it was as if Miss Drew had come and yet had not come. Instead of the brown-and-white-checked shirt and beige gabardine skirt or brown corduroy slacks which were Miss Drew's camp uniform, she wore stockings and a wool suit of some somber color. She talked with Mattie and Laura's parents about living in upstate New York and sometimes about the world situation, and Mattie's father had said once it was difficult to "draw Eleanor out," and her mother had laughed and said yes, these Sunday lunches could be awkward. It was only during those moments after lunch when Miss Drew and Mattie were alone in the study, and Miss Drew asked if there was anything Mattie wanted to say to her about the coming summer, that the real Miss Drew materialized. Then the camp director looked deep into Mattie's eyes. She spoke in the husky contralto which was not like the voices of other adults. *Shazam!* Mattie thought, and her knees were weak with love.

"Don't you think," Laura said to Mattie on the Sunday of Miss Drew's visit the year Mattie was eleven, "don't you think it sounds *peculiar* when Dad and Mother call her Eleanor?" Laura was thirteen, which was the age of the oldest campers, and this would probably be her last summer.

"I don't like it," Mattie said. "It makes her seem like everybody else."

Laura chewed thoughtfully on a strand of her hair. "I think I do like it. I think it's nice that she knows people who call her Eleanor."

"I'll never call her Eleanor," Mattie said fiercely, "not even when I'm old." It confused her when Laura demystified Miss Drew. She slumped down in the armchair in Laura's bedroom and watched her sister dress for church. This year, Laura was allowed to wear nylon stockings. Mattie thought Laura was beautiful, but not because Laura had recently acquired a waist, whereas she, Mattie, went straight up and down like a sturdy tree, and not because Laura had breasts, which were small enough not to make much of an impression anyway. Laura was beautiful because she was thin and blond. *If I were thin and blond, I would have no problems.* Thin was significant. Thin meant that Laura was one of the campers selected by Miss Drew for Extra Nourishment at eleven in the morning, and Mattie, who was hungry all the time, thought how fine it would be to go to the camp kitchen in the middle of the day for milk and cookies. It meant that Laura could scamper goatlike up the mountains while Mattie trudged at the end of the line, panting and weary. Thin meant that Laura did most things right. *I do them right too, but I do them right on the inside and no one can see that. No one knows. Except Miss Drew. Miss Drew knows about me-on-the-inside.*

She had discovered this the evening Miss Drew read the waterfall poem aloud on Glacier Rock. Mattie had been nine then and in her first summer at camp.

Mattie's first summer, her roommate was an albino child with cottony white hair and remarkably tiny teeth who, secretly during Rest Hour, ate candies sent by her parents. She did not offer any to Mattie. Since candies from home were meant to be given to the counsellors and then shared by all, Mattie decided her roommate had a weak moral character, stemming from lack of pigment. Mattie knew from Laura that it was important for Miss Drew's campers to have strong moral fiber, although Laura had explained that the youngest campers were not expected to have much fiber yet and not to worry. Laura was eleven that summer and drifted shadow-thin and graceful across Mattie's vision, on her way to and from Extra Nourishment.

Nonetheless Mattie worried—especially on Sundays. Sunday afternoons, in the outdoor chapel, Miss Drew stood behind a birchbark lectern which she gripped tightly in both hands as she spoke to her campers about how God loved his children. One Sunday, the little girl in Miss Drew's sermon came to a fork in the road. "One branch led down to a broad and sunlit meadow bright with wild flowers," Miss Drew said, "while the other was crisscrossed with roots from the great trees on either side. This path twisted steeply upward and the end was lost in cold mists." When the girl started down the easy path, Mattie drew in her breath. She hated climbing mountains, but clearly the upward trail was the right choice if you had moral fiber. At the close of the service, Miss Drew led them in a recitation of the camp poem. Mattie's heart thumped in her chest. She spoke loudly and clearly so that Miss Drew would know she was going to try harder not to talk during Rest Hour, not to lag

behind on the trails, not to leave articles of her clothing all
over camp.

"Be strong," Mattie intoned.

We are not here to play, to dream, to drift,
We have hard work to do and loads to lift,
Shun not the struggle, face it, 'tis God's gift.

Her voice rose above the collected murmur of the other
campers. It left her throat and soared to where the wind
moved on wings of sunlight in the pine boughs and birch
leaves. The child beside her poked an elbow into Mattie's
rib. "Not so loud," she hissed.

After chapel that Sunday, Mattie changed from her white
middy blouse and skirt into the everyday uniform and went
to Glacier Rock. In an hour a bell would ring and campers
and counsellors would gather at the Rock for a picnic supper, but for now Mattie could be alone in her favorite place.
Glacier Rock went from the woods to the lake in a long
smooth river of stone. Two-thirds of the way down, a trans-
versal crack ratcheted across the stone, and where the crack
was at its widest, a low, flat-topped boulder had come to
rest. Sunday evenings Miss Drew sat on the boulder, the
lake on fire with light behind her, and read aloud whatever
thoughts or stories or poems campers had written earlier in
the week and placed in the birchbark box by her office door.
Mattie sat alone at the top of Glacier Rock. The sun hung
above the mountains on the western shore and splinters of
silver skittered across the water. Mattie shielded her eyes
against the reflections as Pale Moon appeared at her side.

"Hello," said Mattie.

Pale Moon had come to Mattie early in the summer, on
the notes of the song which bore her name. Mattie liked that
song because although she knew it was about the moon, not
about an Indian maiden, the words turned them into the
same thing. Pale Moon's skin was the color of a dark summer tan, and she had shoulder-length black hair which she
wore in a pageboy. She looked very much like the dance

counsellor, Miss Jill. Mattie admired Miss Jill because she could leap across open spaces with her toes pointed, in time to music. Mattie could leap like that in her head but not in her body. This did not matter to Pale Moon, who thought Mattie was a very special person.

"You have been chosen to be on the Inner Council," Pale Moon told her. She was wearing a white deerskin dress with long fringes. "I will initiate you into the rites. I will present you to the Council when the north star shines directly overhead."

"Will you teach me to fly?" Mattie asked. "The way you do—from one side of the sky to the other."

"In time. First there are tasks, some of them dangerous," Pale Moon warned, "but I will be with you."

"What will my role be in the Council?"

"You will write our songs."

Mattie moved her lips, speaking very softly for both of them. She hugged her knees to her chest. "I wrote a poem this week," she said. "I put it in Miss Drew's box before chapel. She'll read it tonight."

"Say it to me." It was a command.

Mattie looked around quickly to make sure no one was near.

"Booming, rushing, swiftly it came,
faster than lightning or hail,
pushing rocks before it in deadly pursuit.
   The roaring of the lion,
   the growling of the bear
mixed together with silvery foam.
That and there was the waterfall."

"It doesn't rhyme," said Pale Moon. "The other campers' poems always rhyme."

"It didn't want to rhyme," Mattie stood firm. "It doesn't matter. And I went in farther with those two lines about the lion and the bear. So it looks almost the same as rhyming."

A bell rang in the center of camp. "I have to go." Pale Moon leaned down and kissed Mattie's cheek. "Remember, you've been chosen." She leapt with pointed toes down the rock and into a birchbark canoe. The wind blew long, dark strands of hair across her face. "Miss Drew will like the poem," she said, saluting Mattie with her paddle.

Sunday nights, when the entire camp gathered at Glacier Rock, the limits of Mattie's world were defined by the stunted pines rooted in the cracks high up where the Rock left the woods, and by the smooth rounded stones that shone beneath the water at the shoreline where it disappeared into the lake. Crimson sparks from the campfire spiralled up and fell down again as ash. As Miss Drew read from the birchbark box, her silhouette loomed black against the strident colors of the evening sky. As tall as the pines she was, and her voice spilled over them, enfolded them, kept them safe. Mattie waited for Miss Drew to pull out the waterfall poem. "Booming, rushing, swiftly it came"—she felt the blood pulse in her temples. She hadn't known, at first, that she was writing a poem. But then the words started coming out in a certain way, and Mattie had to find the right shape for them upon the page, and when she had finished, she wanted to put the pencil down and run for miles, or shout. And now there was a quality in Miss Drew's voice, something like respect, something which made her poem sound the way it had promised to sound when the words were still caught inside her head.

"That and there was the waterfall." Miss Drew paused. "This is a poem by Martha Townsend, one of the youngest campers." The camp director looked over the eighty children assembled on the Rock in the lengthening shadows. And when she found Mattie, she gazed at her long and hard. Mattie looked back. *Here I am. This is me, Mattie.*

"I'm going to read this poem again," Miss Drew said.

"I love Miss Drew," Mattie whispered to her cottony-haired roommate as they got ready for bed. Mattie did not like her roommate very much, but her sudden and overwhelming allegiance to Miss Drew was too big to keep unspoken. She stood by the window of their tiny cabin and shone her flashlight into the night where small insects bumped against the mesh screen. Her roommate, already in bed, pulled extra blankets up to her chin. She was always cold. "Turn off the flashlight," she said sleepily, "you'll bring mosquitoes."

Mattie's first summer had been Laura's third. And at the end of camp, Laura was one of a very few of the younger children to be awarded a camp Letter. The camp Letters, like the minor awards, were emblems cut from white felt, but they had nothing to do with physical achievement. They symbolized honor, selflessness and loving hearts and were sewn in the center of the camp sweater, not on its sleeves. Mattie envied Laura's sweater with its many minor awards running down the sleeves and the Letter glowing in the center. Their mother folded the girls' camp clothes into a special linen drawer each fall. She perfumed the drawer with a small balsam-filled pillow Mattie had made in Crafts. The uneven green stencilled message on the pillow read, "For you I pine and balsam." From time to time, during the winter, Mattie opened the drawer, held the pillow to her nose and inhaled deeply. It was like holding a conch shell to her ear—the same imprisoned whispering to the senses.

She was eleven now, this would be her third summer and it was exactly the middle of the century. Laura had won her Letter when she was eleven and in her third summer. All the omens were good. She waited impatiently for Miss Drew to arrive.

"What do I do to get my Letter this year?" she asked Laura. Mattie hadn't gotten her Letter the summer before either, but then neither had Laura, so she hadn't minded. Laura was in Upper Camp now where Letters were much harder to win.

Laura stared into the mirror, bared her teeth and carefully unhooked the small rubber bands from her braces.

"Mother will make you put those back in," Mattie said. "Do I have to volunteer for things or what?"

"You don't have to do anything," Laura said patiently. "It's a kind of sacrament, like confirmation." Laura was taking confirmation instruction that winter. She pointed to the passage about sacraments in the prayer book.

"The outward and visible sign of an inward and spiritual grace," Mattie read.

"Getting your Letter isn't something you work for. It's something that happens as you . . . as you grow into being a better person." Laura gazed pensively at her younger sister. "Maybe it would help if you were neater. You lose everything. You even lost your bathing suit last summer, and you only had two to begin with."

"I worked like crazy for my Letter last summer," Mattie admitted. "Maybe that was the trouble."

Which Miss Drew confirmed later, when she sat in the study and called first Laura and then Mattie in to speak with her.

"You're a talented child, Mattie Townsend," Miss Drew said. "I have high hopes for you." Mattie flushed. Did she say that to everyone? Had she told Laura she too was talented?

The disguise of the woolen suit and stockings and pumps fell away. The high energy of Miss Drew's presence radiated throughout the room. "You are so intense, child. You worked hard for your Letter last summer. I knew that. All the counsellors knew that. But we finally decided you should wait a little longer. A Letter isn't something you strive for, Mattie." She placed her hand on Mattie's shoulder. "You just come back to us this summer and be yourself." Where her fingers rested, a sudden warmth blossomed. *I would die for you, Miss Drew.*

"So you see," said Mattie, "she gave me permission."

"Permission to do what?" Pale Moon asked a little

crossly. Mattie had not had much time for Pale Moon that summer.

"Permission to be me," Mattie said. "I thought I could only be me-on-the-inside, or when I was with my family. I've had to be so careful when I'm not at home."

"I think you should still be careful. Miss Drew isn't your family. She doesn't have to love you the way they do."

"Miss Drew wants the play I wrote to be performed for the parents on the last weekend. And when Laura and I did the skit on the Fourth of July, where I was Miss Drew teaching Laura how to swim, she laughed louder than anyone. I've written a poem every week too." None of her recent poems came from the place of the waterfall, but she had decided that didn't matter. They had rhyme and meter and were intended to remind Miss Drew of Mattie's inward and spiritual grace. This week's poem was called "The Stag at Eventide."

Pale Moon and Mattie rode their horses along a mountain ridge. They rode with neither saddle nor bridle. Mattie's palomino responded to the slightest pressure of her hands on his arched neck. Far below, she could see the crescent of the camp beach where the twenty or so campers who had not signed up to go on either the Junior or Senior Hiking Club tryouts were having a free swim.

"I think," said Pale Moon, "you should have signed up for the tryouts. Look who stayed back at camp with you. Jane's the only other one in your cabin group who didn't go, and Jane cheats. She steals things."

"I don't like hiking."

"Who will write the trip song?"

"Someone else, for once. I've written all the songs this summer. All the best ones, anyway." She threw her arms out wide, and felt the muscles of her horse quiver beneath her leg. "I am so happy," she said, "I think I might explode."

Jane's voice broke in upon them. "You've got this goofy

look on your face," she said loudly. Pale Moon slipped away. Jane stood in front of Mattie.

"You do that sometimes—get a goofy look," Jane said. Her tone was one of dispensing information, not criticism, but Mattie flinched. She did not want Jane looking at her face when she talked with Pale Moon. She did not like Jane. She wished Jane were not in her cabin group and most particularly she wished Jane did not stand directly in front of her in the Chapel Line. In the Chapel Line, campers were arranged from smallest to tallest. Mattie was uncomfortable being paired with Jane on all the occasions for which the camp lined up by height. Jane did not have a loving heart, and she was neither selfless nor honorable. Mattie felt that having to stand next to Jane so often put her somewhat at risk herself.

"Why didn't you go on the hiking tryouts?" Jane demanded. "Is it because you're fat?"

Mattie thought she probably hated Jane. She crossed her arms over her firm round stomach. She wasn't fat. It was just that she wasn't thin. Jane was thin, but this didn't lend her grace. Jane was sharp and knobby, like a twig. Her hair hung about her face in a wild dark tangle. She almost never smiled.

"If you could ask me any question in the world," Jane said, "what would you ask?" She was standing right in front of Mattie, blocking out the sun.

Mattie could think of several. Why do you steal? Why do you make sarcastic remarks about the counsellors? Why did you come to camp in the first place? The last question didn't seem too risky.

"What a dumb question," Jane said. "You're lucky I'm not a genie from a bottle." She bent down and itched an insect bite on her calf. "My mom needs a break from me. Usually I go to Dad, but he's just gotten married again and is," she sneered lightly, "on his honeymoon."

Mattie stared at Jane somewhat in awe. Jane, then, was a Child of Divorce. She had a secret sorrow. She looked at

Jane with increased interest. Now that she knew of Jane's sorrow, maybe she would become her friend and change her from the nasty person she was into someone nice. The counsellors would notice the transformation. She resolved to be kind.

"Don't you like being here?" she asked.

"Camp is camp," said Jane. "It's okay."

"I love camp," said Mattie.

"You love Miss Drew," Jane said. "The way you look at her—honestly." She turned her back and waded out into the water.

By three o'clock, Mattie had wearied of the Jane Project. The two girls had been together through Rest Hour, Writing Period, Crafts and Ping-Pong. Now they went into the central hall of the Main Building to wait for the hikers to return. They played jacks on the smooth pine floor. Jane moved one of her jacks into better range with an imperceptible flick of her thumb.

"You cheat," Mattie said disgustedly.

"Sometimes," Jane agreed. "You were getting too far ahead."

"Well, I quit," said Mattie.

"Fine by me," said Jane. She went up to the mantelpiece over the fireplace on which the Camp Cup was centered. Except for the simple silver chalice, the mantelpiece was bare. The Cup shone in the slant of late afternoon sun. It embodied the spirit, the essence, the true meaning of everything the Letters stood for—sacrifice, selflessness and love for others. It was awarded at the end of the summer to one of the oldest campers. The counsellors and the girls in Upper Camp voted for the Cup girl on the Sunday evening after the Cup Sermon in which Miss Drew told them how the Cup had been beaten by hand, and still carried the marks of the silversmith's hammer. Its beauty is in its simplicity, Miss Drew told them, and the child who wins the Cup embodies this beauty, this simplicity. Only those who had won the Cup were allowed to touch it. On the Sunday of the

Cup Sermon it was carried into chapel by an aide or counsellor who had been a Cup girl.

Mattie and Jane, who were still in Lower Camp, were not eligible to vote. Mattie was relieved. She knew she would have voted for Laura and she doubted Laura was a symbol of Love for Others.

Jane stood in front of the mantelpiece. "What do you think Miss Drew would do if someone hid the Cup?" she asked Mattie.

Mattie's breath froze in her lungs. "You can't hide the Cup," she gasped. "You can't even touch it."

"Says who," said Jane.

"Well you *know*," whispered Mattie. "You can't, that's all."

"It's a bunch of hooey," Jane said. "That part about not being pure enough to touch it." She turned around and looked at Mattie. Her eyes were green and hard and flat as pebbles. "Dare me," she said.

Mattie said nothing. She knew what she was imagining couldn't possibly happen. Jane would not be pulverized into dust, the Cup would not turn black, defiled by Jane's prints.

Jane stood on her tiptoes and reached up toward the mantelpiece. Her hand hovered near the slender base of the Cup. It trembled there for seconds, and then fell back to her side.

"I'd have done it," she said to Mattie. "But you had to dare me."

Toward the end of August, parents and brothers and sisters invaded the camp in large numbers. For Mattie, the integrity of the summer was breached as soon as they stepped onto the grounds and reclaimed Miss Drew's children as their own. They came in multicolored clothing and spoke in loud voices. They attended the Waterfront Show, the Dance Pageant, the Camp Play. They milled around the edges of everything which all summer had been funny or sad or inconsequential or imperative and was now impossible to explain.

On the last Sunday, Mattie and Laura's parents took them to lunch at the local inn.

"You've lost weight, kiddo," her father said. "You look wonderful."

"What's this about the Good Camper," asked their mother. "Is that instead of the Letter?"

"No. It's stupid," Laura said. "Miss Drew decided this year to have three kinds of Major Awards. You can get Good Camper, or Good Camper with Honorable Mention or your Letter. It's dumb. I don't know why she did that."

"Probably to stop all the crying," their father said. "For five years now, I've come to camp for Major Awards and sat on that rock surrounded by little girls in tears." He looked across the table at their mother. "Little boys aren't like that."

"Some of the parents complained, I guess," said Mattie's mother. "No doubt it's a good thing."

"It's not a good thing," Laura insisted. "No one wants to get a Good Camper. Only the Letter counts, isn't that right, Mattie?"

"That's right," Mattie agreed, but she didn't like talking about the Letters. She thought about Saturday night, and the waves of applause at the end of the play. "Matt-ie, Matt-ie," the campers had shouted. She had come to the center of the stage. She felt stretched and translucent with the happiness within, as if her skin were the skin of a balloon that would burst with one more breath.

"Cross your fingers for me," Mattie said to Laura when they returned to camp late in the afternoon. "I'll cross mine for you."

"It'll be okay," Laura said. "You were great in the play last night." She started up the path to Upper Camp. At the top of the hill she waved both her hands in the air, and Mattie saw she had crossed her fingers.

The center of camp was unusually still, even for a Sunday. The children were in their cabins, packing to leave the next morning. Nothing would happen now until evening, when parents would follow the trail to Glacier Rock, find a place to sit and wait for the Chapel Line of campers in their Sunday whites to emerge singing from the woods. *It's over,* Mattie thought. *The decisions have been made. There's nothing more I can do.*

At the far end of the clearing, Miss Drew was sitting on the porch of her office, her head bent as if deep in thought, and her eyes appeared closed. But Mattie knew they weren't. No matter what Miss Drew was doing, if you stepped within range, she would sense your presence and look right into you. *The last weekend is hard on her,* Mattie thought suddenly. To have to share her children with outsiders, at the very moment she had made them most truly hers, it was hardly fair. Each night all summer the camp drew silently together in a circle after the final song. When the stillness was complete, Miss Drew said, "Good night, everyone," and her voice hovered over them like a blessing. "Good night, Miss Drew," their voices chorused back. But now the parents were there in the evening, and the silence was never perfect. The children were impatient to break out of the circle and hug their mothers and fathers good night. "When will you be back?" they asked. "Are you coming for the Pageant tomorrow? Are you coming in the morning for the free swim?" *She must hate it.*

The birchbark box hung on its nail by the office door. But there would be no readings this Sunday, so Mattie had not written a poem. There was a picture of Miss Drew as a young counsellor in the Main Building, but the tall, awkward woman in the photograph who wore a headband Indian fashion around her forehead appeared no younger to Mattie, looked no different from the Camp Director sitting on her porch that afternoon. She remembered Laura's being glad there were people who called Miss Drew Eleanor. *Laura thinks Miss Drew needs friends. But she doesn't. She only needs us.* Mattie came closer and Miss Drew looked up at once.

"Hello, Mattie."

"Hello, Miss Drew."

"You'd better hurry and change into your whites. The bell will ring soon."

"Yes, Miss Drew." She wanted to say something which would acknowledge the bond between them. *I ought to have written a poem for free. For when we're not here.*

"Run along, Mattie," Miss Drew said gently. Her eyes were very tired, her face lined.

At sunset, the campers lined up to march to Glacier Rock. Most of the parents had gone on ahead but a few still dawdled in the center of camp. Some took pictures of their daughters, who wrapped their arms around the waists of the girls nearest them and leaned heads together. Mattie was glad her parents had already gone to the Rock because she did not want to put her arm around Jane.

Mattie and Jane were small for their age and were in line with children younger than they.

"We should be lined up by cabin groups. We don't belong with these little kids," Jane said.

Years and years ago, Alumnae House had been burnt to the ground and no one had ever discovered who the arsonist was, but the fire was believed to have been set by an angry camper. Mattie knew it couldn't have been Jane, but she thought maybe it had been Jane's mother. Jane was the kind of person who would burn something down if she got mad.

When it was time to begin singing, each camper placed her right hand on the shoulder of the girl in front of her. At first, Mattie touched Jane's shoulder as gingerly as possible, but then Jane looked back at her and grinned and Mattie smiled too. A very big feeling was lighting her up inside. It was as if her hand connected her not only to Jane but to all of the children in front of them and to all those behind, all the way back to Laura, whose fingers were crossed for luck. And the connectedness went down through her body into her feet and into the ground she walked on. It went far beneath the ground to the bubbling lava center of the earth.

The colors had bled from the sky by the time the front of the line reached the Rock. Counsellors stood at intervals along the path, shining flashlights at the campers' feet so they would not trip on roots or stones. "Come along with me," the campers sang, "by the light, by the light of the moon." They had to sing the refrain twenty or thirty times before all the children were lined up on the Rock and the signal was given to sit down. The first pale stars glimmered above Miss Drew's head. She spoke briefly to the parents about the significance of the Good Camper, the Good Camper with Honorable Mention, and the Letters. Then at last she began to read the lists of names. Mattie closed her eyes and prayed. "Please, God, don't let me get a Good Camper, please, God, don't let Laura get a Good Camper." The list of Good Campers was a long one and Mattie expelled her breath in a sigh of relief when Miss Drew came to the end. She repeated the prayer throughout the list of Good Campers with Honorable Mention, but this time, when Miss Drew reached the T's, Laura's name was called. Mattie sagged with her sister's disappointment. She watched Laura rise, step over and through the lines of campers and take the emblem from Miss Drew's outstretched hand. In the light from the campfire, Laura's braces shone in her polite smile. Miss Drew had gone on to the W's. Mattie's heart was racing. *Now she'll read the Letters. Only the Letters are left.*

The final list was much shorter and the T's came and went. For an instant Mattie thought Miss Drew had skipped her by mistake. It was fully night by then and she was reading by flashlight. But Miss Drew's voice ground on through the V's and W's. Inside Mattie, it grew very cold and dark. What had she done? Everyone else in her cabin group had gotten at least a Good Camper, except for Jane. *But Jane steals things!* The camp stood for the last song and in silence the circle was formed.

"Good night, everyone," Miss Drew said.

"Good night, Miss Drew." There were a few sobs.

Mattie's eyes were dry. The children marched single file back down the trail. Once out of sight of the Rock the line

broke apart and campers sprang like startled deer in every
direction, in search of parents and friends and roommates
and counsellors. Mattie plunged into the woods. Low
branches scratched her face but the pain felt good so she
continued to run. What had she done? Once she fell, and
when she stood up, her knee was bleeding. She ran almost
down to the lake. She could see pieces of it glinting beyond
the trees. She could hear the small waves as they lapped
against the shore. Mattie leaned up against a white pine and
the rough bark cut dully into her shoulder blades. The sap
stuck to her skin through her blouse. She thought back on
the summer of skits and songs and poems. *I was being me.
All summer long.*

Mattie cried then, but her tears were brittle shards of glass
and she drew them up from deep in her throat and spat them
out with horrible barking noises.

"Mattie?" her mother said.

Mattie shoved her back harder into the pine tree. "Don't
touch me." The words came out in unintelligible bursts. She
covered her face with her hands and retched and coughed
and gasped until there were no more sounds left in her to
make.

"Come back with me now," her mother said. She held
out her hand, but Mattie didn't move, and after a while her
mother turned and left.

Eventually Mattie began to shiver. She went back to camp
and up the hill to her cabin group. Jane came toward her.
"It's just a crummy piece of white felt," Jane said. "I didn't
get anything either." Mattie drew back into the shadows.
If you come any closer, I'll hit you. Disoriented, she headed
down the hill again.

The light was on in Miss Drew's office and Mattie's
mother stood on the porch. Mattie crept closer. "My child
is down by the lake in hysterics," her mother was saying.
Her mother's face was tight, her lips drawn very thin.
"She's having hysterics, Eleanor."

The light in the office sent Miss Drew's shadow long and

thin through the screen door and across the moonlit boards of the wooden porch. "I'm very sorry Mattie is upset, but you must understand. Mattie was always performing, always calling attention to herself. Many of the counsellors felt she was showing off." Miss Drew spoke quietly, but each word seemed to echo in the clearing. "The Letters reward those who think first of others."

"What happened tonight was wrong." Her mother's voice shook. *Are you going to cry now too? That would be dumb.* Mattie walked away quickly and Miss Drew's response reached her from a long distance.

"Wrong? I think not. Children also learn from failure."

She no longer knew where to go. Her knee throbbed and her eye stung where a branch had scratched it. She wandered back toward the lake. Would they come looking for her? She stood on the beach where the sand was white beneath the stars.

Pale Moon stepped out of her canoe.

"Look at that," she said to Mattie. She pointed to the edge of the lake where a small, stocky child shoved her back into a tree trunk and made gasping, retching sounds.

"She's pathetic," Mattie said.

"Yes," said Pale Moon. "She has to go."

"Absolutely," said Mattie. "We'll kill her."

"That won't be necessary, she'll leave by herself."

"How?"

"In the canoe."

Mattie looked at the child at the edge of the lake. "Stop crying," she said coldly. "You're a mess. Get in the canoe."

The girl looked at Mattie. "Now?" she said. "Forever?"

"Yes," said Mattie. The girl moved toward the canoe which rested on the bright sand. She pushed it into the water. "I have no paddle," she said.

"You don't need a paddle," said Mattie. Then, because she couldn't bear it, she added, "Pale Moon will go with you."

And Pale Moon stepped into the stern of the canoe while the other one huddled motionless in the bow, and the canoe moved out into the lake until at length only the light on the water remained.

The Ring at Yarrow

Jane Yolen

You take the pail,
I the jug,
and we will to Yarrow
where the fairies dance
all in a ring
by the burnside.

We will offer them the drink,
whiter than milk,
redder than blood,
sucked from the nipple
closest to the heart.

We will dance all night,
our shoen worn through,
the little bones sticking
through the sole
like thorns on a rose.

Their stained glass wings
beating above us,

they will hold our necks
in their icy hands;
they will pump us
like small koo.

Our mouths pricked with kisses,
sharper than serpent's bite
sharper than gnats' teeth,
sharper than the venomed dart
of a southern tribe.

You take the pail,
I the jug,
And we will to Yarrow
this night and the next
and all the nights
till the moon burns down
behind our backs
and we leave our burnished bones as warning.

Still Life with Woman and Apple

Lesléa Newman

You have been wandering around Gal's Gallery for barely an hour, yet museum fatigue has already set in. There is a stiffness about your neck and shoulders. Your feet are dragging as if through mud and your eyes are glazed over as though you have been up all night watching television. You park yourself on a hard bench in front of a painting: *Still Life With Woman and Apple.* You stare at the woman sitting on a maroon couch, one arm resting along the back of it, one leg crossed over the other, gazing at an apple on a small white dish on the table in front of her. Just for fun, you decide her name is Lilith.

From the way Lilith is looking at the apple before her, you know she is thinking about sex. Lilith thinks about sex all the time. Sex sex sex sex sex. Lilith thinks sex once a day keeps the doctor away. Lilith greets you on the street by pinching your ass and asking, "Getting any?" when a simple, "Hi, how are you?" would do. Lilith's philosophy is, straight people think we do it all the time, so why disappoint them? Lilith says if they're going to scream insults at us and throw rocks at us and take away our jobs, our houses, our children and our lives because of who we have sex with, we better make sure we're having a damn good time to make it all worthwhile.

There's a clock over Lilith's head. Both hands have stopped at the 12. It is always midnight in Lilith's world, never noon. She is always dressed in black leather from head to toe: boots, pants and a jacket with lots of zippers, all of them unzipped.

You know this is Lilith's cruising outfit. You imagine her knocking at your door just as you finish unpacking your last carton of books, or right as you are placing the last cast-iron frying pan on its hook in your new kitchen. She has left her Honda purring in your driveway, and invites you out for a ride. Reminds you to hold on tight as she takes you up the mountain to a secluded spot under a full moon and a sky speckled with stars. She teases you with a midnight picnic. "Want a hunk?" she'll ask, offering you a wedge of bread. "Take my cherry," she'll say, extending a fistful of fruit. After the meal, she'll lie back on the grass, her hands under her head. "I'm so hot!" she'll exclaim, stripping off her boots, pants and jacket. All she'll have on underneath is a black leather G-string and a tiny rose tattooed on the left cheek of her ass.

Her body gleams in the moonlight. "Aren't you hot?" she'll inquire. You try not to let on that you are sweating profusely. Museums are always so stuffy. Stifling. No air. You can scarcely breathe. You loosen your collar. Unbutton your shirt. Shed your clothes as gracefully as a snake sliding out of her skin.

You approach the painting and place your foot on the bottom of the frame for a leg up. You hoist yourself into the portrait and stare at Lilith. She has not moved. She is still gazing at the apple in front of her. Her eyes reveal her hunger. She is starving. Ravenous. Famished. She has been staring at that apple for a very long time.

Just for fun, you decide your name is Eve. You lift the apple from its small white dish, take a bite and chew voraciously until it is gone. Devoured. A part of you. You lie down on the table. Lilith has not moved. She is still still. She stares at you. At your red rosy cheeks, your breasts like two apples, the long stem of your neck, the apple blossoms of your hair. She is hungry. It is midnight. You have never been so still in your entire life. You know you are delicious. You wait for Lilith to bite. You will gladly wait forever.

The Perfectly Round Bagel

Robert Abel

Joe Levy opened the freezer door and removed a package of frozen bagels. He untwisted the tie and shook a bagel onto the kitchen counter.

By chance, the bagel landed on its edge and began to roll. Joe made a grab for it, but the bagel rolled smoothly down the counter and hopped off onto the floor.

Joe growled. "Just my luck, a perfectly round bagel." He threw the other, un-round bagels back into the freezer and made a dash for the rolling bagel which had already crossed the kitchen and was heading for the cellar door, which was open. Joe snatched at the bagel again, but missed again, and the blasted thing hopped down the basement steps like a rabbit or a frightened mouse. Joe clambered down in hot pursuit.

"Stop that bagel!" he called to his wife, who was hauling laundry out of the washing machine.

Sarah looked up with a quizzical expression, but just in time to see the little bagel scoot out the door which she had opened just a moment before to be able to carry her laundry out and hang it on the line. It was a beautiful spring morning.

Joe stopped just for a second. "The only perfectly round bagel in the world, and who gets it?" he demanded, then shot out the door. Sarah dropped her laundry and ran after Joe and the bagel.

"Let me catch it!" Sarah called. "Think of your heart!" She soon caught up to Joe, who was not a great runner.

The bagel zipped across the lawn, throwing off little green sparks, and down a slope onto the road. Some of the neighbors were coming out to their cars to go to work or to the commuter station, and they watched in dumb amazement as Joe and Sarah ripped by in rapt concentration on what was, maybe, a hockey puck, or some kind of donut-looking gadget. Was this the latest exercise thing? Joe *had* been putting on a little weight.

The bagel ahead of them leaned into the rotary curve in the center of the subdivision and then took a wide and wobbly right turn.

"It's the path of least resistance," Joe said to Sarah, panting.

"It's gravity," Sarah said.

Their feet slapped the pavement in a unified rhythm, then became chaotic, then rhythmic again.

The bagel rolled full tilt down Glennwood Lane. Joe and Sarah realized that if the little bagel topped the rise by the stop sign, it would hit a long, sloping straightaway into the center of town. Joe surged forward in a burst, hoping to nab the bagel before it crested the knoll, and his fingers just brushed it—but too late! The bagel hopped down the hill, gaining speed with every bounce.

Joe and Sarah slackened their pace a little. One of the neighbors pulled up beside them, rolled down the car window.

"Nice morning for a run?"

Joe pointed down the hill. "Run, nuts! We're trying to catch that bagel!"

The man looked down the hill skeptically. All he saw by now was a little leaping dot. "You want a ride?" he asked.

"Please!" Joe said. He and Sarah piled in the car. Joe leaned forward intensely, breathing hard. "It's taking a right on Cranberry," he said. "Step on it!"

The neighbor floored the gas pedal and the big car squealed down the hill toward town. In a few minutes, they were in sight of the bagel again, which was arcing in and out of traffic, sometimes disappearing for a moment as it rolled under a car or truck, only to reappear a moment later, bouncing merrily along the sidewalk or zipping catty-corner across intersections right beneath and between the feet of the pedestrians.

"A perfectly round bagel," Joe said to his neighbor. "Would you believe this could happen to me?"

"It's Monday," the neighbor said laconically. He groaned and stopped for a red light. "You'll do better on foot downtown here." He glanced at his watch. "Besides, I'm late for work."

"Right, thanks." Joe and Sarah piled out, running hard. They couldn't actually see the bagel now but reasoned it had made a right on Grosvenor Avenue because they saw a wave of pedestrians part as if to let something tiny through. And when Joe and Sarah steamed onto Grosvenor they saw they were right.

"There it is!" Sarah said, sprinting. "Right behind that taxi." The bagel was a mere thirty yards ahead now, and seemed to be losing momentum. Now Sarah gave it everything she had, and Joe fell a little behind, cheering her on. Sarah gained stride by stride on the bagel, stretched out her hands, leaned precariously forward, her fingertips coming within inches, then fractions of an inch, fell back to an inch and a half, then to three inches and then the bagel wobbled over onto River Road and gained a little speed as it rolled toward the sea. Then it revolved into the future, no stopping it. Joe and Sarah pursued relentlessly, with an aching devotion, determined to catch the perfectly round bagel. Night fell and still they pursued, following the sound of the bagel spinning along in gravel, humming over tarmac, whispering along on asphalt highway. Day came, and they ran still, and the perfect bagel rolled on. The bagel, and the Levys pursuing, rolled across continents, across time, across mountain ranges, over bridges, and down sunny country lanes, through rain and hail and snow and thunderstorm, through blinding sandstorm and blizzard. The bagel rolled on. The Levys ran after.

The neighbors complained: ''Look at that lawn! It hasn't been mowed for years!''

Owlswater

Pamela Dean

For the first three days of the journey westward, the conduct of Shan's fellows was exemplary. The cat killed and brought him rabbits. The eagle killed and brought him pigeons. The dog was not by her nature inclined to kill things, but she brought back a rabbit too heavy for the cat. Shan was not by his nature inclined to kill things, either. But, his talents not yet encompassing the restoration of life, he was grateful for the addition of meat to his dry fruit and hard bread.

Shan had neither the conceit to take credit for their preposterous harmony nor the humility to consider himself merely lucky. But he did have the temperament to hope that he would come, in the time allotted him, to the battlefield, and do what was required of him with grace if not with perfection.

On the fourth morning this hope became a contented certainty, and the dog chased the cat up a tree. Shan rebuked her, and she rolled enormous injured eyes at him and hid on the other side of the mare. Shan coaxed the cat down, although he had to use his voice, as if this rare and valuable animal were no more than a pet kitten.

They had gone on a mile or so through a belt of skimpy pines, when the dog chased the cat up one of those. From the fourth skimpy pine it was chased up, the cat refused to come down. Shan's inward self became welted with scratches and his outward throat raspy. With a twinge of something that was almost fear, he realized that he could grow to hate this.

He sat on the prickly ground in the mild, crisp smell of autumn, and thought. Speaking words aloud to the animals made them react as if they were no more than animals, and was viewed with grave displeasure by those it was his business to please. Thinking words at the animals, although no one had told him not to, seemed to confuse them. Thinking pictures at them always produced results, but seldom the results he wanted. His mental pictures were not clear at the best of times, and the clearest were most clear in details irrelevant to his fellows. Only a day or two ago, trying to keep the dog from rolling in a patch of poison ivy, he had pictured with exquisite clarity the fine red of the leaves. He was balked in his present attempt by an inability to remember whether cats climbed down headfirst or backwards.

The cat sat high above his head, like a piece of bracket fungus. The mare, which was not a fellow but just a horse, shifted from one foot to another like an impatient child. Shan felt more sympathy for her than for all his fellows together. Shan sighed and pulled at a saddlebag. He had tried thinking about food, but perhaps giving the cat a real whiff of the real viands would help.

He paused in the midst of unbuckling the bag. "Dear heaven," he said, as if he were saying something much worse. Where was the eagle? He moved from under the obscuring trees and turned slowly in a circle, searching the pure autumn sky.

At his first touch of panic, the eagle came sailing out of the north. Its flying shape was distorted. As it came closer, Shan saw that it carried something in its talons. Well, one of his fellows still behaved as if they were a fellowship.

Shan moved further from the mare, which had been dubious about the eagle from the beginning. The dog, who had gone to sleep in the grass while Shan tried to coax the cat down, raised her head, leaped up, and joined Shan in the middle of the road.

"Wherefore shouldst thou have aught?" he said to her. He tried, in a quick series of pictures, to convey to her that so long as the cat was up in the tree, she got none of the eagle's gift. She could bring that cat down in the time it took her to wag one wag, if she chose. The two of them, for all their immemorial enmity, inhabited the same inner landscape, one to which Shan was still a stranger.

But she was a stranger to the conditional mood. She wagged her tail at him, as if she were confident of being fed simply because she was there. She was a black dog of no particular kind except large: the top of her head was level with his elbow. Her tail and legs were feathery, and she had tangles of hair on her drooping ears that caught every burr and bramble the road offered. But the rest of her coat was short and sleek, and her feet were webbed. At Shan's reproachful look, she poked her nose into his stomach and wagged again.

Shan looked hopefully at the tree. The orange splotch that was his cat was moving. Shan scratched the dog between the eyes, and the eagle swooped upon the horse.

There was a perch, attached to the saddle, that the eagle had always disdained. Now it landed there with great delicacy, dropping a bloody rabbit onto the saddle. The mare put her ears back, flared her nostrils as if to make sure of what she smelled, let out an agonizing half-scream, and reared. The rabbit flew from the saddle and hit Shan on the foot. The dog snatched it up and trotted off into the trees.

"Mudface!" yelled Shan, as soothingly as possible. He ran for the mare, which reared again to dislodge the shrieking eagle and then pelted down the road. Shan reached for it with his inward voice, but the horse had no inward ear.

"Dragons take thee and all thy ilk!" said Shan to the

hovering eagle. He prudently said this with his outward voice, the language of which the eagle did not understand. It circled twice over his head and flew away westward.

The dog came pelting out of the trees again, dropped the rabbit back on his foot, and put her cold nose into his hand.

"Course well, my brindled hound," he quoted bitterly, from the song he followed. The knight in it had animals far more obliging than Shan's. He pulled a new burr out of the dog's right ear and added, "Fetch me the mud-brown mare." She wagged her tail. As far as she was concerned, "fetch" meant that he would throw a stick for her to chase. He would get more good out of giving her to his younger brother.

She whined at him, possibly because she had caught some echo of this thought, and possibly because she wanted to eat the rabbit.

" 'Twere better by far," he told her, "that thou fetch me the fire-red cat."

She licked his wrist. He thought at her, hard: his fellows were more important than his horse. Without the horse he would be late; but without the cat they would all be powerless.

If he could get the cat down quickly, they might be able to catch the horse up. Surely no animal that answered to the name of Mudface could have a glimmer of adventure in its heart. Giving up on the dog, Shan trudged through goldenrod to the tree's foot, squinted up, and drew in his inward breath.

The day was warm, but the year was old and sunset came early. It found Shan, the dog, and the cat only a little further advanced on their journey. Stopping at every farm to ask after his horse had slowed them considerably, and having the dog and cat made much of by every child on the way had slowed them more. The eagle had not come back.

Shan found a flat stone on the western slope of a hill and took his map from his sleeve. It was a pity he hadn't kept his food there as well, or at least his firebox. He had let the cat and dog share the raw rabbit. He sighed and flattened the map out.

The clump of farms they had passed was called Greenwell, the hill they sat on Brightbarrow, that smear of trees on the horizon Apsinthion's Wood. Shan traced with dreary familiarity the windings of the West Road through hill, bog, briar, and village, until, on the very edge of his stained and crumpled map, it drowned in the Owlswater.

Past that there was no road. But if the dreams of his teacher were true, the Owlswater would border on a nameless battlefield, and would take him past it, through the pass called Hallowstone in what mountains nobody knew, to the gray lake and the goldenrod and the world's desire. Shan sighed again. That the world's desire was not his was just another small joke of the Cocchinoi.

The cat bumped his hand out of its way and spilled itself into the middle of the map, purring. In the red light of sunset the deeper colors of its fur were almost luminous, and the white of its paws and chest faintly pink. It was a very long cat, but not a heavy one. Its ears and feet were so much too big for it that Shan thought it was not yet full-grown. It soothed him to think that some of his trouble came from the perversity of the cat's youth.

"Wretch," said Shan, scratching the top of its head. He looked out across the darkening air and sighed once more. He ought to have asked for food—or at least a firebox—at one of the farms. His red robe and a polite word would bring him all the kindness to be had.

His dog, who had been nosing around at the bottom of the hill, came tearing up it, sat on his feet, and barked. The cat hissed. Shan looked down the hill and saw a child in a green smock and soft boots exhorting a cow and two goats to do something they were not doing. Shan knew how she felt. As he pulled the map from under his indignant cat and began to fold it, she looked up and saw him.

"Hark!" she said. Shan looked for whatever strange thing

she was calling his attention to, and then remembered that people in these parts used the exclamation as a greeting.

"Hark," he said, feeling foolish.

"My mother asks whether you'll have some milk," called the girl. She was breathless from tugging at the cow.

"Tell thy lady mother," said Shan, putting the map away and scooping up the cat, "that I will indeed."

"My grandsire's a carter," yelled the child. The goats began to sidle away, and she took a halfhearted whack at the nearest with the stick she held.

"An his daughter have the grace to offer me milk, she is lady enough for me," said Shan, whose grandfather had earned his living as an indifferent musician.

He nudged the dog off his feet and stood up. The dog ran before him down the hill and barked at the little girl, who laughed and said, "What's this one's name?"

"She hasn't told me," said Shan, trying to match her diction.

"The goats don't tell me, either. But when I say Incense, and Ambergris, they know I'm talking to them."

"Well, the dog is a fellow, and must tell me her name in her own time, if she chooseth," said Shan, blinking a little at the names of the goats.

"What about the cat?" she asked.

"The same." She looked so exasperated that he added, "I haven't had them long."

"You're only an apprentice, then."

"Aye," said Shan, ruefully.

"I don't suppose you know about the Fountain of Youth, then?"

"Not to find it, no."

The cow and goats began to move down the road. Shan and the little girl and Shan's animals followed in a disorderly clump. Shan's dog, without instruction, kept the cow and goats from blundering off across country. Shan wondered who had taught her that, and whether he would ever teach her anything.

"Are you looking for the Fountain of Youth?" the child asked him.

"No," said Shan. "On no account."

"I would," she said, wistfully.

Shan looked at her. She had level brown eyes under straight, thick brows, a small sharp nose, wide cheekbones, and a pointed chin; altogether a most unsentimental countenance. "You might make application to be of my order," he told her. "My masters know more than I of these things."

"How old must I be?"

"Sixteen," said Shan. She looked grieved. "The same age at which you may go for a soldier," he explained.

"My brother's thirteen, and he *has* gone," she said.

They turned off the road onto a rutted track, Shan's dog harrying the cow and goats along.

"They ought not to have taken him," said Shan. "Is there war in these parts?"

"Away west," she said.

Shan was startled. What could it mean, that news of his teacher's dream-battle should come to the outer world? "Is he gone to that, then?"

"No," she said, dimpling wickedly. "They made him stay just one village over, and mind the farms, that true soldiers might go west."

Shan laughed. "So 'twould be for thee," he told her, "shouldst thou come to my teachers before thou'rt of age. Thou shouldst grow herbs while others sought thy dream."

"I do that now," she said, sourly. They had come over the crest of a hill, and vague in the twilight below them Shan saw a stone cottage, a wooden shed, and six fruit trees. "I have to take care of my mother," said the girl. "I'll bring you something in a moment."

The cow and goats began to move more quickly. Shan's dog ran after them, barking, and the little girl ran after too. Shan looked at the cat, which minced along in the middle of the track, nibbling an occasional weed and rubbing its head against an occasional rock. Shan ambled along with the cat. It was the first time since he joined the Cocchinoi that he had not been hurrying.

When he reached the cottage the girl was sitting on a stone bench under the fruit trees, and handed him a pottery mug full of milk. It was goat's milk, but she had put cinnamon in it, which helped a great deal. He wondered how so unprosperous a family had come by any spice at all.

"My thanks for the cinnamon," he said.

"My cousin's a sailor," she said.

"Hast charged him to find the Fountain of Youth?"

She shrugged. "He doesn't believe in it." She looked at him sharply. "Do you?"

"I know not," said Shan after a moment. "But look you; I think that, were it true, it would be a very great evil. And evil being a more likely thing than good, I do therefore perhaps believe in't after all."

"Evil!" said the child, outraged. "Why?"

"Thinkst thou not that unending life would be a great weariness?"

"I think," she said, "that it would give you time to do everything right. My brother should have stayed home to help me look after Ma, but he didn't have time to both be a soldier and look after her, so he left. And I don't have time to be a sorcerer and look after her, but I can't leave."

"Thou speakst of longer life, not unending. Indeed, child, the sorcerers will take thee at twenty or at sixty, an thou hast the will."

"How old are *you*?" she said.

"Nineteen," said Shan.

She looked surprised; Shan could almost feel her measuring him with her eye. He raised an eyebrow at her, and she grinned. "Well," she said, apparently abandoning whatever it was she thought of him to resume the argument, "something would always get in the way of whatever you wanted to do, if you only had *some* time and not all the time there was."

Shan wondered if she had had this argument before, with her brother or her cousin, or with herself.

"Why do you think it's evil?" she asked again.

"Where is honor," asked Shan in his turn, "where risk is not?"

She snorted. Shan had thought her to be perhaps ten, but she was sounding older as their talk went on. Maybe disappointment had matured her. "Thinkst thou life is good without honor, then?" he said.

"If my brother didn't want honor he'd have stayed with us."

"True honor," said Shan sharply, "had stayed where duty bid it and not gone howling for's own good only."

"Well, that's what I thought," she said, "but my mother and my cousin didn't."

"They are wrong," said Shan, before he thought he might be just as wrong to bring more dissent into her family.

She shrugged again. "My mother said, if I liked the look of you I was to say you could sleep in the barn. The cat and the dog, too, if the cat doesn't fight with our cats. There's clean hay."

The cat was asleep under the bench, and Shan had never seen it fight with anything larger than a blowing leaf. He looked at it with envy, and at the barn with longing.

"I must catch up to my horse," he said.

"You've got a horse, too?"

"Not a fellow," said Shan.

"Well, where is it?"

"Ahead of me on the road," said Shan, hoping she would not realize that he had let it run away from him. "Perchance thou sawst it; a horse the color of mud?"

"I saw one horse on the road today; it was brown."

Shan remembered that the mud in these parts was red. "My horse is brown. Whither went this horse?"

"West," she said. "Very briskly."

Shan began to doubt that it had been his mare, which was no more brisk than his cat was hot-blooded. But he had better not take the risk. "I go west also," he said, "and needs must find my horse ere I arrive. Thanks for thy kindness; I must go."

"Are you going to the battle?"

"No," said Shan, handing her his mug and nudging the cat with the toe of his boot.

"Where, then?"

"To the place where all dreams come true."

He thought she would speak again of the Fountain of Youth, but instead she shook her head. "All of them? That's awful."

Shan, after a brief puzzlement, knew exactly what she meant. He said, "Do you have bad dreams?"

"I have one," she said. "Skeletons come and take all the people. They have great iron cauldrons, and the people they put in the cauldrons turn to skeletons too, and they go out and find their friends and put them in the cauldrons. If you get out quickly only part of you will be bones."

Shan's spine crept. "And no weapon availeth against them?"

"Well, if you beat them all apart with a stick and bury all the bones in different places, they don't come back. But it's hard. All the bones rattle together again the minute you stop beating on them. And they howl and the others come to help them."

Shan shivered outright. "Heaven send I meet them not," he said.

"Do good dreams come true there, too?"

"So they say. Should I learn aught of the Fountain of Youth, I will send thee word."

"Or the skeletons," she said. "If anything works better than sticks."

"Or the skeletons." Something that had been in her voice made him add, "I must pass this way on my return. Shall I bring thee word myself?"

"Yes, please," she said, politely. Shan wondered how many promises made to her had been broken, but he could think of nothing to say. He thanked her again, and she went into the house.

Shan picked up his limp cat and looked thoughtfully at the dog. She would come to a whistle, but his masters frowned on that also. Shan closed his eyes and imagined a whistle with all the strength he could muster. The dog came galloping up to him and barked. Shan, delighted, bent and hugged her with the arm not holding the cat, and they walked away under the early stars.

Before they reached the main road, the cat had climbed upon his shoulder, draped itself around his neck, and gone back to sleep. The dog stayed well enough with his unambitious stride, but she sighed heavily now and again to show him that she was suffering. He cast out an occasional inward call to the eagle. He was beginning to worry.

"Apprentices to the School of Green Sorcery," he said to the dog, "must by their own contrivance, but according to the rules of their Order, make new things to grow, or old things to grow where by nature they do not. Those of the Yellow School must master the winds. Those of the Blue must brave High Castle in the Hidden Land and bring from its secret armory an enchanted weapon to serve them. Even those of the Brown must do things very great, if very terrible.

"But we of the Red must have no such adventures. I, look you, but go with a gaggle of unruly animals to a battle told of in a dream of a song, find there a certain knight, and do what? Naught but to observe what doth befall him, with the very comment of my soul, and thine, can I force thee to that," he said to the dog. His voice had risen sharply, and she barked at him.

"Think you," he said to her, more quietly, "that any knight will suffer a boy and a dog and a cat and a bird to so deal with him? Most particularly when all the boy can say to his Why is, My teacher dreamt a song about you, and wisheth to see if what befell in the song will befall in fact?"

She had nothing to say to this. Shan felt the prick of a vast but distant anxiety and decided that he had upset her. He put a hand on her neck, and the prickling dwindled.

"The old man dreameth true," he said to her. "But an he dream a song, meaneth this aught but that truly there is such a song? Wherefore should the song also be true? Do I go to find a battle and a witch, or but a wandering minstrel with a half-tuned harp? He tells me I go to find the battle. Is it part of my test to understand that this is not true?"

She slobbered amiably at his wrist, but had no comment.

Shan sighed. One did not question one's masters until one had returned from one's first pointless quest; and one did not, in the city and school of Asteococchinon, discuss one's quest with colleagues. He had discussed it with himself so much that now he found himself talking to a dog about it, and wishing he had mentioned it to the little girl. Neither of them could be of much help, but at least the girl would have talked back.

Shan had been filled full of stories of the communion achieved between masters of the Red Sorcery and their fellows. He certainly had achieved no such thing yet. Worse, he was not sure he would like it. He had always loved the talking animals of story. The feeling animals of fact were not what he had had in mind when, eight months ago, he knocked on the gate in the brick wall and professed himself able to answer the riddles of entrance.

"What's thy name?" he said to the dog. He knew a hundred things he might call her if she were a mere dog and chattel. He knew what he would have liked to call the cat. It would have sped the dragging hours of his journey to contemplate what one ought to call an eagle. But the little instruction given him before he went away had dwelt sternly on the folly of naming animals that knew their names already and would, when he had earned their trust, make him free of those names.

"None hath asked thee to earn my trust," he grumbled at the dog.

He was instantly swept under a wave of sorrow so vast

that it threatened to become his own. He remembered his sister's telling Cari next door, but not Shan, the surprise she had contrived for their mother's name-day; the puppy's preferring Mother to himself, only because it was Mother who remembered to feed it; Father's hushing his excited tale of an otter in the stream, to listen to an old neighbor's ramblings about someone who was getting married. He rubbed his eyes and came out of these inward waters.

His dog was plodding down the road ahead of him, her tail trailing in the dust. Shan had hurt her feelings. It had not occurred to him before that, in this communion he was supposed to seek, hurting her feelings would also hurt his own.

They did not find Mudface, that night or in the days that followed. The eagle did not return. Shan was able to be sanguine about the latter: it had been flying in the right direction when it left, and it knew as much about their object as he did. He did not know how it thought, or whether it thought; but a mind capable of that jape with the rabbit might well choose to reappear only when its presence would be most welcome.

If he had lost it altogether, the Red Master would have something to say to him. Shan thought, in the long sunny hours of trudging, that he might have something to say back, about the wisdom of sending people out untrained, unadvised, unaccompanied except by the words of a song and a bunch of valuable animals whose value was only a burden.

The cat, in the eagle's absence, or perhaps through some unpleasant memory of that last rabbit, began to bring him pigeons. Shan begged other food from farmhouses. Even those inhabitants unwilling to speak to him would usually throw out a bone for the dog, which left more pigeon for Shan. The weather was cool and dry, and the goldenrod burned in the fields and ditches. It was a fine month for a walk.

But he understood his animals very little better than he had when he began, and the eagle was gone. On that day when the horse would have brought him to the brink of the Owlswater, he was still two days' journey from that enigmatic river, coaxing the dog away from some stinking mess she had chosen to roll in, and trying to persuade the cat to walk instead of being carried. He had begun to sing and whistle the song under his breath, that he might not forget it in his irritation. The cat, who hated music, put a huge soft foot over his mouth and grumbled at him, but still insisted on being carried. The dog had not yet howled at his singing, but looked as if she would like to. Shan felt growing in him a profound distaste for all living things, including himself.

On the seventh day of what ought to have been a six days' journey, some difference in land or air made itself felt to all of them. Dog and cat pricked up their ears, and Shan straightened his back. Sounds multiplied in his inner hearing, though he could not make out what they were.

He muttered the song to himself. "Pale was the wounded knight That bore the rowan shield. Loud and cruel were the ravens' cries That feasted on the field." He listened, both within and without, for those cries. He heard only the wind, in the outward grasses and in that inward place he could not see.

Two hours before sunset on the ninth day of the six days' journey, they came slowly to the top of a hill and saw the road running down its other side to a little clear stream. Across the stream there was no road, and the sky was full of black birds, circling and diving and circling again. Shan could not see what they circled over; there was a vast gray shadow on the far bank of the stream. The croaking of the birds came only dimly to his ears, as if they were very far off. He and the cat and the dog went down the hill even more slowly than they had come up its other side. The dog kept herself pressed against the calf of his left leg, and the cat began to growl.

Shan stopped walking. A clamor was rising in his inward

ears, and he was afraid it would make him forget what he must do. If there was a way to shut out such inward noise, he had not yet found it.

He considered his task once more, and began to laugh. It had not occurred to him before that to find one wounded knight on a battlefield would be like catching one particular raindrop out of a thunderstorm. A man with a rowan shield to whom the ravens talked: for all Shan knew, every knight in the battle had borne a rowan shield and been worthy of such converse. And he was late. Had the ravens spoken already, the hare delivered its counsel and the owl its challenge? He had thought his quest absurd from the beginning; would he find it also impossible?

Shan shrugged, and went on. When they came to the bank of the stream, his inward ears were assaulted with such violence that he clapped his hands over the outer ones. Voices both smug and ravening chorused at him, fading in and out, obscuring one another. *Where shall we gang and dine the day, oh?* they inquired of him. *Nevermore,* they answered themselves. *I wot there lies a new-slain knight,* they said hopefully. *Your true love will die by your own right hand,* they offered. *And naebody kens that he lies there but his hawk and his hound and his lady fair,* said they, adding in heavily ironic tones after a moment, *God send every gentle man fine hawks, fine hounds, and such a leman.* And in a monotone that gradually drowned all the other voices, they chuckled, *Beck water cold and clear will never clean your wounds. There's none but the Maid of the Winding Mere can make thee hale and sound.*

This was the place. Shan scooped up his rumbling cat and stepped into the water. It was not quite knee-deep. The cold of it struck through his boots; he might as well have been barefoot in snow. His dog splashed happily along beside them. He was glad one of them liked water.

The mist slid around them and he could no longer see her even when she bumped his leg. The cat went on growling; the water sloshed; and inside his head the ravens gloated. *O'er his white banes when they are bare, the wind sall blaw for ever mair.* Shan willed them to be still, and they subsided into mutterings.

Just ahead of him in the impenetrable mist, something howled. The dog burst out barking and leaped away from him, showering him and the cat with water. The cat kicked him in the stomach and was gone from his arms. Right in front of him he heard a chaos of angry animal noises: cat, dogs, and birds. It seemed he must step into their midst with his next stride, but he waded on through the blank air and the running water.

Shan reached for his fellows, frantically, and caught for the first time in days the sharpness of the eagle's thought. He hoped earnestly at it to stop the cat and the dog. The cat's voice rose to a furious shriek, and thick silence fell.

Shan splashed on, and still heard nothing but the water. Could he have turned aside and be walking up or down the stream? It seemed to buffet him from all directions at once. If he lost those animals, nothing he could say or do would make it up.

He must be walking down the middle of the stream instead of crossing it. He changed direction, too suddenly. A stone turned under his left foot and he fell sideways into the bitter water, landing hard on his left knee. His dog began to bark again, still just ahead of him.

Shan was too cold to say what he felt. He put his hands down to the stream bed, not trusting the knee to hold him, and peered through the brown curling water for a stone that would not betray him. Between his hands he saw another hand among the stones.

Sourness rose in his throat, and then he saw the arm in brown leather. He crawled forward, keeping his eyes on it, and sunlight fell about him. He had found the other bank of the stream, a long flat stretch of round rocks on which lay the owner of the arm.

"Pale was the wounded knight," said Shan, just managing a whisper.

The wounded knight was worse than pale. Even Shan,

who had in his life seen a handful of dead birds and a few curled-up spiders, knew that this man was dead. *To go we know not where; to lie in cold obstruction and to rot,* said a voice in his mind.

Still kneeling in the cold water, Shan looked up over the knight's body. Three brindled hounds sat just beyond it and stared at him, the hair standing straight up on their long necks. Someone had told them to sit, and they were sitting. Shan's own dog, dripping, and his cat, fluffed up like a seeding dandelion, sat at the knight's head and glared at the hounds. Someone had told them to stop, too, but they were hoping the hounds would lose patience.

Shan thanked the eagle as well as he could. He was afraid to look for it, to look away from the hounds. They made his dog seem like some child's drawing of an animal. He wished at her to calm down, and at the other dogs to stay where they were, but he could not find the others with his inward self; no part of them lived where it was.

Beck water cold and clear will never clean your wounds, hissed the ravens in their inward voices. Shan looked from the hounds to the dead knight and felt fury begin to take possession of him.

The knight's hounds had no inward ear. What a rowan shield meant in this shadow-place between dream and deed he did not know; but in the lands he came from, it meant a sorcery not of the mind, but of the hands, that took the virtue in this wood and that stone and bound it to the hands' will. No man with an inward ear had need of a rowan shield. The knight's hounds had no inward ear. Shan was sure beyond mere scraps of evidence that the knight had had none either.

But the ravens who came to tell him what his salvation was spoke only with an inward voice.

Shan sprang to his feet, scattering water and pebbles. None of the animals moved. "So course well, my—his brindled hounds," he said; over the pounding of the blood in his ears he could not hear in what tone he said it. The words of

the song came more easily to his tongue than cursing. "And
fetch me the mountain hare Whose coat is as gray as the
Wastwater Or white as the lily fair."

He had just sense enough to add a sharp inward admoni-
tion to his own dog to stay where she was; even as she rolled
a reproachful eye back at him, the three hounds got up.

"Go, then," said Shan; and they did.

Shan watched them, and saw for the first time the mountains that stood up against the sky westward. The ruin of the
battle seemed to stretch to their lower slopes. Shan swallowed; other things were also making themselves known to
him for the first time. His dead knight was not the only one.
He seemed freshly dead, but from the heap and tumble of
the battlefield rose a stench that seemed more than a smell,
tangible as the dipping ravens.

*You'll sit on his white hause-bone, and I'll pluck out his bonny
blue eyen,* they sang to Shan. He looked down at the knight.

The man's eyes were closed, but the hair spread among
the stones was fair. Shan's cat slid up and delicately sniffed
at the knight's forehead, then sprang away, spitting, from a
raging shape that dived on it like a streak of lightning.

At first Shan thought his eagle had gone mad. But there
was no towering anger in his mind from it, only the distant
prickle of a never-sleeping vigilance. This fury was all in the
outer world. Rest ye, my good gray hawk, he thought,
crazily. But the hawk, like the hounds, had no ears for this
language. It sat on the knight's chest beating its wings and
shrieking.

Shan found his cat within; it was astonished almost
beyond fear, but it was not hurt. His dog gave him a sense
of resignation so thorough that for a moment he wondered
if it was not from his dog at all, but from some other man
nearby with the inner voice, one dying perhaps. *The rest is
silence,* said a voice neither his nor the ravens'. He looked
wildly over his shoulder, but there was only the bland face
of the mist.

He looked back at the hawk. He knew nothing about such

birds. But its screeches were making his head hurt, which in turn upset the dog and the cat far more than the screeches themselves; his animals' defensive indignation buffeted him. And this in its turn would bring the eagle. He had better do something quickly.

"Rest ye, his good gray hawk," he said, hopelessly; and the hawk folded its wings and turned one empty yellow eye upon him.

Shan stared back, feeling the waves of indignation and impatience from his animals recede along the edges of his inward hearing. He thought of the hounds. What manner of creature were they? They had no inner ear; yet no ordinary animal would answer to poetry.

He knelt beside the knight. The hawk abode motionless. Shan tried to pick up the rowan shield. It was too heavy for him, but the mere touch of it made his fingers sting and prickle. This was sorcery, though not his sort.

His dog barked, for his inward ear only, and he looked up quickly. Before him sat a mountain hare; behind it the three brindled hounds threw themselves panting to the ground. The hare paid them no attention. It was almost as large as Shan's cat, and regarded him with a much more intelligent eye. The season being what it was, the hare was neither as white as the lily fair nor as gray as the Wastwater, but mottled with both colors.

Shan reached without thinking for its inner ear, and was rewarded. Its silent voice was snug and close, a great refreshment after the distant tangle of his own animals and the horrible clarity of the ravens.

It said, *Green moss and heather bands Will never staunch the flood. There's none but the Witch of the Westmerlands Can save thy dear life's blood.*

It was looking, not at him, but at the dead man. Shan's own dear life's blood pounded in his ears. He had almost forgotten how angry he was. He felt embroiled in a conspiracy against the innocent deaf.

Why comest thou so late? he demanded, laying his hand

on the knight's chest. The hawk there stirred, but made no sound.

The hare still looked steadily upon the dead man, and spoke again with its inward voice. *So turn, turn your stallion's head Till his red mane flies in the wind And the rider of the moon gaes by And the bright star falls behind.*

Shan remembered how, on first committing the song to memory, he had been grateful that it was the knight, not he, who must follow these perplexing directions.

What use are thy instructions? he shouted within.

His dog stood up; his cat laid its ears back; the hounds, the hawk, and the knight never moved. The hare put back its delicate ears rimmed with white, wheeled clear around, and went in huge leaps back towards the mountains.

Shan swore briefly. He did not even have the mare he had set out with. The deathly air was still. The moon was not up, and would not be until late. And even if all these things had been according to his desire, there was still the knight.

There were other dead men on this field; he had not even looked straight at them. But he could not bear the thought of leaving this one lying. It was this one who should have risen hale and sound, with the sun high in the day. For a moment he considered; if he could find some war-horse and deceive it into accepting an authority he did not have, he could sling the dead man across it. It would soothe his heart to bring this body to the malicious maid in the song, who, it now appeared, sent salvation in words none who needed it could hear. If she could raise the dead, well and good. If she could not, he would at least distress her.

But nothing moved in that whole landscape except the devouring ravens. Shan straightened and looked at them. They were still silent after his rebuke. A voice not theirs said sweetly, *Call for the robin redbreast and the wren, Since o'er shady groves they hover, And with leaves and flowers do cover The friendless bodies of unburied men. Call unto his funeral dole The ant, the field mouse, and the mole, To rear him hillocks that will keep him warm, And, when gay tombs are robbed, sustain no*

harm. But keep the wolf far hence, that's foe to men, Or with his
nails he'll dig them up again.

If Shan had had a sword, he would have drawn it. He had
been told by the sorcerers of his school that for every outward possession that he had, he could find the inward, if he
dared. But the instructions for this inward discovery were
far in his future, and depended upon his solving, in a manner agreeable to his teachers, the dilemma that now con-
founded him. There was no sense in groping about for an
inward sword. But that lovely voice, being bodiless, and
seeming to have found out his thoughts, frightened him
more than the ravens'.

He repeated the words thoughtfully in his own inward
voice, which had never pleased but had no power to frighten
him. They were certainly advice of a kind. He could not take
the dead man with him, and as his anger ebbed again he
was just as pleased that he could not.

There were no stones large enough to build a cairn. But
there were animals here who took their orders in the form
of poetry. He looked at the hawk. Well, the hounds had not
eaten the hare. He would have to hope for the best.

"Hawk," he said. "Call for the robin redbreast and the
wren."

The hawk turned an expectant eye upon him. Shan
thought he knew what it wanted, but the leather glove they
had given him for the eagle was in Mudface's saddlebag. He
looked around him. The knight's bare right hand lay still in
the useless water, but on his left he wore a heavy glove.

Shan walked around the body and gently tugged at the
glove. The knight's wrist was still warm. Shan, gripping the
unfamiliar muscles and pulling harder at the glove, thought
that this must have been an accomplished warrior. Shan's
own wrists were mostly bone.

The glove came free, and Shan saw that the knight wore
a ring on the first finger of his left hand: a twisted band of
silver set with a blue stone. Shan stared. An accomplished
warrior, but a mere apprentice in the school of Blue Sorcery.

He had chosen an enchanted shield, rather than a weapon so enhanced; being, perhaps, already accustomed to a plain weapon. Shan wanted to talk to him.

He jerked the glove onto his left hand. It was too big for him. He held out his wrist to the hawk. It gripped fiercely with its talons, but did not prick through the leather. It was very heavy. Shan stood carefully, secured his balance, and flung up his arm. The hawk went smoothly from it and, as his eagle had done, beat away westward. Shan hoped that it would be back in time to gather the goldenrod. His heart quailed at the thought of asking the eagle.

He sighed. All three hounds stood up.

"Well, then," Shan said to them. "Call unto his funeral dole the ant, the field mouse, and the mole." The smallest of them barked, but they did not move. "And keep the wolf far hence, that's foe to men," Shan told them, "or with his nails he'll dig him up again." He shivered, and they looked at him with their sorrowful brown eyes. "Go, then," said Shan, and they went.

Shan pushed the hair out of his eyes, wondering when last he had combed it. His comb, of course, was with his horse. He hoped that a wild and unkempt appearance would be more daunting to that false witch than the sudden eruption from the wilderness of someone civilized and clean. Had any wounded knight ever found her in the gray lake? Well, she should think one had found her now. If he could not follow the knight, he must be the knight. That was as close as he could now come to watching what would have befallen, had the knight heard the ravens' cries and ridden to find the witch.

Whether what he contemplated was really in accordance with his instructions, he did not stop to consider too closely. His anger demanded some action. His dog and cat were becoming restless. He looked around, wondering how far he should carry this charade. Probably he ought to take the rowan shield; and the silvery sword, if he could find it.

The thought of staggering through difficult country burdened with weapons he could hardly carry, let alone use, stayed his hand. He had been a fool to lose Mudface. Somewhere in his inward hearing, words formed, and he spoke them aloud unconsidering. "A horse; my kingdom for a horse."

There was a drumming in his outward ears, and looking up he saw a red horse striding across the battlefield. It came to the other side of the dead knight and nosed among his scattered hair.

A great fear coiled to cold life in Shan's stomach. In plain fact he had no kingdom. But he knew the old stories: folk promising, for present jubilation, their future treasures, and paying later in bitterness; or not paying and suffering for it. Women who meant not to marry promising a firstborn child; men who had lost what was most precious to them blithely promising what they thought not to have again. If he took this horse, it was certain that he would somehow gain a kingdom; and no doubt it would become most dear to him before those with whom he had bargained came to claim it. He knew now what he had never been sure of: that some store of happiness awaited him. Such powers as he now dealt with did not barter with the empty-handed.

The horse moved from the knight to the water, startling Shan's cat and dog before it, and began to drink. Shan, still divided in his mind, searched for the horse's inner presence. It had none. If he should want to take it, then, he must use poetry.

Warily, he listened.

Farewell the neighing steed, and the shrill trump. When I was on horseback, wasn't I pretty? Steed threatens steed, in high and boastful neigh, Piercing the night's dull ear. When I was on horseback, wasn't I gay? Gallop apace, you fiery-footed steeds, Towards Phoebus' lodging. Why should a dog, a horse, a rat, have life And thou no breath at all? Give me another horse! bind up my wounds! Hast thou given the horse strength? hast thou clothed his neck with thunder?

Shan's whole inward self bellowed, *Stop!* His cat and dog,

who had been cautiously advancing on the horse, stood still and stared at him. Their reproaches came back to him with the echoes of his command. Through its dying waves he felt the cold bewilderment of the eagle. He apologized to them, and the cat came and rubbed against his ankle.

The horse, being unequipped to notice these things, lifted its dripping nose from the water and blew vigorously. Shan's dog, showered with water, bolted back to Shan. He pulled one of her ears and looked at the horse and sighed.

It turned and looked back. The shape of any horse's head will make almost any of its glances seem supercilious. But Shan had never felt so acutely measured since he stood before the Master of the Order of Red Sorcery and tried to explain why that Order ought to include himself.

The horse, as if it had made up its mind about him, sank suddenly down upon its haunches, and sat there like an oversized dog. Shan had never seen a horse do such a thing, but he recognized an invitation when he saw one. He looked along the body of the knight, measuring it with his eyes. Yes: the knight had not been a tall man. Shan was not tall himself, nor, they told him, very likely to be. He was stricken with fellow-feeling for the knight, and pity, and a return of his rage.

He looked at the sunken face of the dead man: the freckles on his nose and the ordered array of his pale eyelashes. Even now, Shan thought, I have more kingdom than this one.

He knelt, heaved up the rowan shield, and carried it, prickling, over to the horse. There should be a place on the saddle; yes, there. The horse sat still under his fumbling.

He went back to the knight. The knight had a scabbard, but it was empty. Shan, after considering for a moment, eased the silver ring off the knight's finger. He did not dare put it on.

The knight had a leather pouch, not much worn, that held a signet ring Shan did not recognize, two folded letters written in an alphabet Shan could not read, and a map of countries utterly strange to him. Shan put these things with the silver ring into the pouch and the pouch into one of the red horse's saddlebags. These should all be returned to the Blue Order.

Shan patted the horse, which did not seem to resent it.

"Have patience yet awhile," he said, and went back to the knight, trailed by his cat and dog.

Shan had not looked closely to see from what manner of wound the knight had had his death, and he did not look now. He searched the stones between the knight and the battlefield, and found with very little trouble those marked with blood. The mountain hare had known precisely what ailed the knight.

Shan cursed the hare and its presumed mistress briefly, and went on. *What are the roots that clutch, what branches grow Out of this stony rubble?* asked a voice not his. Shan made a gesture as if to scratch the inside of his head, and went on. As he came to the region where the corpses were more thickly strewn, and began to wonder how much longer he could go without throwing up what little food he had eaten, he found what he sought.

Hilt and blade alike were thick with blood, but the blue stones winked at him through that covering, their color only a little altered. Shan held his breath and grasped the hilt firmly, and almost dropped it. He had been prepared for the stickiness, but not for the sudden feeling that his hand had fallen asleep. He turned the hilt in his hands, wondering. The knight was more than an apprentice, then. He had braved High Castle and found his sword.

Shan, having made his way back to water, took the sword belt from the dead knight, stood up, and looked once more at his face. He had a scar on his forehead and a sunburn. "Fear no more the heat o' the sun," Shan told him, "nor the furious winter's rages." He stopped, twitching himself as if to shake off an intrusive insect.

The words followed him as he went back to the horse. *Quiet consummation have, and renowned be thy grave.*

"I will make it renowned to one at least," muttered Shan,

buckling the belt around his waist and shoving the sword into the sheath. He was obliged to take it off again and bore a new hole in the belt with the knight's knife. Like everything else of the knight's, it was far too big for him. After a moment the way his cat came and sniffed at the scabbard made him think, and he took the sword out again and washed it in the stream. The blood ran away in the water as if it were paint. He dried the sword on his cloak and put it back once more.

Then he ran through the old man's song in his mind, and searched again. Yes, a small horn hung from the knight's belt. Its mouthpiece was silver; it was bound with broad bands of silver; and in the widest of these were set two of the blue stones. Shan unhooked the baldric, gingerly, and felt again the sting and prickle of sorcery. He had never heard of an enchanted horn; and he had certainly never heard of anyone so young as the knight bearing three enchanted objects. He wondered if the knight had overreached himself. He wondered if he would be overreaching his own self if he dragged these belongings about this peculiar country.

The horse still sat, looking down its nose at him. Having put the horn into the saddlebag, Shan called his cat. It consented to settle inside his cloak, and he clambered awkwardly into the saddle. The horse heaved itself to all four feet and waited. The dog looked as alert as she was able. Shan took up the reins and grinned suddenly.

"Turn, turn your stallion's head," he said to the horse, "till your red mane flies in the wind, and the rider of the moon goes by, and the bright star falls behind."

The horse wheeled around with a violence that snapped Shan's teeth together and went like the river itself along the stony shore.

Shan was appalled. No horse ought to be able to go at this speed on such ground, and no rider ought to let it try. But its gait was utterly smooth. He might do more harm by distracting it than by leaving it alone. A sweet and mocking voice followed him, saying, *Smart lad, to slip betimes away From fields where glory does not stay.*

He was about to swear at it when he caught the desolation of his dog. She had easily kept up with Mudface, but this horse was beyond her. Shan looked behind, and could not see her at all. He felt as soothing as he could, and wondered desperately if she could track them by scent. She was a retriever, insofar as she was anything. He did not know how good their noses were. He did not know how to tell her to use her nose if she did not have the sense to do it. Shan leaned forward and took a huge, reeking breath of the horse's mane. The sense of desolation dwindled, whether because he had made her understand or because of the distance, he did not know.

"Fool," he said aloud to himself. The inner voices were silent. His cat had gone to sleep.

He had almost gone to sleep himself, which was also foolish, however smooth the horse's gait, when someone murmured in his inward ear.

Why do you ride this way, and wharfore cam' ye here?

The horse stopped, still smoothly, and Shan looked around.

They had kept the water on their left. Sitting in a little gnarled tree to their right was an owl. The moon had risen, and by its light Shan saw clearly the heart-shaped white face of the owl and its great round eyes that glinted yellow even in the bleaching moonlight. It was not the owlet of the song, but a full-grown, even over-grown bird, much too large for its type: larger than the eagle, when it should have been smaller than the cat. It looked capable of carrying the cat off if it chose. Shan gripped his fellow firmly, and took a steadying breath.

I seek the Witch of the Westmerlands, he said inwardly, blessing the insistence of his teachers that he know the song even in his sleep, *That dwells by the Winding Mere.*

Then fly free your good gray hawk To gather the goldenrod, answered the owl. Its voice was quiet and furry, but there was an undertone of irony in it. Shan thought it knew very well that the hawk was not his, and was not with him. He waited. *And face your horse into the clouds Above yon gay green wood,* said the owl. It rose suddenly from the tree and flew softly away, over the glimmering river and towards a dark patch that might, in a kinder light, be a green wood.

Shan's cat hissed. Shan blinked and looked at the sky. He was reassured to see that the pale moon was clear, and that the brightest star was below the hills. The owlet had obeyed the song. The Red Master would be pleased.

"Mark thou the sky," he said to the cat, which purred and tucked its head under his arm.

The horse stood still. Shan thought for a moment. "Fly free, his good gray hawk," he said, so loudly that the cat started, "and gather the goldenrod. And face, thou horse, into the clouds Above yon gay green wood."

The horse ambled down to the water's edge, seemed to consider it for a moment, went slowly along the bank for a little way, and splashed suddenly across.

There was a dim gray light over the land when they came to the wood. As Shan looked at the clouds above it, the hawk swooped down from them and dropped a great bundle of goldenrod impartially over Shan, the cat, and the horse. Shan and the cat both sneezed, and the cat began to wail. The horse only stopped. Shan, who was still wearing the knight's glove, held out his arm quickly. The hawk landed on his wrist and stared the cat into silence.

Shan worried over having neither poetry nor fresh meat with which to reward the hawk. He hoped he was not spoiling it for further use. It seemed contented, but how could he know its mind? It could, like the owl, collect his cat if it had a mind to.

He listened cautiously for the inward voices. *When the wind is southerly,* they snapped at him, *I know a hawk from a heronshaw.* Shan stopped listening at once, and they were silent.

He bundled as much goldenrod as he thought would be

useful under the sword belt, and brushed the rest off the cat, the horse, and his hair. Then he looked at the wood. He had never ridden a horse through a wood. "Well," he said to the horse, "face thyself into the clouds above this glum green wood."

The horse went along the edge of the wood until it found a spot that suited it. They followed the Owlswater through the wood. The ground grew steeper; the river flowed more quickly; and the horse slowed.

" 'Weary by the Owlswater,' " said Shan. The hawk was already wearying his arm. The horse snorted. Shan was beginning to suspect it of possessing considerably more intelligence than he was able, with his scanty stock of poetry, to find out.

None but love shall find me out, said a bodiless voice, to his inward ear. *There's no art To find the mind's construction in the face. Go and find out and be damned, dear boys.*

"For heaven's sake!" cried Shan. He had been free of the voices unless he willfully listened to them, until now. "What is this place?"

No voice inward or outward gave him any answer. But as he rode on, growing more and more sleepy, the mist from the river crept round and engulfed him. The horse strode on undeterred, but Shan, having nothing to look at, began to listen the more, and heard for the first time music as well as poetry. *And it's weary by the Owlswater,* sang a myriad melting voices, *and the misty brake fern way, Till through the cleft of the Hallowstone The winding water lay.*

Shan jerked his head up, but he saw neither singers nor pipers in this outward landscape. The light was brighter, but still gray. He was in the clouds above the gay green wood, which was beginning to show faintly green, but every leaf of which hung motionless and dripping. A few feet ahead of him the wood grew up against tall gray rocks spotted with moss and lichen, the moss so green it almost glowed in the dull air. The horse was plodding steadily towards a cleft in those rocks. He could hear the Owlswater off to the left, but saw only the sodden trees.

As the horse moved under the shadow of the cliffs, a chill fell on Shan that was not all of their making. He could not stir up the coals of his anger to warm him. Its cooling remnants took from him the delight of meeting such a creature as the Witch of the Westmerlands, but gave him no courage in return.

The cat stirred in his arm and poked its head out of the cloak. Shan wondered about his dog, and then looked up. But the clouds were close above and around him, and he did not see the eagle.

The sound of the horse's hooves on stone quieted suddenly. They had come out onto a little lawn of grass and goldenrod. Beyond it the slope dropped very swiftly, and through ribbons of mist Shan saw the winding water laid out before him like a sleeping snake, striped with waterweed and bordered by purple loosestrife and the ubiquitous goldenrod.

Shan cleared his throat. "Lie down, his brindled hounds," he said, though they were not there to hear him. "Rest ye, his good gray hawk. Thee, his steed, may graze thy fill, for I must dismount and walk."

The horse promptly lowered its hindquarters to the ground. Shan slid off, put the cat down, and flung the hawk into the dim air. It did not fly high, but circled below the clouds.

"But come when you hear his horn," shouted Shan, "and answer swift the call, For I fear ere the sun shall rise this morn Ye will serve me—him—us—best of all."

The horse stood up and shook itself. Shan, remembering what he would need, went up to it as it grazed and took the shield from its place and the horn from the saddlebag. The horse paid him no mind. He put his right arm through the strap of the shield, and took the horn in his left hand, and walked down the hill.

He felt already light-headed from little sleep and less

food. The pricking and shivering that the enchanted shield made in his right arm, and the horn in his left, seemed to meet in his heart. The weight of apprehension lifted from him, but left him light and empty. The shield was no longer heavy nor the sword in its sheath awkward. The only outward sound was the brush of the grasses against his cloak. His inward landscape was utterly silent.

He stopped at the water's brim and tucked the horn under his arm so he could pull the goldenrod from his belt. The water was flat and shining, but it was not clear. He tossed the goldenrod out over it and watched the sky's reflection break into pieces.

Where the goldenrod had disturbed it, the water did not grow smooth again; it grew darker, and little swells ran from the darkness and brought a sprig of goldenrod back to his feet. Still in silence, a streaming blackness formed itself from the water. It was so encumbered with tangled black hair that he was not sure of its shape. It had a white face and eyes as big as the owl's. It looked ungainly, but when after one wild look at him it leaped from the water to the shore and ran away through the goldenrod, it went fast and fleet. "One half the form of a maiden fair," said Shan aloud, "with a jet-black mare's body." The Red Master would indeed be pleased.

Shan put the horn to his lips and blew as hard as he could. Then he staggered: it rang in his inward as well as his outward ears, and much more loudly there. The red horse came down the hill as fast and fleet as the thing he had called from the lake. Behind it, barking furiously, leaped the brindled hounds. Shan scrambled into the saddle and, as the horse surged forward without being told, he looked up. The hawk was there.

"Course well, his brindled hounds," he cried. "Fetch me the jet-black mare. Stoop and strike, thou good gray hawk, And bring me the maiden fair." What maiden? he thought. Where would her other half come from?

There was a brief confusion of galloping and barking, and

he saw the hawk streak like a falling star across the face of the clouds and stoop upon the black shape with its flying hair. A voice fell upon his inner landscape that was more than a voice. For the first time, his four other inner senses woke to full life. Sunlight and water flooded his being: he felt the light's warmth, he saw it glint and waver on water, on distant leaves; he smelled wet rock and dry rock and the sun on summer grasses; he tasted cold spring water.

These things all said to him, "Pray sheathe thy silvery sword. Lay down thy rowan shield. For I see by the briny blood that flows You've been wounded in the field."

He had closed his eyes, but some echo of this speech in his outward hearing made him open them again. He still sat on the horse, which had stopped at the water's edge. A ripple ran across the lake and brought another yellow sprig to the shore. Right there at the horse's head, holding the reins Shan had foolishly dropped, stood a woman.

She stood in a gown of velvet blue, bound round with a silver chain, just as she ought. But Shan's first thought was that it did not become her. She was so tall that she could have mounted the horse without its kneeling, but she was very slender. The velvet looked too heavy for her. So did the blue. She had perfectly black hair, dark eyes, and very pale skin. The blue picked out only the veins in her throat and temples and sicklied over what beauty she might have had.

She looked at him with an expectant patience, absently rubbing the horse's neck, and said nothing. Shan was at a loss. The song had no more words for him to say. She might kiss his pale lips once and twice and three times round again, if she liked. Or she might be less inclined to this once she had seen him try to get down from this horse, which showed no inclination to kneel. He had just set horse and hounds and hawk on her; why should she be peaceable? Shan wondered also what she would say when she found that his briny blood was safely in his veins. He had somewhat to say to her on the matter of blood, but he could not remember what it was. The baked smell of the grass and the welcoming lap of the lake water distracted him, and a sweet taste he could not name.

The woman was still looking at him. Embarrassment drove him to what fear might have disdained. He listened for words he might use to her or to the horse. *Down on your knees,* they said to him, *and thank heaven, fasting, for a good man's love. When thou dost ask me blessing, I'll kneel down, and blessing ask of thee; so we'll live.*

Shan let his breath out impatiently; and when she frowned a little, said the first thing he could think of.

"Lady, what is this place? Why is the air full of voices?"

"These are the grazing-grounds of the Unicorns," she said. "Words are their food and their drink is music."

Her manner of saying this reminded Shan of the way in which his sister had explained to him that cows ate grass, and gave him the comfortable feeling that, not only was she speaking the truth, but there was nothing out-of-the-way about it. Her voice was low and somewhat husky, like the owl's that had challenged him.

While they looked at one another, the sun had come up behind her. By its kindly light he saw that she had black hair, but brown eyes, and more color to her than he had thought. She wore a red jewel at her throat, and when the sunlight had kindled it, he thought blue a most becoming color. Over her great eyes, the black brows were arched like the ears of a cat. She raised one of them at Shan, and he knew he must speak.

He found words waiting. "Ask me no more where Jove bestows, when June is past, the fading rose; for in thy beauty's orient deep these flowers, as in their causes, sleep." He stopped, nonplussed. The words could not be his, for he could hear also what followed them, and the ones that followed were wrong. *Ask me no more whither doth stray the golden atoms of the day; for in pure love heaven did prepare these powders to enrich your hair.* And her hair was black.

"What powders to enrich my hair?" she asked him.

Shan felt the welling up in him of an enormous warmth.

No one had ever before known what he was talking about or what he wanted. His family thought he had chosen his particular branch of sorcery because he liked animals, when the fact was that, as creatures irrational or extrarational, beyond words, they frightened him, and the discovery of a part of himself made to speak without words astonished him. His fellow students thought he had chosen sorcery for the power, when power frightened him more than animals. Even the child with the goats had thought he must be seeking the Fountain of Youth, when in fact he did not want length of days, but glory.

She must be answered. What powders to enrich her hair?

"Ash of a most precious thing," he answered at last, greatly daring. And what came next? For once, the voices did his wish and not his bidding. *Ask me no more whither doth haste the nightingale when May is past; for in your sweet dividing throat she winters and keeps warm her note.* No; not to a lady who spoke like the inward voice of an owl. He looked to see if she shared his amusement, but she had heard only his outward words.

"Ash of adamant?" she said, her face alight. "Of porphyry? That were a potent blaze indeed, my lord."

"It is indeed, my lady. But I am not your lord." *Ask me no more where those stars light that downward fall in dead of night—*

"Am I not, then, thy lady?"

Ask me no more if east or west—

"That, madam, is by your choice," said Shan, with a stiffness and formality he had often wished for, and now wished as earnestly away.

The Phoenix builds her spicy nest—

"Then to be my lord must be by thine."

For unto you at last she flies and in your fragrant bosom dies.

"What is thy name?" he asked her; the melodic din in his inward ears made any more graceful response impossible. She seemed to find this the best of all answers; she smiled at him. Shan wished she had a hundred names, that he might ask for them one by one.

"Melanie," she said.

The horse knelt down, and Shan slid from its back and stood before her. She took him by the hands. He thought he saw only her eyes, but long years after, with a most unwelcome clarity, he could remember the heavy thud of the rowan shield and the softer sound of the horn as he let go of them, and the cold glare his cat gave him before it made its stately way through the goldenrod, padding back up the hill and eastward.

"What is the Phoenix?" he had occasion to ask her later. All her rooms were hung with green and gray; her carpets were like moss, and every torch- or candle-flame wavered as if it were its own reflection. But she herself was most solid and most clear to the gaze.

"I know not," she said, " 'tis not my song."

" 'Tis so far true," said Shan, burying his face in her throat, "that here is a most fragrant nest."

"Search lower," she said, laughing.

"Nay, but that's not i'the song."

"What? That not my beauty's orient deep?"

"And what is Jove?"

"I tell thee, I know not."

"He hath my most potent gratitude for what he bestoweth," said Shan, and promptly forgot the bestower, as the recipient let him know that there had been words enough.

Shan knew that he had forgotten something. Sometimes the inward voices brushed on its far edge, brought it just to the border of remembrance. Had he been able to follow the convoluted path of his thoughts and memories unmolested, he could have dragged the matter securely into his inner landscape and recalled it. But if the inward voices did not wing away on their own wild trail of chance associations and foolish jokes, taking his inner thoughts with them whether he would or no, there was Melanie.

She had distracted him once by building up the fire, and

once by demanding what he had done with the pepper, and once by catching him in the eye, stingingly, with a lock of hair as she whipped by him on some hurried business; by kissing his hand, by pulling his hair, by pouring his forgotten mug of cold tea in his lap and laughing like a six-year-old, she had made him take his inward eye from the thing he sought.

He could not be angry with her. He had never been the sole focus of anyone's attention, and her attention, even giving full weight to its annoying aspects, was more gratifying than any he had ever wished for. Except for the first words she had spoken to him, he had never found any part of her in that inward landscape from which she so consistently distracted him. She never spoke to his inward ear, and if he called inwardly to her she did not hear him. She could hear the bodiless voices speaking poetry, and in fact could hear them singing, which he could not. She knew all the poems and songs he heard, and when he repeated them aloud to her she could finish them for him; but she did not hear them when they spoke to him.

She was so accomplished that she frightened him, and so silly that, had it not been for certain clear evidence to the contrary, he would have thought her eight or nine. She looked his own age, nineteen, and he might have believed her to be as much as five-and-twenty. She was the best harpist he had ever heard, he who had spent his childhood in the company of musicians far better than his grandfather. She sang as though she had been studying it for more years than she could have lived. She knew more natural history than he had thought there was; but in the midst of a learned disquisition on the habits of the muskrat, she would suddenly begin telling him absurd and fanciful things, as if she did not know the difference between scholarship and children's tales. If he let her brush his hair, she would braid beads into it, or dry grass, or feathers. She knew some sorcery to make the seeds of the wild grasses fall meekly into her cupped hands; but she then took this largesse into the kitchen and blithely burned it. Shan was not much concerned with food while he lived with her; but on considering the matter afterwards, he thought they had subsisted largely on lake water and dried fruit, and in his more melancholy moods attributed their hilarity to this lopsided diet.

He was not much concerned with sleep at this time, either. They spent a great deal of time in bed, but very little in sleep. Sometimes he thought he did not sleep at all; if he dreamed, it was only of Melanie and the gray lake and the fluffy spikes of the goldenrod, burning against the dull water. He had no need to separate sleep from waking.

One sunset, however, by means Shan did not care to inquire into, Melanie killed a goose. She plucked, and singed, and drew it, and stuffed it with the wild grass seeds, and roasted it, quite as if she had been cooking, and expertly, for all her life, instead of having only that morning boiled two ducks' eggs until a child could have played at dodge ball with them. Shan had been unwise enough to make this observation aloud, and Melanie immediately threw hers at his forehead, where it burst open, showering him with dry fragments in a way, as she happily explained to him, that a child's ball would never do. Shan had hurled his egg back, since the inside of Melanie's made him disinclined to eat his own; but it had missed Melanie and hit the stone wall behind her, where it still clung damply while she dealt with the goose.

Having eaten the goose, they built houses of its bones. This provoked a flurry of deathly poetry from the inward voices and, Shan thought, gave him dreams that were, for the first time since his arrival, different from his waking life. He dreamt that skeletons came to his town and took all the people. The skeletons had great iron cauldrons, and the people whom they put into the cauldrons turned to skeletons as well, and went out and found their friends, and put them into the cauldrons. Some struggled out of the cauldrons before their work was done, and limped about on bony feet, or nursed an arm of bones.

Shan spent an agonizing time convincing the elders of the town, all of whom looked like his teachers in Asteococchinon, to try beating the skeletons apart with sticks and burying each bone far from its fellows. This method was effective, but difficult of accomplishment: the bones rattled together again when the beaters stopped for breath, and the skeletons howled as they were beaten apart, which brought more skeletons to their aid.

Shan, standing in a shower of bones and beating them apart as fast as they assumed the semblance of order, bethought himself suddenly of the inward voices. They had words for every other occasion; perhaps they had some for this one.

He knew the anguish of the marrow, they told him earnestly, *the ague of the skeleton; no contact possible to flesh allayed the fever of the bone. Behind this mortal Bone there knits a bolder One.* As an assessment of the matter, Shan thought, these were not pleasing. He thumped an assembling rib cage with his stick, and had the pleasure of seeing two of the flat bones break and fall to the ground. He listened again.

Arise from my bones, avenger of these wrongs! Well, that was a command, but of perhaps the wrong sort. *Peace to her bitter bones. Can these bones live? Dogs bury bones in hideaways.* Shan snickered, and was thumped on the head by a thighbone for his inattention. He ducked and smacked it, frowning.

The mention of dogs made him uneasy. Dogs had something to do with what he wanted to remember. Perhaps he should suggest to the elders that they use dogs to battle the skeletons. The dogs could bury the bones in hideaways. *Cry havoc,* suggested the voices, *and let slip the dogs of war.* Shan smashed a skull to bits and watched them shiver together again before they hit the ground.

"Havoc!" he cried, but nothing happened. The bones continued their dance. *Oh, ye dry bones, hear the word of the Lord. Full fathom five thy father lies; of his bones are coral made.*

"Stop!" said Shan, exasperated, and smashed an assembled hand into flinders. *They are not a pipe for Fortune's finger,* the voices told him severely, *to sound what stop she pleases.*

"Quiet, I beg of thee," gasped Shan, ducking a femur and bouncing his stick off a collection of vertebrae. "Or speak to me of bones."

The knight's bones are dust, and his good sword rust; his soul is with the saints', I trust.

"Quiet consummation have," shouted Shan, triumphantly, "and renowned be thy grave."

The bones fell down in a clattering cloud. He put his arms over his head, and when silence came and he looked up, he was kneeling in the bed and Melanie lay grinning at him, the dying firelight caught in her hair and in her eyes.

"What dream was that?" she asked.

"The latest dream I ever dreamt," said Shan, slowly, "on the cold hillside. I saw pale kings and princes, too, pale warriors, death-pale were they all: They cried, 'La Belle Dame Sans Merci Thee hath in thrall!' " He grimaced, and hit his forehead with the palm of his hand, but the voices had already stopped.

"What is this hath me in thrall?" he asked her. "What is la belle dame sans merci; what folk speak so mincingly through the nose?"

"Nay, I know not. 'Tis not my song," she said, as she always did when he asked her about the voices.

"What is thy song, then?" he said, for the first time.

"What? Hast thou heard it not? How camest thou here if thou heardst it not?"

"Play it for me, then," said Shan, who did not want to go back to sleep.

Melanie flung the covers over his head and bounded across the room. He disentangled himself and watched her take the harp from the case. It was the only thing she took consistent care of. She pushed her hair back over her shoulders, and the light of the dying fire ran along it like water. She plucked a string, turned a peg, plucked again, and

began to play. The fine hairs rose along the back of Shan's
neck. He knew this music.

    Pale was the wounded knight
    That bore the rowan shield;
    Loud and cruel were the ravens' cries
    That feasted on the field.

    Beck water cold and clear
    Will never clean your wounds.
    There's none but the Maid of the Winding Mere
    Can make thee hale and sound.

Shan sat perfectly still while she sang. The Red Master, in
a voice still very fine, had sung this to the assembled apprentices on a late summer evening. Shan had sung it to
himself on a long autumn journey. He had lost his horse on
the West Road; he had met a little girl who wanted him to
look for the Fountain of Youth, and who had nightmares
about walking bones. He could tell her now what to do about
them. He ought to ask Melanie about the Fountain of Youth.

He walked over to where she sat by the fire, and put his
hand very gently across the harp strings. This was not always safe, but this time she only smiled at him. "I had
thought thou hadst known it," she said.

Shan knelt at her feet and laid his arms across her knees.
She was as warm as the embers of the fire. "I prithee tell me
one thing."

"What thou wilt."

"Where is the Fountain of Youth?"

The laughter slid out of her face, and she looked at him
with eyes as cold as opals. "There is a great virtue," she
said, precisely, "in the blood of a Unicorn killed by treachery." She leaned the harp against her stool, on the side away
from the fire.

Shan stood up and took two steps backwards; not from

her eyes, or from her voice, but from the knowledge she gave him.

"Surely such a thing could bring only great evil," he said.

"It hath brought thee me," she said. She stood up also, a head taller than he.

"Wherefore came ye here?" he asked her.

"You know that only a makeless maid shall tame the Unicorn?"

"Aye."

"Know you of the Unicorn Hunt those of the Secret Country hold at summer's waning?"

"No."

"This is but a mock show; the Unicorn leads them a hard chase, and when it chooseth, or when they tire, lays its head in the lap of the maiden. The hunters play at killing, and the Unicorn at dying. Being a maid, I went one year on the Hunt and lured the Unicorn; but my father and my brothers did in truth kill it and bathe in's blood, and did anoint me also."

She stopped. Shan, colder than he had ever felt, only looked at her.

"For that I had the benefit of this murder," she said after a moment, "and the knowledge, and made no move to stop it, though I contrived it not, I was made to give the benefit to others. And for that I had used my innocence to trap the Unicorn, I was made to give this benefit at cost of my innocence."

"And thy father and brothers?"

"I know not. I was set here, and now and again the wounded knights come."

"How many?"

"Thou art the twelfth," said Melanie, smiling at him, though not quite as she was used to do, "and the last. After twelve I am free."

"I was no wounded knight."

"Oh, fear not," she said, still smiling. "Thou hast the benefit e'en so."

Shan, thinking a lewd jest out of place in this hideous

spate of revelations, blinked at her. He felt, after that infinitesimal gesture, as if he had just opened his eyes upon morning after a night of vivid and conflicting dreams. The very light was clearer and less rich. He stared at Melanie, and saw for the first time that she had freckles.

The dream, the song, and her face came together as the broken bones had done. His joy went from him like a cloak whipped away in a high wind. He remembered what had brought him to this place. He saw the young knight, with his freckles and sunburn, sleeping too soundly upon his stony bed. He felt the sudden purity of a just rage. He took a step forward.

"And what of one that lies by the Owlswater, tended by beasts and attending on worms?"

"What meanest thou?" The firelight made her face fantastic; he could not see what look was on it.

"That knight thou tookst me for, he with the rowan shield and the silvery sword. He that lieth by the Owlswater, bled to death, for that he had no ears for thy most diligent messengers."

"I have no messengers." She was neither afraid nor indignant; she was merely explaining the natural history of the Maid of the Winding Mere.

"What? Not the ravens, nor the mountain hare, nor the owlet?"

"What meanest thou? I am not of thy Order; no beast attends me; to them I have neither speech nor language. Those are the minions of the Unicorns."

Shan wrapped his arms around himself. Oh, dear heaven, he thought, so clearly that he knew the words were his own, the wind that hath taken my cloak of joy is bitter cold.

Melanie said, "Hast thou lost a friend by their machinations?"

"I know not," said Shan.

"Indeed I am sorry. 'Twas none of my doing."

"I know," said Shan, absently. He was still unsteady from what he now saw as his disenchantment. Some glamour had been lifted from his sight; he had been angry with Melanie; he had remembered what he was. He wanted to go to her and bury his face in the summer smell of her hair, but he was afraid of her now. If he were to love her, he must do so with an unclouded mind. If she could cloud it at her will, what then?

"I think we must leave this place," she said, still standing on the other side of the hearth. "If thou hast dreamt of thralldom, the virtue of the lake diminisheth. Why should it last beyond the twelfth knight?"

"I am not a knight," said Shan.

"So much the better; I have had my fill of them." She grinned, but less wildly than was her wont.

Shan looked at her. Did she want to go with him? "I must seek my fellows," he told her. "Recall you that when I met you first, I bore a cat?"

Melanie shook her head. "I remember thee only." She grinned again, more naturally. "And thy most obliging horse."

Shan looked at her with sudden hope. "Was the spell upon me of thy making, or of the Unicorns'?"

"I have cast no spell; the change I have made in thee goes to the bone."

Shan stared at her. "But it hath lifted even now."

"Not what I have done," said she.

Shan could not ask her what she had done. He felt that he trembled on the brink of ruin. Had these wild days been all of his kingdom, and was the payment due so soon?

Melanie took two steps towards him. "There's none can harm the knight who's lain with the Witch of the Westmerlands. Thou hast found thy Fountain of Youth."

"I'll none of it," whispered Shan.

" 'Tis too late to say so," she said. In her voice was only grave speculation. "But for all else we have world enough and time."

"And so infected, am I to plague others wi'this fever?"

"No, thou hast no such power. Why art thou angry? Didst thou not come seeking this very boon?"

"Of all terrors in earth or sky," said Shan, "I'd have fled this one fastest."

"Art thou mad? In immortality, thou art safe from the greatest terror, thou art free of envious and calumniating time."

"Oh, aye; and free of honor, glory, virtue, effort."

"The paths of glory lead but to the grave," said Melanie, and then shook her head in the manner of one betrayed by inward voices into defending the wrong side of the argument.

"E'en so," said Shan. His own voices were silent. His inward landscape was full of shadows.

Melanie put her left hand on his head, with so formal a gesture that he did not flinch from it as he would have from a caress. Her touch was light and exceedingly cold. "You have risen hale and sound, the sun high in the day," she said. "Ride with your brindled hounds at heel, and your good gray hawk in hand."

Shan felt, from very far off, the first touch of an inward pain, as if some warrior far more skilled than he had slashed him with an inward knife. He turned from Melanie before he could take a last look at her. He gathered up his boots, one from beside the fire and the other from beside the bed, found before the search became awkward his other garments in their various locations, bundled his cloak and the silvery sword atop it all, and went out of her house.

It was a bright autumn morning, not long after sunrise. There was no wind. Shan dressed himself with his back to the house. Then, having ascertained that his reluctance to look at it derived not from delicacy but from cowardice, he turned around. The house was not there. The dark water lay in just such a wilderness as he had seen when first he flung the goldenrod into it.

Shan looked down. To his left in the grass shone the little horn; to his right lay the rowan shield. Though sun had

shone and rain fallen and the wind howled while they lay
there, they were not worn, nor weathered, nor gnawed by
worm or mold. Like himself, perhaps, they had put on immortality. Shan hung the horn on the dead knight's sword
belt and heaved the shield into his arms. He was no better
able to carry it now than he had been at first; but now he did
not need it. Horn and shield stung and prickled his flesh, but
in the middle of him where their forces had met before and
lightened him, there was a weight like a stone that they
could not move.

Shan walked a few hard steps with the useless shield, and
felt a breath on the back of his neck. He started violently,
hitting himself in the mouth with the shield, and with great
difficulty prevented himself from beginning to cry. He
turned around. The red horse gazed down at him as if it
wondered whether he was worth the trouble of stepping on.

"Down on your knees," said Shan, in a cracked voice,
"and thank heaven, fasting, for a good man's love."

The horse sat down for him and allowed him to mount it,
but managed to give the impression that it did these things
at orders other than his own. Shan listened for the inward
voices, but they were still silent.

As he retraced his path, he found one by one the brindled
hounds and the hawk, but saw no sign of his fellows. He
rode with the knight's animals down the Owlswater to the
battlefield. He found the battlefield only by the odd mound
of leaves and earth and flowers on the stony bank of the
water. The robin redbreast and the wren had done their
work well.

Shan frowned even as he thought so. Was he, after all, in
the right place? The mound looked settled; the leaves were
from other autumns; the flowers grew in the earth. He
thought he had been several months with Melanie; if it were
autumn, he must have stayed a year; but this mound looked
as if more seasons than that had worked on it. Shan rode a
little way in the direction of the westward mountains, looking for the dead. He found one staring skull in a clump of

rocks, but it was grown through with some autumn-reddened vine.

He turned the horse and looked at the wall of mist above the Owlswater. He listened once more for the voices, and this time he was rewarded. He, like Melanie, could hear them singing.

> The Flowers of the Forest, that fought aye the
>   foremost,
> The prime of our land, lie cauld in the clay.
> We'll hear nae mair lilting at our ewe-milking;
> Women and bairns are hearless and wae,
> Sighing and moaning on ilka green loaning:
> The Flowers of the Forest are a' wede away.

Shan shivered, as though someone were walking over the grave he would never lie in. One thin voice said, *And after many a summer dies the swan. Me only cruel immortality consumes; I wither slowly in thine arms.* Shan thumped his heels into the horse, which considered for a moment and then stepped into the water. Behind them the voices dwindled and died.

He rode east holding a perfect stillness about his heart, but some small part of his mind wondered idly at the weather, and tried to calculate how long he had spent with Melanie. He wondered, with a sudden hope, if he had dreamt his doom in the merest instant. He pulled the horse to a stop.

The shivering of the enchanted sword met the shakiness of his hands and stilled it. He held the blade out in the sunshine for a moment and then brought it deliberately down upon the top of his left arm, just below the joint of the elbow. It hurt more than he had expected, and the blood ran faster. But even as exultation caught him, the flow of blood slowed, the gaping lips of the wound pulled together, shriveled pink, and grew smooth again.

Shan dropped the sword and wept into the horse's neck.

* * *

He was of two minds about stopping at the farm where the little girl lived, and the mind that wished to pass by was uppermost when he rode over a rise and saw cottage and sheds below him in the light of early afternoon. But as he passed the narrow road to the cottage, a black streak and an orange one burst out of the underbrush and leaped up and down in the middle of the road. The hawk rose from Shan's fist, shrieking. The three hounds barked and yelped. The horse stopped dead; Shan slid off it, before it could kneel, if it was going to, and sat down hard in the dust; and the black dog and the orange cat swarmed over him.

In the untraveled shadows of his inward landscape, their forms took on solidity. To his inward ear, the dog spoke to him.

"Most gracious greetings," she said. "What hath so potently unveiled thy inner understanding?"

"Great sorrow," said Shan, shortly.

"This is often so," she told him. She had the most mellifluous voice he had ever heard.

"What's thy name?" he asked her.

"What thou wilt," she said.

He looked at the cat, with some peculiar doubling of inward and outward vision. "What of thee?" he said.

The cat purred thunderously, but disdained to speak. Shan tried to remember the names he had thought of for the dog.

"You're not dead," remarked a voice above his head.

Unwelcome as this observation was, Shan shoved the dog's slobbering head away from his and squinted up. A tall young woman in brown smock and skirt and boots stood and grinned at him.

"Did you find the Fountain of Youth?" she said.

Shan felt his jaw hardening, and spoke before he thought.

"There is great virtue," he said, "in the blood of a Unicorn killed by treachery."

She took two steps away from him, looking sick. The dog

climbed out of his lap and sat down at her feet. Shan, realizing that he would have longer than most people to regret anything he said or did, pressed his hands to his eyes for a moment and then looked at her.

"I cry you mercy," he said, "but in truth, in all my travels, that is the manner of immortality I saw or heard tell of. Look not so sickly; I've not done the deed. How's thy lady mother?"

"She died the year after you came," said the girl, "and I guess I'm glad. I don't think I could kill a Unicorn. But she didn't finish her book. She named the dog and the cat, though; she said we could change the names when they got around to telling us the right ones."

"Why art thou not at the School of Sorcery?"

"I have to take care of the animals. I can't walk up to the brick wall with a cow, a horse, a dog, an eagle, two goats, and seven cats."

"A horse?"

"The color of mud," she said, trying to smile.

Shan looked at the red horse, the three brindled hounds, the hawk.

"What's thy name?"

"Chalcedony," she said. Shan thought he knew now who had named the goats. If he had been able to wish for anything, he might have had a fleeting regret at not having met the girl's mother.

"What hath she named the cat and dog?" he said.

"Sumac and Elderberry," she said.

Shan gave up. "Thou and I," he told her, "may pass through the brick wall with a cow, a hawk, an eagle, two horses, four dogs, two goats, and seven cats. I have had travail enough on my journey; they may but begin to pay for't do they take thee and all thy stock."

He stood up, and she began brushing the dust from his robe. She was taller than he was, but still thin; neither so tall nor so thin as Melanie. He wondered, not very much, how

many years he had been away. He had no more need to
count them.

He coughed a little in the dust and thought that he must
still count time for others. The dead; the living; the ever-
living: he had duties to each and could only determine the
order of performing them. He must see this girl settled soon;
he must return the dead knight's belongings to his Order
before his Order forgot him. His real business, if he had any,
lay with the Unicorns. But they, like he, would always be
there. With a tiny but potent shock, like the barest touch of
an enchanted weapon, he realized that Melanie too would
always be there. He could not end anything, ever. He spoke
quickly to Chalcedony.

"I have found also," he told her, "what doth vanquish
the skeletons. Thou must speak to them in poetry, and
they'll do thy will."

"Do you know," she said, slowly, abandoning his robe
and holding out her hand for the brindled hounds to sniff,
"I haven't dreamt of them since you first came?"

Shan was silent.

"I've grown eight inches," she told him. "You haven't at
all, I don't think."

"No," said Shan. "Not at all."

After Centuries

Donna J. Waidtlow

Gravity worked
on the angel's jowls
and her body
sagged earthwards
between each wing beat.

Passage

Gardner Dozois

Sven left the midnight forest, and turned down the slope toward the sea. Where the tall sea grass ended and the path slanted down the shingle toward the beach, he stopped to put his dark-lantern down on the hard-packed scree; he dared not take it near Them. He plunged his dagger to the hilt into the ground, next to the lantern. Nor cold iron. He shifted the weight of the bag on his shoulder and continued down the path.

As he came over the lip of the slope, where it steepened to the sea, the world seemed to open up before him, more felt than seen. The sea was restless, a dark breathing immensity that opened to the horizon, with here and there a white phosphorescent gleam edging a wave tip, like a knife blade briefly shown and then hidden away again. The water was oily and black and rolled in slow oily surges into the shore, making no sound. You could smell the salt. Far behind, on the distant point of the cove, you could still see one or two flickering yellow lights in the darkened town, and when the wind shifted for a moment to gust from that quarter, ruffling his square-cut rufous beard, you could smell woodsmoke and dung, and hear the scrannel yapping of a dog.

Sven paused for a moment on the steep slope, and the heavy bag thumped against his back. The moon had been half shrouded in tattered black clouds, but now they parted, and there was the moon, smoky-bronze, as full and round as a shield, bigger than he'd ever seen it before, bigger than seemed possible. Hunter's Moon. Thin lines of black cloud streamed across it, flying with the wind, and he heard a clamoring overhead in the sky, iron-tongued voices barking and baying and snarling and quarrelling, drawing nearer, then fading slowly away out over the dark expanse of the sea, and he knew that the Wild Hunt was abroad this night, coursing through the sky. Big as he was, he shivered. He made the Sign of the White Christ; then, for safety's sake, Thor's Hammer. After a moment, he went on down the slope, his tangled blond hair snapping behind him in the wind, digging his heels in, little rivulets of sand and pebbles whispering down before him to the beach.

Then he was on the strand. Sand crunched underfoot, and rats and other nameless scurrying things fled away from him as he walked, rattling the tough beach grass. Nearer the waterline, his feet sank into the dark sand, making a slight sucking noise as he pulled them free again, and he could imagine his footprints filling slowly with cold water behind him, in the dark.

More black clouds boiled up around the moon, as though it were being cooked in a black cauldron, shrouding it again.

The Ship loomed ahead, at the edge of the oily black sea. The masts and rigging were dark—you could just make them out, black against the lighter blackness of the sky, like clouds almost-seen at night. The masts seemed to stretch far taller than the masts of the ships of mortal men. He couldn't see their tops. The hull was like a wall of black cloud. A milky silver light shown low, from a gangway set near the waterline.

Nimbly for all his bulk, he scrambled up the jetty and onto

the pier, the wood groaning under his boots. The pier was old and sagging, the wood slimed with moss and barnacles, slowly collapsing into the bay. You could smell the green rot in the wood. Then he was on the pale shining gangplank—never a sound to be heard now, underfoot—and then he was in the Ship.

The room was lit with an even, sourceless silver light, like autumn moonlight on ice. He could just make out the Elf, sitting at a table, his hands flat before him, motionless. He was very much taller and more slender than ordinary men, with fingers as long as flutes. If his face knew how to make expressions, they were not expressions that Sven knew how to read.

Sven put the bag down on the table. "Here's your bagful of heads," Sven said.

The Elf looked at him. His eyes were tunnels through his head to someplace black and cold and far away—at the very bottom of them, a faint gray glimmer came and went, like a swordblade thrown into a lake and gleaming coldly beneath the moving surface of the water.

He closed his long fingers around the bag and took it possessively into his lap. The heads shifted wetly in the bag, rolling like melons inside the rough flax cloth.

Sven bit back guilt. The Ship for Elfland wouldn't sail again in his lifetime—this was a cheap enough price to pay for immortality. He dared not think—and could not—what they wanted them for.

The Elf was still staring at him. His face was cold and radiant and pale, and almost too beautiful to look upon.

In his voice like a bell ringing under ice, the Elf said, "Now go get us a bagful of hearts."

On his way out, Sven passed a sallow, rat-faced man with pockmarked skin and a scruffy beard, a bag thrown over his shoulder.

They eyed each other warily, uneasily, as they passed on the pier. They didn't speak.

I wonder what *he* brings them?, Sven thought.

The Hound of Merin

Eleanor Arnason

There was a lineage named Gesh, which held land in the hill country at the western edge of the Great Central Plain. The land was good, with plenty of water and timber. The valley bottoms were flat and arable. But the Gesh were not lucky, especially when it came to war. They became involved in a struggle with one of their neighbors, a large and powerful lineage named Merin. The struggle went on for years. At times there was peace, but it never lasted. In the end there was a decisive battle, and the men of Gesh lost.

Imagine a fortress town overlooking a valley deep in the hills of Gesh. There are high walls made of stone covered with pale blue plaster, narrow streets and houses built around courtyards. Sunlight enters, filling the courtyards, slanting into shadowy rooms. The women of the lineage go about their business more quietly than is usual and with only a few jokes. Their children are with them. One of the children is a boy named Hala, thirteen or fourteen, not quite old enough to go to war.

Days pass. It's autumn. The fields have been harvested, and the trees on the hilltops are changing color. Finally a message comes, brought by a single man. His *tsin* is stumbling with exhaustion as it comes through the gate. The man can barely stand once he has dismounted.

He tells the women, his aunts and senior cousins, that everything is over. The men of Gesh are dead, killed by the enemy or by their own weapons. The Merin are a day behind him at the most.

What mourning they want to do will have to be done now, along with preparations to greet their new relations.

After he delivered the message, the last man of Gesh went into an inner courtyard. There he knelt in the dust and sunlight, taking out his knife. The women and children were safe from harm, and there was nothing more he could do for them. No man willingly falls alive into the hands of the enemy.

The boy Hala followed the man to the courtyard. A balcony went around it on the second story, roofed over but open toward the courtyard. The boy stood there in the shadow, looking down at the man as he cut his throat.

A body empties itself as it dies, releasing whatever is in the bladder and bowels. Most likely this happened, but the story does not tell that part. It speaks of red blood rushing from the wound in the throat, and how the body of the man collapsed onto the dusty white pavement. Gesh Hala decided then that he would never belong to Merin.

He left the body for the women to care for and went down to find the man's riding animal. That afternoon he cared for the *tsin*. In the evening, he led the animal out of the fortress. It could not yet be ridden. He walked through the fields, over the dry stubble, leading the *tsin*, then up into the hills.

He spent the night there, hidden by the forest. In the morning, he went on, still leading the animal. It was still too weak to ride.

He did not see the soldiers of Merin arrive or the greeting they received from his female relatives. The mourning was over by then, the body of his cousin cremated. Surely there had been time for that. The children had been dressed in their best clothing and told how they must speak to their new uncles and cousins.

Most likely, Hala went east toward the Great Plain. He would have kept to the high ground, where the forest would protect him. There were trails made by animals. The men who had known the trails, who could have followed him, were dead, and the animals were shy: no danger, unless he did something really stupid.

Imagine him, moving through the shadows below the trees. Around him the foliage is green and blue-green, copper-red, the rich brown of weathered bronze. The ground is dry. The air smells of autumn, whatever that aroma may be on this planet and in this country.

The *tsin* follows him, a large quadruped that looks something like an antelope. Its horns have been cut off close to its head and capped with metal. This was always done to the animals used in war. Most likely, the *tsin* is striped. The animals with solid coloration are rare and expensive.

We don't have a description of Hala as a boy. I see him as tall and thin, maybe a little gawky. At a distance, he'd pass for human, except for the fur that covers him. It is short and thick and grey. When he moves through a patch of sunlight, the fur shines like silver. He wears the usual costume for a male of that era: a kilt and sandals. There is a knife in a sheath at his side.

This is how I imagine him, as he leaves everything he knows behind: the land of Gesh, his family, his name and his childhood. It's unlikely that he understood what he was doing. He acted in response to grief and rage and maybe to some odd trait in his personality. How could he possibly, at the age of fourteen, know what he was getting himself into?

There are many versions of the story of Hala. Some are brief and stick to known facts. Others elaborate, filling all the empty spaces. These long tales, which are known as *tsugalin,* or "lies," tell us what happened next in detail. But it's all made up. All we know for certain is that the boy was on his own.

This was the age called the Unraveling, when there was almost continual war. Old families were destroyed. Old alliances were torn to pieces. The world was full of people who no longer had a lineage. They were outlaws—thieves, beggars, prostitutes and mercenary soldiers—living as best they could. Living badly, for the most part. Life has never been easy for people without a family. Hala became one of these people. He lived among the shadows for more than fifteen years.

When he comes back into the light, he is a man of thirty, a soldier employed by Eh Manhata, war leader for the new alliance that by now has begun to dominate the Great Central Plain.

By this time Hala has his nickname. He is called *Sul,* after an animal which the People use for hunting. The animal is large, fierce, relentless and loyal. The closest equivalent animal on Earth would be a hunting dog. So Hala's name can be translated as Hound-Hala. According to the histories, he was a respected captain in the army of Eh Manhata.

His old enemies, the Merin, were allied with Eh, as they had been for several generations, and they had troops in the army. The man leading the troops was a son of Merin named Ie.

So now the two main characters in the story have been brought together. At this point most of the stories describe Hala for the first time.

He was tall for a man of the People, which probably means his height was somewhere in the area of 175 centimeters. His body was broad and powerful-looking. According to many of the stories, "it was evident that his life had not been easy." This probably means that he was scarred. His fur was pale grey. His eyes were ordinary blue.

(Remember that these "ordinary" eyes would have been entirely blue, with no white showing, and the pupils would have been rectangular and horizontal like the eyes of a sheep or squid.)

The stories tell us that he was a good comrade and an

excellent soldier. Men liked him, though "he was one of those people who always keep their ideas in back." He kept secrets, this means. He was not forthcoming.

When he spoke, he was to the point. When he moved, his motions were rapid and decisive. But he knew how to wait, and it was no problem for him to be silent.

Merin Ie was a few years younger, about the same height as Gesh Hala but more slender. His fur was dark grey. His eyes were blue-green. He was the favorite son of a powerful lineage: well-nourished, confident, happy with a quality that the People call *kahtiad*. It means upright, in-front, clearly visible, sincere: a person who says what he thinks and goes in a straight line toward his goal.

According to the stories, he was a good soldier, though not as good as Gesh Hala, and a good leader. His directness made it easy for him to deal with other people, and he was intelligent and observant. An ardent young man, but not a fool.

He had several nicknames. One was "Malachite" and referred to his eyes. Another was "The Beautiful." A third was "The Well Adorned." This last probably refers to the way he dressed, but there is a possible double entendre.

Both men held ranks that put them on the army council. It was not possible for Hala to avoid the son of Merin, though he must have wanted to, and Merin Ie had no idea that Hala was (or had been) Gesh.

The old quarrel lay between them like a sword covered with blood. But Merin Ie did not know this, and he fell in love with Hala Sul. No one knows exactly why. What could have been so attractive about this tough soldier-for-hire? This man out of the shadows?

Most likely, Merin Ie was not especially serious at first. It would be a camp romance, lasting a few days or maybe a tenth of a year. How could it be anything else? Hala was nameless. Not the kind of man one would choose for a longtime love affair.

But when he approached Hala, the man said no.

This is the part of the story which the People find really hilarious. It is their version of a rolling-around-on-the-floor joke.

Hala Sul was nameless to other men, but he knew that he belonged to one of two lineages. If he was Gesh, then Ie was an enemy. If he was Merin, then they were relatives. In either case, they could not be lovers.

He could not explain to Ie what was going on. If the Merin decided he was Gesh, they were almost certain to kill him. If they decided he was a cousin—well, he still had no desire to be one of them, though his anger had almost vanished over the long and difficult years. Now, more than anything else, he wanted to make a decent living and stay out of trouble.

The other aspect of his problem was this: Hala was in love with Ie.

This also strikes the People as very funny.

The situation was impossible. Hala did his best to avoid Ie. When they had to be together, Hala was polite and unfriendly.

It did no good. Ie's affection, which had not been much at first, at least according to the stories, grew strong now. He became crazy in love. Whenever Hala turned around, there was the son of Merin.

The stories about Hala treat this period in one of two ways. Either they emphasize the romance, describing how the proud and beautiful son of Merin is pushed back (i.e., brought down) by love.

Or they emphasize the humor. Isn't it funny to see Merin Ie make a spectacle of himself, languishing in a conspicuous fashion around the camp?

Isn't it funny to watch Hound-Hala push away the only man he has ever loved?

This went on until Eh Manhata called Hala to his quarters. "Why don't you go to bed with this man? Then maybe he will be able to think about something except your body, and we can all get back to the important business of war."

Hala can do nothing except tell him the truth.

This may be the moment to speak about Eh Manhata. He led the alliance which became the Ten Wound Together and then the Weaving. In the end, this turned into the government of the planet. Insofar as the People have a Founding Father, he is it. They respect him for his religious piety, which no one has ever questioned, and for his devotion to his family. He was a loving son and brother who never went against the women of his lineage. No one can argue with his skill as a soldier. No one can fault his drive to power. But he is a disturbing man.

There is no evidence that he cared for anyone except his mother and sisters. He had many male relatives, who fought alongside him for years and died in his campaigns. No stories tell of his affection for these people. He had allies outside his lineage, but no close friends. The first descriptions of his sexual behavior date from a hundred years after his death and may not be reliable. They say, when he decided he needed sex, he would point to one of his officers—someone who was not a relative—and tell him to spend the night. His officers accepted this as one of their duties. It was not an especially difficult one. His sex drive was not strong, and there was nothing perverse about his sexual habits.

This is the man who listened to Hala's story: a man who understood nothing about love.

He had never been interested in Hala's past. Why should he have been? The world at that time was full of people without families. Some were like Hala, refugees from lineages that had been destroyed. Others had been driven out of their families. The age bred many criminals. Manhata didn't ask the men he hired where they had come from or what crimes they might have committed.

But now he became furious. Hala had kept secrets from him. Hala had injured his plans. This was a betrayal, and—in any case—he could not leave Hala in the camp, in front of Merin Ie, driving the man even further into craziness.

He told Gesh Hala that he no longer had work in the army of Eh. "If I ever see you again, I will have you killed."

Then he told his soldiers to beat Hala and throw him out of camp. This was done.

In a day or two, Merin Ie noticed that Hala was gone and asked about him.

"He is a man of the shadows with no loyalty to anything. He has left us. He will not return."

According to many versions of the story, Merin Ie tried to find Hala, questioning people in the camp. He found out nothing. The soldiers who knew what had happened kept quiet out of fear. Later on, the stories say, whenever Ie sent messengers anywhere, he told them to ask about Hala. But it was years before he got any news.

At first, he moped, having trouble paying attention to anything except his own unhappiness. But his relatives told him this was unmanly and disloyal. He had to pull himself together, they told him, and get back to thinking about the war.

"The man left without saying a word. He has no interest in you, cousin. Let the wind take him and blow him away! Don't think about him any longer."

In the end, the son of Merin listened to his cousins. Though he did not forget Hala. He merely put that memory off to the side.

What happened to Hala? The most reliable stories give no information. He goes back into the shadows and is not seen again for almost five years.

The lying stories describe many adventures.

According to the most famous tale, he was found—almost dead—by a camp follower. This person was a woman, who made her living by divination and prostitution. The divination was, of course, a legitimate activity. The prostitution was the worst possible kind of crime, since her customers were men who felt a need to have sex with a woman.

This story is unlikely. Eh Manhata is famous for his absolute hatred of heterosexuality except for the purposes of

procreation. He would certainly not have allowed a hetero-
sexual prostitute to follow his army, though how he would
have gotten rid of her is a bit of a question. Manhata was
very traditional. He would have found it difficult to coerce
a woman and impossible to harm one.

But there would have been no problem with any man who
visited a female prostitute. Manhata would have had the
man killed in the most unpleasant way available.

But if the story is unlikely, it is also entertaining. It says
that the prostitute nursed Hala back to health. He would
have died without her. The soldiers had done a good job of
beating him.

When he had recovered, he asked what he could do for
her. She said her work was dangerous. A man who was
willing to have sex with a woman was capable of anything.
She never knew when one of her customers would turn on
her, driven by guilt and horror at what he was doing or had
just done. She needed a bodyguard.

The story says Hala took the job and remained for some
time in the shadow camp which followed after Eh Manhata's army. The people there were diviners, gamblers,
prostitutes, dealers in drugs and *halin,* criminals of every
variety. They had little loyalty to anything and little honor.
How could they? Loyalty and honor are like trees which
grow from a great root system. The root system is kinship.
When it is no longer healthy, the trees that grow out of it
must die.

Hala liked the woman, though not in a way that was
sexual, and he felt grateful to her. In any case, where did he
have to go? Though it was dangerous for him to stay so close
to Eh Manhata.

He told the woman about this problem. She boiled up a
dye and combed it into his fur, turning him from grey to
black. Hah! It was strange to have a woman touch him, who
was not a relative! But it had to be done. Now the soldiers
coming into the shadow camp would not recognize him. He
was no longer Hala of the shining silver-grey pelt. Instead,

his fur was drab, and his eyes in contrast seemed brighter and paler: no longer ordinary. He kept out of sight as much as possible, especially during the day. At night, the woman's customers arrived, some to learn their fortunes, others to have sex. Hala stayed close to the woman's tent, listening for any sign of trouble. It was not work that he found pleasant.

But the People have a proverb, which is very close to "Beggars can't be choosers."

"There are few choices beyond the firelight."

In the end, the story tells us, the woman became pregnant. There was always the risk of this, though the woman knew as much as anyone about ways to prevent conception, and most of the men who visited her did not ask for "the act which causes procreation." For one thing, it was a lot more expensive than the other things she did. For another, there are degrees of perversity. Most of her customers were willing to be satisfied with less extreme versions of the crime. (Some no doubt were repelled by the idea of doing for pleasure what should be done only to create people. Others may have lacked imagination: they wanted to do with a woman what they had done with men.)

In any case, the woman got pregnant. Think of what this meant in this society. Remember that these people drew— and draw—a line between sex for pleasure and sex for procreation. Sex for pleasure is between people of the same gender. Sex for procreation is (of course) between members of different gender. It is not something done casually. Children do not come out of nowhere, by accident. Children come from families. They are the product of negotiations between lineages and of matings that have been formally arranged. If a woman without a family becomes pregnant, it is almost certainly evidence that she has done something immoral.

She tried every way she knew to end the pregnancy, but nothing worked, though several of the methods made her sick. The foetus remained inside her. She decided she had to tell Gesh Hala what was going on.

It's hard to explain how disturbing this situation was to him. For one thing, the People keep their men firmly away from the concerns of women. Men belong on the perimeter, guarding the lineage and its land. What happens at the hearth is not their business.

If the women decide now and then that an abortion is necessary, most likely because something has gone very badly wrong with the pregnancy, the men are not told about it. If certain children die as soon as they are born, the men are not given details.

So now Hala was faced with the worst possible kind of problem: a problem that belonged to women. What he knew—what he'd been told his entire life—was that his first duty was to keep women and children from harm. Even in the shadows, this lesson had not been forgotten.

He was horrified that the woman had tried to kill the child inside, since she was healthy, and there was no evidence that there was anything wrong with the child. But that, in the end, was not his decision. He had no right to an opinion about the making or raising of children. Everything he had ever learned told him that he could not let the woman deal with her problem alone.

So they discussed the problem, Hala feeling more uncomfortable than he had ever been in his life. The woman knew a midwife, who'd be willing to help her, but this person was not close. They would have to leave at once, while she was still able to travel.

They bought two *tsina:* lazy bad-tempered animals that cost far too much. The good animals had all been bought by the army of Eh Manhata.

They rode south and west. Once again it was autumn, but this time the season was rainy and cold. The roads were muddy tracks. There were few other travelers. The war had produced too many criminals. It was dangerous to leave home.

Often, when they reached a caravanserai, they found it half in ruins and empty, except for themselves. The local families had forgotten their old duties: there was no wood or food in the storerooms. Even the supply of water was uncertain. Wells had fallen in. The ceramic pots designed to hold rain had broken. Once they found the body of an animal floating in a water storage pond, huge and bloated. Hala could not tell if it had gotten there on its own or been put there.

A long hard journey. They made it finally to the village where the midwife lived.

Her house was gone. Nothing remained except burnt pieces of wood. Hala left the woman in a thicket and went to ask questions.

"That witch and pervert! We drove her out and made sure there was nothing for her to come back to."

"You did that to a woman?" asked Hala.

"You could scarcely call her a proper woman. She belonged to that horrible new religion, which says that the Goddess has two forms. We couldn't have that in our village."

The world was becoming a truly bad place, thought Hala. He went back to the woman and gave his news.

It was true, the woman told her. Her friend had been a follower of the religion that says the Goddess has a mate, equal to her. Together, they had created the universe. In this religion, sex between men and women was tolerable and maybe even holy, since it was a replica of the act between the Goddess and her Other Self.

Hala felt as if he was sinking deeper and deeper into excrement. He was not the passionate and romantic boy who had left Gesh more than fifteen years before. He had done things he did not like to remember and lost some— maybe most—of his faith in the honor and decency of people. Even his faith in the Goddess was not what it had been. But he had not become entirely cynical. He still could tell the difference between right and wrong, and there were certain kinds of behavior which would never be acceptable to him.

"Why did you know this person?" he asked the woman.

The woman said that she was a follower of the same religion.

"Why?" asked Hala.

"Because, if I don't have that, I have nothing. The old ways don't work beyond the perimeter. You know that, Hala Sul. The old Goddess who spoke to me when I had a family has not said a word since I moved out of the firelight. I must believe in something. I will not believe that my life is entirely empty and wrong."

No question about it. He had gotten mixed up with a whore, a pervert and a heretic. When he died, he would certainly turn into one of those unhappy ghosts who roam the world, complaining about their past and trying—without success—to undo or remake their lives. He might even become the worst possible kind of ghost: one that was deliberately evil. Hala shivered and noticed how cold the thicket was. Ground and air were damp, and the woman was coughing. She had begun to develop an ugly-sounding cough several days before.

That brought Hala back to the situation at hand. He was going to have to find a dry place and some firewood. Maybe the villagers would give him some food—or sell it. He had a silver bracelet that he'd managed to hold on to this far. He rose and went to get a blanket for the woman.

They went north from the village, looking for some sign of the midwife or other people who believed in the heretical religion. Several times, Hala asked the woman if they could stop. They had lied before, using the name of a lineage far to the west and saying they were brother and sister, caught in the war and trying to get home. Let them do it again, said Hala, and stay in a village till she had recovered her health.

"I want to be with people I trust when I have the child," said the woman.

By this time, she was probably a little crazy from illness. But Hala didn't know this. All his training told him that women's problems had to be left to women. He had no right to interfere. His job, only and always, was to guard. One morning he could not rouse the woman. He felt her skin where it was bare, on the palms of her hands and the soles of her feet. It burned. Her lips were dry and cracked. He looked at her, her belly swollen till she looked like the animal floating in the pond, and he listened to her breathing. The sound was harsh. He could tell she was struggling. The sickness in her lungs had gotten suddenly much worse. Well, this was the end to their argument. The woman would have her child wherever he could find people. Hala cut branches and made a litter to sling between the *tsina*. They didn't like this innovation, and he had to beat them. They were not the kind of animals that listened to reason. Finally, they quieted down, and he lifted the woman into place. He led the animals down out of the hills.

As he'd hoped, there was a village at the edge of the plain: twenty tumbledown houses belonging to a lineage he'd never heard of. The people looked gaunt, even though it was harvesttime, and they were not happy to see strangers.

But they took the woman in. What else could they do? And she had her baby and died. This took several days. In the meantime, the baby was nursed by a woman in the village. Gesh Hala waited and tended his animals. Finally, the woman he knew—the diviner—was gone. The villagers said they could not care for the baby. Times were hard. The winter coming on looked bad.

Where could he take the child? Gesh Hala asked.

The next village to the north was more prosperous, and the people were odd. Who could say what they would do?

He went north, carrying the child. The weather had cleared by this time. The sky over him was blue, and the wide plain began to dry, though there were still pools of water in low places.

He came finally to the village of odd people. They seemed ordinary enough to him, and their houses were kept up, and their gardens looked orderly. He told his story, as much of it as was decent.

They listened and said they would keep the child. Did he want to give the little girl a name? He thought for a moment, then said, "Geshani."

They said fine. The name would be given. He lay down to sleep, not worried for the first time since he learned that the woman—his friend—was pregnant.

In the morning, an old woman came to him, thin and bent over, her fur as white as snow.

"You said that you were searching for a midwife."

"Yes," said Hala.

"I am that person. Tell me who the woman was."

He gave his friend's name.

"Hah!" said the old woman. "Now, tell the real story, the entire story."

What did he have to lose? He told the story. The old woman listened, looking interested and grave.

Finally, he was done. The old woman said, "Everyone in this village follows the new religion. We believe that this division between men and women is contrary to the will of the Goddess and her mate."

Hala made some kind of noncommittal answer.

"And we believe that the world is coming to pieces, because people have ignored the true wishes of the Makers of Everything. Surely, this is the last age. Surely, something new and different has to happen."

"Maybe," said Hala. "But that isn't my concern. I have done the best I could for the diviner and her child. Now, I think I ought to go and find a new job elsewhere."

He waited until the child had been named in a ceremony that made him uneasy. There were two people officiating, one a woman and the other a man. They were called "mother" and "father." This seemed perverse to him.

But the child got a name which meant "woman of Gesh." That gave Hala a kind of satisfaction. He rode north, skirting the plain, and came finally to the town that was not held by

Eh Manhata or his allies. There he found work as a guard. Time passed. The war continued, but Hala was out of it. Sometimes he heard news of Eh Manhata or Merin Ie. That world, of the army and the war, seemed almost as remote as the world of his childhood. Now he lived in a world of petty merchants and little caravans. He made enough to live on, and after a while, he stopped fearing the son of Eh. Who would ever find him in this dusty unimportant town? Or in any of the towns he visited, when he guarded traveling merchants?

Now the story moves to the meeting which young men love. Hala is traveling with a caravan. It stops for the night in a caravanserai. Great stone walls shut out the windy plain, and for once there is wood in the storerooms. They build a fire. The merchants start drinking. Hala watches his soldiers to make certain they remain sober.

Another group of travelers arrives, coming in through the iron gates: a war band, their clothes glittering with gold. Is there a problem here? Gesh Hala walks toward them. When he gets close, he realizes that the leader is Merin Ie.

He stops, hoping that the darkness will hide him.

Ie moves forward. "I think I know you."

"Is that so?" asks Gesh Hala.

The son of Merin moves closer to Hala and grabs his shoulders, turning him so the firelight shines in his face. "Hound-Hala!"

There was nothing for Hala to do except admit that he was himself.

The war band dismounted and made camp within the walls of the caravanserai, and the son of Merin invited Hala Sul to join him for a jug of *halin*.

What could Hala do? It would have been discourteous to say no. And hah! The son of Merin was lovely! His fur shone like steel. His eyes were like malachite. His clothing was richly ornamented with gold.

They settled at a distance from the fires. (There were two

now. One for each company.) For a while they drank and spoke about neutral topics.

Finally, when he was a little drunk, Merin Ie said, "Why did you leave? I tried to find you year after year. I just heard about a soldier in the west, a man named Hala who might be you. I thought I would go and see." He reached out and touched Hala gently on the shoulder.

It was time to explain, Hala thought, and told his story, though he did not talk about his interview with Eh Manhata, and he said nothing about the diviner. Only that he was Gesh or maybe Merin.

"Let's get up and walk," said Merin Ie.

They went through the gate. The sky was full of stars. The flat dark plain stretched to the horizon.

"Do you want to kill me?" the son of Merin asked.

No, said Gesh Hala. As far as he was concerned, the old quarrel was over. He could get up no enthusiasm for it.

"I have not forgotten you, Hala," said Merin Ie. "And I haven't met a man I liked more."

Gesh Hala tried to explain about his lineage a second time. If he was Gesh, they were enemies. If he was Merin, they were cousins, and a love between them would be incestuous.

Merin Ie listened patiently, then said, "If you had been adult when the Gesh came to an end, we would have been enemies. My family would have killed you. If you had stayed one day longer with your female relatives, you would have become Merin, and we'd be cousins. But neither of those things happened, and we cannot make them happen now. No one can change the past, not even the Goddess.

"You aren't Gesh. That lineage no longer exists, except in the minds of people and barely even there these days. You can't be part of something that has no real existence. That is like—what? Sailing on a ship that burned and sank a generation ago. Or living in a house out of a dream. It can't be done.

"Life is life, Hala Sul, and ideas are ideas. You have been mixing them up.

"As for Merin, I think the time when you could join is over, but maybe not. I'd sooner have you as a lover than as a cousin, Hala, but if you want to belong to Merin, I am willing to speak to my female relatives. It's possible that they will make an exception. Families have been known to adopt adult men in the past."

No, Gesh Hala said. He did not want to be Merin.

"So," said Merin Ie, "what's the problem? You are a person without a family, which is sad. But in this age, many people have no family."

They stopped and faced each other. Merin Ie took hold of his shoulders again and pulled him close and kissed him. It was not the superficial kiss of friendship, but rather the deep kiss of love.

After a while, they went back in through the gate and gathered blankets and went up into one of the towers. There they made love. Hala wasn't certain it was morally right. But something had broken inside him, some wall or locked door. Instead of moral questions, he thought of Merin Ic's body and his own loneliness and desire.

In the morning they parted. Hala escorted his merchants to their destination, then quit his job and rode to join the son of Merin. The two of them were together through a summer of military campaigns. In the autumn, the war slowed down for a while and Hala went to Merin with his lover.

Hah! This was difficult! He was afraid that one of his old relatives would recognize him. But over twenty years had passed, and the middle-aged soldier looked nothing like the boy of Gesh. Fortunately for him, Hala was a common name, and the world was full—as Merin Ie had told him—of people without families. No one was suspicious.

It's possible that the son of Merin consulted with his female relatives, and they told him he was right: Hala belonged to no family. Or maybe he kept the whole thing a secret. This isn't known.

The two men stayed together for close to thirty years, and Hala fought with the Merin in the endless war. Eh Manhata never did anything to either man, in spite of his threat to Hala. Maybe he decided the original problem had been solved, and if he killed Hala, he would have another quarrel on his hands. He had plenty to occupy himself.

In time, Hala's nickname changed. He became Merin Sul, the Hound of Merin, and that is the way he is known to history.

He never had a family name, though other lineages offered to adopt him, as years passed and he became famous and the Merin increasingly powerful. He refused them all with courtesy.

Merin Ie died at the age of sixty of a minor wound that became infected. He made it home to Merin, though he was no longer rational by the time they reached the big main gate. Hala got him off his *tsin* and carried him up to a bed, helped by other men. Then the women took over, though Hala was always there, sitting next to Ie, holding his hand, talking to him. Ie never answered or said anything that made sense.

After he died, Hala got up and stretched, rubbing his cramped arms and hands. People spoke to him. He ignored them and went down to the stable. His favorite *tsin* was there, a big male with red and white stripes. He got the animal ready to be ridden and led it into the main courtyard. More people spoke. He brushed past them and mounted the *tsin*, turning it toward the main gate. One of Ie's sisters stood in his way.

"Will you move?" said Hala.

"Where are you going?" the sister asked.

Hala shook his head, trying to clear it. Grief filled him like a great, heavy stone. His tongue seemed incapable of motion. There were no ideas in his mind.

"If you want to ride out and be alone for a while, that is fine. I'll let you. But if you are trying to leave us, Merin Sul— No! You'll have to ride over me."

"It is over," he said finally. "I am done with you."

"What did you love?" asked the sister. "Not the son of
Merin! You know if he'd been able to, he would have asked
you to stay. Do you think we want the dishonor of sending
you out into the world? Do you think we want the pain of
losing you as well as Merin Ie?

"And how can we replace both of you? What kind of
situation will you leave us in?"

"You don't know," said Hala. "You can't understand."

"You have lived among us for thirty years, and fought in
our war band, and stood—always!—next to my brother.
This is what I understand. I will not let you go."

Hala sighed finally and dismounted, leading the animal
back into its stable. Men came to care for it. He walked back
to the room where Ie's body lay. He sat down in a corner and
wrapped his arms over his head, remaining there motionless and silent. The women of the house moved past him,
getting his lover's body ready for cremation.

The next day Ie was burned. His ashes were buried on the
hill above the Merin fortress. Hala watched all this without
expression. When it was over, he walked off by himself and
was gone until evening.

When he came back, he went to Merin Ie's sister, who
was the leading woman of the lineage.

"I'll stay," he said. "I'll do what Merin asks of me. I
want one thing only in return. When I die, bury me in the
graveyard by the old fortress of Gesh."

The sister looked at him for a moment. "This tells me
something I didn't know before."

Hala waited.

"It will be done," the sister told him.

"Good," said Hala, and left.

He stayed with the Merin until he died at the age of a
hundred. He was in good health until his last days, and he
kept traveling until he was past ninety. He had gotten in the
habit of going places when he was young.

When he was almost eighty, he made a trip onto the Great

Central Plain. By this time, peace had been established in most areas, and Hala didn't need more than a small retinue. They stopped one evening in a caravanserai. It was in good repair, he noticed. The storerooms held wood and food. They built a fire and settled down for the night. Then a second group arrived: soldiers wearing the insignia of Eh.

Hah! They were curt and efficient. They searched the building, then said, "You can't stay here tonight, old man."

One of the soldiers of Merin started up and opened his mouth. Hala raised a hand and asked, "Why not?"

"Someone important is coming. We can't let him share this building with the likes of you."

"Very well," said Hala, and stood up, his joints making noises. The soldiers of Merin gathered around him, looking angry.

"Be patient, children," Hala said. "And think of who must be coming."

They led their animals out onto the plain and made a second camp.

After a while, more soldiers arrived, coming out of the twilight. They entered the caravanserai. Hala watched them. He saw no one special among them.

Night fell. He drank a little *halin*. His body was aching more than usual, and the *halin* helped. The soldiers of his retinue talked quietly. They had been with him long enough to know when he needed to be left in peace.

Finally, a shape came out of the darkness. A harsh voice said, "Hala Sul."

Hala lifted his head and then his hand in greeting.

"My men said they had pushed an old man out into the night. What old man? I asked. They didn't know, they told me, but the men who traveled with him wore the sign of Merin. Fools, Hala! I am surrounded with people who cannot think. Come in."

He got up and followed Eh Manhata through the gate.

The soldiers had built a fire in one of the inside rooms. There were chairs, old but in good repair, and a table with a big crack going through it, still usable. The walls had been painted with a scene: a battle. Hala could make out that much, but no more. The paint was badly faded and great patches had flaked off.

Manhata waved him into a chair.

Hala settled and groaned.

"Right enough," said Manhata. "You are almost as old as I am. How could they possibly not recognize the Hound of Merin?"

"One old man looks like another," said Hala. "Except you, of course, Manhata."

Manhata made a noise which indicated disbelief. He was still impressive, his fur as grey as iron. There was no white at all in it. (Hala by this time was the color of snow.) His body had lost muscle and fat, so the big heavy bones were clearly visible. His face still wore an expression of command, made—if anything—more evident by the years.

He settled opposite Hala and filled two cups with *halin*. They began to talk, two old men in the firelight. By this time, Eh Manhata was beyond a question the most powerful man in the world. He was also alone. His last sister had died. He had no one to turn to for advice. In a year or two, he would make a stupid mistake and find himself in a trap, and then he would be dead, killed by enemies who got nothing out of his death.

Hala had twenty years to go. He would die in bed in the fortress at Merin. His lover's nieces would keep the promise their mother made. Half the promise, anyway. His ashes were divided. Part was buried in the graveyard at Merin, and part went to Gesh to the hill above the ruins of the town where he was born.

But none of this was known to the men, as they talked in the caravanserai. The meeting seems actually to have taken place, but there are only lies and speculations about the conversation.

One story has Eh Manhata asking if the two of them—he and Merin Ie—had ever been sexually involved.

"Once or twice," Hala Sul answers.

"I can't remember," says Eh Manhata.

Hala smiles. He has kept most of his teeth. "It wasn't worth remembering, son of Eh."

Manhata asks Hala what happened after he was beaten and thrown out of camp.

"A long story," Hala says. "I found out that life is even more complicated and difficult to understand than I had already suspected. And I refound Merin Ie."

"You could have saved me trouble if you had decided to have sex with him earlier. What difference would it have made? The problem you had with him—I can't remember what it was—something to do with your families. Isn't that right?"

"Yes," said Gesh Hala.

"It stopped being a problem, and you ended in his bed. For how long?"

"Thirty years, and fifteen years in Merin since he died."

"Such a long time!" Manhata turned his cup, looking at the fire. He said nothing for a while, then began to speak of the past: the battles and campaigns that had made him the foremost man alive.

Hala listened and commented from time to time.

Finally, Manhata grew tired and a little drunk. He dozed off in his chair. Hala went to find the soldiers of Eh.

"This happens," one of them said. "He is no longer the man he used to be. We apologize for the way we treated you, Hala Merin Sul. We didn't recognize you."

Hala said it wasn't important and went out to where his men were camped and settled by their fire.

When he got back to Merin, he told the senior women about his meeting with the son of Eh.

"His own men say that Eh Manhata is failing. I don't know if he'll go quickly or slowly, but Merin needs to be ready."

The women agreed with him. Plans were made and instructions given to the men who led the Merin war bands. (There were three by this time.)

When Eh Manhata was trapped and killed, the soldiers of Merin knew how to act. They did not become involved in the struggle that broke out as soon as Manhata was dead. Instead, they pulled back to guard the boundaries of their own country and consulted with other lineages, the ones they were especially close to, and waited to see how events would go forward.

In time, it became evident that Eh was not going to produce an adequate leader. So the Merin threw in with Ahara, and this turned out to be a wise decision. All this happened because of Hala Sul.

As mentioned before, he died in Merin when he was almost a hundred years old. His mind remained clear until the end, and there wasn't a lot of pain. The women of the lineage took care of him. The men came in to pay their final visits, full of respect and grief. When he looked out the window, he saw the hills of Merin, their foliage autumn brown and green.

It was a good death, the stories tell us, and a really fine joke. Although he was a quiet man, he had a good sense of humor, and he must have enjoyed the situation. What an ending for the boy of Gesh!

After he was gone, the Merin began to name their sons after him. "Hala" became their favorite name for a male child, and other lineages began to make jokes about the number of Halas in Merin.

This habit has continued into modern times. Even today there are so many men named Merin Hala that nicknames have to be used. But no one is ever called Hala Sul.

It Comes Lightly Out of the Sea

William Stafford

At night lifting in silence it becomes its own
self through miles over the land. Milder than fog,
invisible except that the eye sometimes blinks, it
won't hurry, touching you soft as a moth
all your life. It will keep you; slight as a moonbeam
it gradually reforms every breath until
you become different, shimmering like the slow
tremor that lives always in even the stillest water.

You can't feel it, but over the years it merges
with your breathing and heartbeat. It feathers
down on your hand. Late at night when you are
most alone it touches you, or in a curl of air
at noon a little signal passes you unnoticed,
until that evening when you almost remember.

By many thin layers, too small to notice, tons of
    influence
accumulate. Years later you say, "What was that
rumor about living near the sea?" And in your voice

the sea will be present. It will surge inside your breast
when you say, "Nothing was there. Nothing came."
  Then
you remember those days when you walked on the
  beach
    and didn't feel anything.

A Boy and His Wolf: Three Versions of a Fable

John Morressy

1. *The Boy Who Cried, Among Other Things, "Wolf!"*

A young shepherd boy with an irritating penchant for practical jokes decided to play one on his neighbors. One day, while guarding his flocks, he began to shout "Wolf! Wolf!" in a terrified voice. His neighbors seized their pitchforks and axes and came running to his aid. When they arrived on the spot, sweaty and red-faced, the boy burst out laughing.

"What's so funny?" one neighbor asked.

"And where's the wolf?" asked another.

"There wasn't any wolf. I fooled you all," the boy said with an obnoxious grin.

The neighbors went back to their work, mumbling and grousing and saying to one another that the boy needed a good thrashing. A few days later, feeling bored, the boy tried the same trick again, and again he succeeded. This time the neighbors were quite irate. They pushed him around, and several of them threatened bodily harm if he tried any more such tricks. The boy was no fool. He promised he would not cry "Wolf!" again.

The very next day, a wolf appeared. The boy was about to call for help when he remembered his promise.

He ran to the hilltop and shouted ''Cantaloupe!'' as loudly as he could. No one came. The wolf finished his first lamb and started on another. The boy screamed ''Shoelace! Hippopotamus! Underwear!'' Still no one came. The wolf continued to eat. Finally the boy cried ''Bear!'' That got a rise out of his neighbors. They came running.

The mayor demanded, ''Where's the bear? It had better be a big one, lad, or you're in for it.''

''There's no bear. There's a wolf, a real wolf!'' the boy cried.

They looked, and saw the wolf, who was just finishing his third lamb and was in a pleasant sociable mood. He waved to them.

''That's a wolf, all right,'' said the village wise man, and the others all nodded their heads and murmured agreement. ''Yes, it certainly is, no doubt about it, definitely a wolf,'' they said to one another.

''Why'd you yell 'Bear'?'' the mayor asked.

''You made me promise not to yell 'Wolf,' '' the boy said.

''So we did. Too bad,'' said the wise man.

''What about the wolf?'' said the boy.

''We didn't come up here to fight no wolf,'' said the village hunter. ''We're out for bear.''

And so they all left. The boy sank down under a tree to mope, and while he was sitting there, a bear came along and ate him.

MORAL: Those who ask for what they don't need may get what they don't want.

2. *The Boy Who Did Not Cry ''Wolf!''*

A young shepherd boy, temporarily out of work, learned of the unfortunate demise of the boy who cried, among other things, ''Wolf!'' and resolved that he would not fall victim

to a similar fate. He journeyed to the late shepherd's place
of employment and offered his credentials.

"You're not about to go shouting 'Wolf' every time you
get bored, are you, boy?" said the sheep owner.

"No, sir," said the boy, touching his cap respectfully.

"Nor anything else, either, like 'Antidisestablishmentari-
anism' or 'Bear' or anything like that?"

"I will shout only what I am instructed to shout, sir."

"You won't have to do any shouting at all," said the
sheep owner, taking a little tin whistle from his pocket.
"There's been altogether too much shouting around here. If
you see a wolf, you're to blow this good and loud. No shouting. Understand?"

The sheep owner's wife, a slender and very attractive
woman, said in a husky voice, "All you have to do is whistle. You know how to whistle, don't you?"

"Yes, ma'am."

"All right, then, we'll give you a try," her husband said.

The boy started next day. He put in a full day's shepherd-
ing, and when he returned to the fold at night, the owner
said, "I didn't hear any whistling today. Good boy."

"Thank you, sir. I decided not to summon help, even
though . . . but there's no need to concern yourself with
that," said the boy, and headed for the showers.

Next day the boy was also silent. When the sheep owner
praised his self-control, the boy only said, "There was no
need to call for assistance, sir. No real need. No *pressing*
need, if you know what I mean."

The owner did not know what he meant, but was not
about to admit it and look dumb in front of an employee. He
nodded and said, "Right you are, son. Nice work."

Every day the boy went out with the flocks and passed the
day without alarm, and every evening he returned and responded to his master's questions with a cheerful, "The
situation is well in hand, sir," or words to that effect. This
went on for several weeks.

One day the owner decided to go out to the pasture and

see for himself what the boy was doing. As he came near, he heard the faint strains of a pleasant tune being played on a whistle. He crept closer, and saw, to his astonishment, a group of wolves sitting on their haunches, or sprawled out on their bellies, around the shepherd boy, who was playing tune after tune for them. Whenever the boy paused too long for breath, the wolves grew restless and began to eye the sheep, who were placidly grazing nearby; but as soon as the boy resumed his playing, the wolves were enthralled.

The owner watched for a time, and the longer he watched, the angrier he became. His shepherd, this boy he paid to guard his sheep, was serving as an entertainer for his worst enemies, amusing them with the very whistle he ought to be using to sound the alarm. "My own shepherd. The lad I pay out of my own pocket," said the owner to himself bitterly. "My own whistle, provided at my own expense," he added, seething.

He looked on at the peaceful scene until he could stand it no longer, and then he burst from his place of concealment and snatched the whistle from the boy's lips. He gave the lad a buffet on the side of the head and shouted, "Traitor! Spy! Double-dealing little sneak!"

"What have I done wrong, master?" the boy asked, rubbing his ear.

"I don't pay you to entertain wolves, I pay you to keep my flock safe," the owner cried, his face reddening.

"But I *am* keeping them safe. You haven't lost any sheep, have you?"

"You call this keeping them safe? You're amusing wolves, that's what you're doing."

"You told me not to shout 'Wolf!' or anything else! You told me to use the whistle, and I used it!" the boy said indignantly.

The owner, in a rage, hurled the whistle to the ground and stomped it into a useless lump of metal. "*That* for the whistle!" he cried. "And now I'm going to do the same to you, you idiot!"

But then he noticed that about half the wolves had gathered around him in a ring, while the rest were heading for the unsuspecting sheep. They were all very big wolves, and they looked hungry.

"Wait a minute, boy," he said. "We've got a problem here."

"We don't. You do," said the boy, who had scrambled up a tree at the owner's threat of violence.

"What am I going to do?!"

"You could cry 'Wolf!' " said the boy, grinning down at him.

"There's nobody around to hear. And even if someone heard, he'd ignore it."

"Try whistling. You know how to whistle, don't you?"

The man looked down at the ruined whistle lying at his feet in the dirt. One of the wolves growled, and the ring began to close on him. The owner gave a cry of terror and made a dash for it. The wolves were too fast for him.

While they were occupied, the boy climbed down from the tree and made off. The wolves did not bother him. They had all they could eat, and besides, they had enjoyed his music, and wished him well.

MORAL: Music hath charms that shouting hathn't.

3. The Boy Who Thought About Crying "Wolf!"

The widow of an unfortunate sheep owner advertised for a boy to watch her flock. An introspective lad from a neighboring hamlet learned of the position and presented himself as an applicant.

The boy did not really want to be a shepherd, he wanted to be a philosopher, but right now there was no work for philosophers. Besides, he believed that he could do a lot of deep thinking while he was watching the sheep, and he liked outdoor work.

"This job is no piece of cake," said the widow, a slender

and attractive woman with a husky voice. "The last shepherd disappeared, and the one before that was eaten by a bear."

"I am alert and quick on my feet, ma'am," said the youth.

"You'd better be. And the rules are strict: you're not to cry 'Wolf!' unless there's a wolf in sight, and you're not to blow a whistle."

"They sound like sensible rules to me, ma'am."

"All right, then, you've got the job," said the widow.

For several weeks, the work was uneventful. The sheep ate and gamboled and slept, the youth watched over them and thought deeply about the purpose of life, the nature of reality, and the possibility of achieving certainty through the evidence of the senses. In the evenings, he pondered the mind-body dichotomy; mornings were given to the question of the real existence of universals. At lunchtime, he thought about girls.

Things went well for sheep and shepherd until one afternoon, just after lunch, when the youth saw something moving in the distance. It was large and grayish black. It had a bushy tail, pointed ears, and long legs.

"That certainly looks like a wolf," said the youth to himself. "If I were not a philosopher, I would probably shout 'Wolf!' at the top of my lungs this very minute, despite the widow's injunction. But I must have grounds more relative than this."

The animal made its way around the perimeter of the flock, nose to the ground, looking very busy and interested. The shepherd followed its movements closely.

"Extremely wolflike behavior," he said to himself. "If I were given to acting on appearances, I would almost certainly shout 'Wolf!' But is the creature really there? Is it not possible that this animal is a hysterical wolf, a delusion arising out of my preoccupation with wolf attacks? It might equally be the result of defective vision. Or perhaps it really exists, but is a friendly wolf. It may even be a dog of some breed remarkably like the wolf in appearance and behavior, in which case I would not only be unjustified, but also inaccurate, to cry 'Wolf!' ''

While the youth studied its every move with intense concern, the animal sat on its haunches, scratched itself vigorously, and then seemed to lose interest in the sheep. It wandered off and disappeared into the trees.

As a matter of fact, the youth had been correct in his final conjecture. The dog was a pedigreed Alsatian, the prized pet of a wealthy circus owner who was passing through the region on his way to the city. In his desperate search for the missing dog, the man came to the house of the widow. He found the animal, whose name was Lance, sitting at the widow's feet while she scratched his neck and the backs of his ears. Struck by such tenderness, and also by her beauty, the circus owner fell in love with the widow, and they ran off together that very afternoon. She left a note for the shepherd which read simply, ''It's all yours, kid.''

Now that he was a sheep owner, the youth became an even more conscientious guardian of his flock. One day he noticed a large dark animal, much like the first one he had seen, exhibiting great interest in the sheep on the outer edge of the flock. It could not be the Alsatian, because only that morning the youth had received a postcard from the circus owner and the widow, sent from the capital city, far away, in which they mentioned Lance. This animal greatly resembled a wolf. It walked with a wolfish gait, its tongue lolled wolfishly, and it sat like a wolf. It was soon joined by two other equally wolfish creatures.

The youth studied them closely, and asked himself, ''What is it to be a wolf, truly and indisputably? What is the wolfishness of wolfness? What is the nature of wolf-as-such?'' This led him to the question of realism versus nominalism, which occupied his mind so completely that he did not notice four additional creatures, very similar to them in appearance, joining the first three.

He pondered the essence of wolfness, and the question of

whether this essence preceded existence as wolf, or wolf-ness was the result of consciously chosen wolfish acts. Un-convinced of the wolf's capacity for pure decision and its ability to make the necessary existential leap, and dubious of wolfish recognition of *le néant* and its susceptibility to objectless anxiety, he found himself unable to decide whether or not he was justified in crying "Wolf!" or indeed in ever doing anything at all.

As he sat deep in thought, the wolflike creatures began to behave in a wolflike manner, snatching up lambs and carrying them off. The other sheep bleated and ran about in panic, breaking into the young shepherd's reverie.

"Perhaps I might cry, 'Wolflike entity!' or 'Perception of a wolflike phenomenon!' without risking inaccuracy," he said to himself, but then immediately saw the problem of the interpretations that might be placed on these outcries.

By this time, the wolflike creatures were nowhere to be seen. The sheep that had not been eaten had run off in all directions. The air was filled with dust and terrified bleating. The youth rose, studied the scene, and concluded that some-thing had to be done. At this point he noticed a large crea-ture standing very close by, attracted by the uproar. It looked very much like a bear.

The youth decided that the time had come to make a definitive statement. While he was deliberating over the exact wording, the bearlike entity ate him.

MORAL: Thinking precisely
　　　　Sometimes serves us nicely,
　　　　But too much contemplation
　　　　May bring extermination.
　　　　When in doubt,
　　　　Shout.

Time Travel, the Artifact, and a Famous Historical Personage

Will Shetterly

Jack was everywhere. He pushed a cart past the end of the baking supplies aisle just as Kate reached for a package of enriched flour in Rainbow Foods. He hurried into the Business and Technology section of the Minneapolis Public Library as Kate, on her way to Art and Music, glanced down from the up escalator. He came from one of Dayton's revolving doors and disappeared into the lunchtime traffic as Kate walked toward the post office. He touched Kate's shoulder lightly from behind as she rode a crowded elevator down from a temp job in a law office, said, "Excuse me," and got out on the third floor. His voice was as accentless as a TV announcer's. She watched his back while the doors closed and did not breathe until the elevator reached the lobby.

She never saw his face in these encounters, but she knew him. She knew his height, his haircut, his walk. When she dreamed, she saw him clearly: medium height, medium build, short brown hair—so common-looking that she could never describe him as an individual when she woke, yet she knew him. She tried to draw him in her diary, but her sketch was of an awkward, elongated, androgynous figure whose smile was a silly leer. She never showed it to anyone.

She knew his handwriting too. Two postcards written in red ink had come with Hell for a return address. The first had arrived a month ago, shortly before she saw Jack in the grocery store. The second came two weeks later. The postmarks said they came from New York City; she did not know if Jack expected her to think they had been forwarded or if he was making a joke. The first said, "I wil be back as sharp as evre. No need for the trade name, you kno who I am." The second said, "You want to use Jack but Jack is to clevr. I am coming from the devle since you invited me so nisely."

After each sighting, after each dream, after each postcard, she told herself that she was too imaginative. The sightings were of ordinary men, the dreams were signs of her obsession, and the postcards were a misguided joke by someone who had heard of the book and did not know how much the postcards terrified her. She could tell David, but he would only worry.

She tried to describe Jack once. Not to David, who would laugh, ask her if the book was getting to her, then recognize what he had done, apologize, hug her, and never understand that this was not enough compensation for his laugh. She tried to describe him to Kenny, who laughed before she finished, but with delight, not condescension. Kenny slapped his new pink sofa and said, "That's your dreamfuck!"

"I beg your pardon?"

"Mr. Perfect. The Candy Man. Your lean, clean, sex machine."

"Kenny, I—" She heard her annoyance and began again. "My ideal man is Prince grown six feet tall. This guy isn't any taller than I am, and he's just as pale. And I don't want to fuck him."

"He sounds cute."

"Cute. Right, Kenny. If I want him, why am I afraid of him?"

"Because you're afraid to admit that you're tired of David."

"I love David!"

Kenny shook his head, grinned slightly, and tapped his chest with both hands. "Did I say you didn't? *Petit moi?* I said you're tired of him."

"I love David," she repeated.

"What's that got to do with anything? When was the last time you seduced him? When was the last time you wanted to seduce him?" When she said nothing, he added, "Face it, you're tired of being Mom for the boy wonder. You want excitement. You want a lover."

"Not Gentleman Jack."

"Why is this Jack? Somebody shows up in your dreams. He's nice-looking. He smiles at you. He's nothing like David."

"David smiles at me."

"Sexy?"

"Well . . . Friendly sexy."

"Right," said Kenny. "And this guy in your dreams, there's no friendly in his smile, there's just sex."

"There's no sex, Kenny. Weren't you listening to me? He *scares* me."

"Weren't you listening to you, girl? Why do you think this guy is Jack?"

"Because I know it."

"Has he got a knife? Does he say who he is?"

"He just smiles."

Kenny nodded smugly. "It's because you're putting together an anthology about the Ripper. You're obsessed, so you decide Dreamboy is Jack."

"Right."

"Hey." He put his hand on her shoulder. "I didn't mean to upset you. Maybe I play shrink too much."

"Maybe."

"Maybe you should talk to someone at the U."

"It's not really bothering me."

"Maybe you should talk to David."

"He's too busy. This book's important."

"Maybe you two shouldn't do the book."

"We signed a contract. A lot of stories are in already."
She smiled. "We spent our share of the advance."

"Oy," said Kenny. "Then do the book quickly, hmm?
And think about leaving David. It might be best for both of
you."

"Right, Kenny. You going to do a story for us?"

"Maybe. A gay Ripper, pressured by society . . . It'd be
interesting to portray the Ripper as a victim . . ." He
shrugged.

"A victim." She patted his knee, thinking that Kenny
would probably never write the story, and if he did, it would
be bad. "That could be interesting."

Walking from Kenny's apartment, she considered leaving
David. That would mean moving into her sister's basement
in the 'burbs and having to take the bus anyplace she
wanted to go. That would mean abandoning the book she
and David had planned to write together. That would mean
that their friends would be divided into his friends and her
friends, because David would not take this well.

She smiled, realizing that she was not thinking about the
most important consequences. What of David? His friends
had said she was good for him, that since they were together, he was less excitable, he washed himself and his
clothes more often, he wrote more than he had in years, he
had finally gained some weight. How would David react?
Did he already suspect that something was wrong?

As she turned onto La Salle, she saw Jack drive by in a
yellow Toyota. A little black kid on a ten-speed bicycle that
was too large for him said, "Hey, lady. You all right?" She
nodded and walked on. She wanted to go straight home, but
avoiding the mail would be the same as admitting that she
was frightened.

There were no postcards in the post office box. There were
three manila envelopes. Two were from writers she did not
know, and one was from Curt. Delighted, she ripped open
the envelope as she walked outside, then sat on the low wall
across the street to read the cover letter.

5/14

David and Kate—

Here's a story after all. Didn't think I'd have time, but when I found a copy of Rumbelow's book on the Ripper, I became a bit obsessed. Hope my story isn't too cute.

Ever so timidly,
Curt

P.S. to Kate: I almost didn't do this. Rumbelow made me realize we aren't talking about Boogeyman Jack, creature of legend, but a madman who killed women in horrible ways. I understand why David's editing this—David would steamroller his grandmother if he thought it would result in a nice metaphor (and sometimes I admire him for that)—but I wonder about your motives. For the last hundred years, Old Leather Apron has probably been the ultimate symbol of violence against women, yet you choose to cash in on his legend?

That's not fair, and I apologize. Of course the Ripper's a richer symbol than that. He's the upper classes preying on the lower, he's the mad herald of the twentieth century, he's knowledge without restraint, he's lust without love, he's the slasher of hypocrisy, he's the dark self in all of us. So I suppose that's how I rationalize writing a story for you. Even if you don't like it, it was fun, I blush to admit.

She stuffed the letter and the manuscript back into their envelope. What sort of hypocrite was Curt to send a story if he felt like that? She walked faster than usual to her apartment. She wanted to return Curt's story unread. His success had come too soon, and he had never learned to behave professionally. His cover letters were smarmy, sloppy, presumptuously intimate. His stories weren't very good either. His characters had no depth, no motivation. Describing his prose as workmanlike was an excess of kindness. She did not need to read his submission. If she rejected it, she could be proud; it would prove that their anthology was constructed on the merits of the stories, not on the writers' names.

If the anthology was constructed on the merits of the stories, she would have to read Curt's. By the time she reached the apartment, she felt calmer. Curt was probably the nicest of David's friends, and God knew none of her friends had perfect social skills. Maybe Curt meant well with his postscript. Or maybe he had rid himself of his doubts by transferring them to her.

Snicker and Doodle met her at the front door. Snicker rubbed against her ankle, meowing as if he had been neglected for weeks. Doodle sat sullenly in the entryway as if annoyed that David was not home, too. Two of David's friends were in town, and he would be drinking with them until the bars closed, talking about writing and not doing any.

Kate closed the thin front curtains. Passersby in the harsh summer light became shadowy figures of unknowable age, race, or sex. She fed the cats and cleaned their box, then began to microwave a leftover slice of pizza Florentine.

Pouring a diet root beer, she saw a note on top of yesterday's mail, still heaped on the kitchen counter. She began to smile, thinking it was from David. The handwriting was strange. The note was written in red ink. It began: "Boss lady—"

The plastic root beer bottle was cold and slick in her left hand. The Flintstones glass was cool and brittle in her right. If she did not stop pouring, the root beer would overflow. The apartment was very quiet. The upstairs neighbors should be fighting by now, since this was a Friday. The kid next door should be playing Metallica on his stereo and trying to turn the receiver up to 11. The kitchen counter had several toast crumbs on it, and a coffee splotch to make Rorschach proud.

Jack had left a note in her apartment.

She recapped the root beer and set it beside her glass. She turned around slowly, completely around. She saw no one. The cats behaved normally, for cats that no one could describe as normal. Would the cats behave oddly if a maniac from the nineteenth century was waiting in her home?

The carving knife lay beside the stove. David had probably halved a bagel at lunch. David often halved bagels at lunch. She ran to the knife and snatched it. The rough wooden handle comforted her, and she realized that if Jack—or anyone—was in her apartment, he was not likely to set out a knife for her.

The phone was in the living room. The back door always creaked loudly, and anyone might be waiting on the back stairs. She had come safely from the living room. She should return to it. She could call the police and say— No. If someone was here, she would not be allowed to finish a call. If no one was here, the cops would be less likely to come later, when—if—she needed them. Since she was more afraid of the back door, she went to it first, and then searched the apartment. The doors and windows were locked, as they should be. No one was hiding in the closets or under the bed.

Halfway through her search, she realized that the note had to be from David, the red ink a coincidence, the letters blocky because David had hurt his wrist, perhaps. She returned to the kitchen and touched the note with the point of the knife to turn it toward her.

Boss lady—

You wil hear that Saucy Jack is operating tonight. Maybe you wil kno it, ha ha.

J.

It was a very bad joke. David had thought it would be funny to scare her. Maybe he hadn't thought that the note would scare her; maybe he expected her to be amused. Notes from Jack the Ripper, ha ha ha. Had David written the postcards, too? Sent them to someone like Curt to mail from New York? Or had Curt created them in collusion with David? She ran back to the living room to find Curt's manuscript.

The envelope had been addressed with the same typewriter that was used for the story. Curt's signature on the cover letter was a quick, graceful scrawl in blue felt-tip.

Someone wrote with a different hand than usual, or perhaps a third person had collaborated with them. Kenny? Was Kenny so desperate to be published that he would help David in a stupid prank?

Curt and Kenny were her friends, and David was her lover. She was being paranoid. Yet the note remained, something frighteningly tangible from something unknown.

The knife remained in her right hand. She realized that her left rested on the telephone. Who could she call? The police? Her sister? Kenny? What would any of them say? You're terrified because of dreams. Oh, and postcards. Who would have your address, then? Hundreds of writers, because you'd put a notice in a writer's magazine that you were in the market for Jack the Ripper stories? It's probably some nut. Why're you so worried about some nut?

Because a note had been placed in her kitchen.

A note. Anything threatening in it? Uh-huh. Anything else strange? The cats cut up into little pieces? Your boyfriend in Baggies in the deep-freeze? Intestines strewn decoratively about your bedroom? No? And your boyfriend isn't home? You ought to talk to him, lady, or to your landlord. Not us. We got a job to do.

She giggled suddenly, and Snicker looked up at her.

David had done stupid things before, thinking to amuse her.

The pizza was warm, and so was the root beer. She took her dinner into the living room and placed Curt's story on top of the two unsolicited submissions.

Curt's story was not as good as she had hoped nor as bad as she had feared. David would be annoyed, because Curt had done a Sherlock Holmes pastiche in which Holmes realized that he had committed the Ripper murders while under the influence of laudanum. Was that too much like David's story about Robert Louis Stevenson and M. J. Druitt, the doctor who was David's favorite candidate for the Ripper? David had Druitt inspire Stevenson to write the Jekyll and Hyde story. Curt's and David's stories weren't that similar, and what David had completed was certainly better-written than Curt's.

The first of the unsolicited stories began:

"I wish to purchase something that belonged to Jack the Ripper," the American said, his bright blue eyes rolling about the crowded interior of the quaint little London shop.

"Blimey, sor," the jolly shopkeeper said with twinkles in his eyes. "We 'ave just the thing. 'Is braces."

"I didn't know there was anything wrong with Jack the Ripper's teeth."

"Wot you'd call 'is suspenders, guv'nor."

She skipped to the end. The American, wearing Jack's suspenders, killed his girlfriend, and then, anguished by his deed, hung himself with the suspenders. The shopkeeper came into the American's apartment to recover the suspenders and smiled with beams in his eyes, thinking that he was Cain and another unfortunate had fallen to the Curse of Jack the Ripper. Kate decided that David did not need to read this one, tucked it into the writer's self-addressed stamped envelope, and turned to the next.

The cover letter simply said, "I have enclosed a story for

your consideration." It was signed J. Noble. The story was titled "Time Travel, the Artifact, and a Famous Historical Personage." Kate began to grin, then frowned. The unsolicited submissions—and a significant number of the solicited ones—fell into three sorts: someone travels to Jack's time or Jack travels to another time; an artifact of Jack has an effect, inevitably gory, on someone; a famous historical person who lived in Jack's time is involved with the Ripper or turns out to be the Ripper. Her favorite of the last sort, already returned to its writer, revealed that Jack the Ripper was Queen Victoria in drag, happily not thinking of England for a few minutes.

Had J. Noble submitted the quintessential unsolicited Jack the Ripper story? Or was this a submission by someone who had heard David mention the kinds of stories they were getting? She looked again at the return address: New York. Curt had mentioned that a friend might send them a story. Curt might have told the friend about the submissions they received.

On the first page, when she discovered that the main characters were two editors who were compiling an anthology about Jack the Ripper, Kate stopped and looked around the apartment. The carving knife still lay beside her, on the coffee table next to the sofa. Snicker slept on a nearby chair, Doodle on the window ledge. The kid next door played the ultimate self-referential rock song; its lyrics seemed to consist solely of "rock, rock, rock." Wishing they had decided to do an anthology about Mother Teresa or Mr. Rogers, Kate continued to read.

The editors, Spencer and Eileen, had two friends, writers who shared an apartment: Benny, who wrote badly, and Burt, who was fairly successful. The editors received postcards written in red ink, apparently from the Ripper. They then received an anonymous story titled "Time Travel, the Artifact, and a Famous Historical Personage."

Its main characters were modeled after Spencer, Eileen, Benny, and Burt: Fletcher and Lisa were the editors, Lenny was the aspiring writer, and Art was the popular one. The postcards received by the editors in the anonymous story were identical to the ones that Spencer and Eileen had received . . . which were identical to the postcards that Kate had received. At the end of the story within the story, the editors, Fletcher and Lisa, were killed and mutilated by Lenny, the unpublished writer, who then wrote the account of their murders and sold it as fiction for a great deal of money.

After reading the end of the anonymous story, Spencer and Eileen, terrified, went to Benny's house and killed him when he denied terrorizing them. In their rage, they mutilated his body with the Ripper's trademarks: slashed ears and nose, organs piled beside the eviscerated body, intestines dragged out of the corpse and looped over the right shoulder. Leaving Benny's house, exhausted but finally feeling safe, they met Burt, Benny's housemate, who said, "You guys get my story? Sorry I forgot to include a cover letter."

Kate placed the manuscript carefully on the coffee table. Night had come while she read. She had not drawn the roller shades, which meant that from the street, this bright room was perfectly visible through the thin curtains. She went to the window, telling herself that no one would have been watching her, and if anyone had, he would only have seen her reading. J. Noble's story, she thought, meant nothing. It was an exercise in bad taste on some would-be writer's part. An exercise in bad taste with flawed logic. An exercise—

Jack stood on the sidewalk, studying the number above the door of Kate's apartment building.

She yanked the roller shade down. Knowing Jack would not be there when she looked again, she looked again. He was not there. Someone knocked at their apartment, and she ran to snatch up the carving knife. "Special delivery," Jack called through their door, his voice cheerful and midwestern.

Kate pressed herself against the wall. Pretend no one was home? Sneak out the back stairs? No. She was mistaken. She had to be mistaken. "What is it?" she called.

"Special delivery, ma'am."

"Slide it under the door."

"You have to sign for it."

"Slide the receipt under. I'll sign it."

"Yes, ma'am." The pink slip appeared at the bottom of the door. As she reached for it, she thought of TV commercials for door locks, in which booted men kicked down massive oak doors with ease.

The slip was for something from New York. She had to hold the knife in her left hand to scratch her name in the appropriate box. After she passed it under the door, a thin envelope in U.S.A. colors came through to her. Jack said, "Thank you, ma'am," and she listened by the door until he had walked away.

The envelope held a small note on pink paper, written in red ink:

Please discard my previous submission. I am revising it. There is a problem that I should have caught: If Burt wrote the anonymous story without intending to terrorize Eileen and Spencer, why would he send the postcards?

In my revision, only Eileen is terrorized by the notes. That is much, much truer to the spirit of the Ripper. In the story which she and Spencer receive, only the female editor is killed and mutilated; the male editor is arrested for her murder; Lenny, the unpublished writer, writes up the story as fiction and sells it for a lot of money. After reading this tale, Eileen waits for Spencer to come home, wanting to tell him of her fears about Benny's sanity. At the end, she learns that the anonymous story and the notes are from Spencer. He is insane, you see, partly from jealousy, partly from frustration. He knows that his career is over. He knows that she stays with him because of his fame, his connections in publishing, and possibly out of some condescending pity for him. He knows she will leave him when she realizes she has no more use for him. Why is Spencer so obsessed with Jack the Ripper, anyway? Why did Eileen never think of this, before it was too late? Those are her last thoughts, before he kills her.

I think it'll be much better this way.

—J. Noble

Kate sat down with the note between her thumb and index finger. She released it, and it fluttered to the floor. Noble. Jay Noble? Jackie Noble? Noble. Jack. Gentleman Jack?

Her thoughts would not cohere. She was being persecuted by Jack the Ripper, as a punishment for exploiting his legend. She was being persecuted by Kenny, who had some mad idea that this would result in a story that he could sell. She was being persecuted by David, who believed she would leave him. What had she done? She had helped David when he had needed help, and now—

If Kenny was responsible, how far would he go for the sake of a story? If Kenny was Benny was Lenny, the answer included her death. If David? She knew how David behaved in the morning when he had not eaten, she knew what he liked when sex between them was good, she knew how he responded to small children and long-haired dogs, but she did not know if he would terrorize, kill, and mutilate her.

If Jack was responsible, it did not matter what she did.

Curt? Curt was fifteen hundred miles away. In "Time Travel, the Artifact, and a Famous Historical Personage," Burt was not responsible for the killings, nor was Art responsible for the killings in the unsolicited story within the story. Kate nodded. It must be Curt because he was the only one without a motive. She forced a grin, suddenly certain this must be the work of a writer in New York, a real person named J. Noble who probably knew Curt. She checked their phone list, then dialed Curt's number.

"Yo," someone said.

"Curt? Kate here."

"Oh, God." His voice was immediately quiet. "I was going to call, really, then I forgot. The kid lost her bike, and we were—"

"What is it, Curt?" Her fear was forgotten as she wondered if something had happened to someone she knew and liked.

"Did David tell you, or did you figure it out? I shouldn't have agreed, I know, but he thought . . ."

"Yes?"

"He thought you were getting cold and distant, and maybe you'd come to him if you were scared."

She didn't think she had been cold or distant before, but she knew how her voice sounded now. "You mailed the postcards for Davy."

"Yeah. And the J. Noble things. I shouldn't have, I know, but he promised he'd explain everything the second you seemed upset. He thought it'd be interesting to get your reaction. He's thinking about doing a story about an editor who gets a submission that's obviously inspired by her life."

"Not the Jekyll and Hyde thing?"

"No."

She listened to Curt breathe on the line.

"Kate? You still there?"

"You shit."

"Kate, he begged—" His voice was cut off as she slammed down the receiver.

The phone rang. She waited, counting twenty-two rings, then decided it would never stop, and picked up the receiver.

Jack laughed into her ear.

She slammed the phone down. She held the carving knife in her lap, one hand on the handle, a finger touching the edge of the blade. She had cut herself, so she put her finger in her mouth.

I'll call my sister, she thought. I'll call my mother. I'll call

Elise in California. I'll call Kenny . . . but Kenny might be part of it, too.

She picked up Curt's submission, the Sherlock Holmes story, to throw it across the room, then stared at the cover letter. He had written it, knowing that he was helping David, and never hinted— Had he giggled as he wrote the postscript?

David would come home soon. Would he be expecting to comfort her? Would he come in trying to scare her? She could imagine him calling, "It's yours truly, Jack the Ripper!" then beginning his shrill, self-satisfied laugh. When she did not answer him, the laughter would break off, and he would call, "Kate? Sweetcakes?" In the dark and quiet hallway, he would finally begin to be afraid that he had done too much. He would run to the bedroom, not knowing whether she was asleep or gone.

Kate walked through the apartment, turning off lights. One light in the living room would suffice; she would not let herself be afraid. In the mirror at the end of the hall, her reflection was familiar and strange: moderate height, moderate build, short brown hair.

One hundred years of Jack the Ripper, she thought. And now, David, Curt, Kenny . . . One hundred years of Jill.

In the mirror, Jack smiled.

Baby Face

Esther M. Friesner

"Fairy what?"

The simplest thing can ruin an otherwise perfect morning. Even an April day in the Green Mountains can have its beauty dimmed if a wandering witling comes knocking at the front door by first light, trying to sell a fool's tale.

"Hey, man, fairy *ointment,* I said." The caller showed large white teeth, slabby as a thoroughbred's. "Don't get me wrong or nothing."

He tucked a long strand of tow-colored hair behind his left ear and leaned his scruffy brown backpack against the doorjamb, effectively blocking his potential customer's means of polite retreat. Casually he undid the top flap and pawed through the rattling, rustling, ragtag contents.

Adam Sawyer, captive on his own threshold, watched the proceedings with all the vacant fascination of an infant attending its first Christmas, too timid or too innocent to do more than watch while miracles and terrors pop out of ordinary boxes.

There were strips of leather and sticks of wood, carved ivories and loose handfuls of rough-cut, blood-drop garnets laid out on the fieldstone doorstep for anyone and the sun to see. Cornhusk dolls did a do-si-do with hand-painted clothespin Santas.

Palm-sized pussycats sculpted from bubbles of fragrant pine gave up the carved kittens nestled in their wooden wombs. One generation of artfully formed mousers yielded the next until a brindled moggy, no bigger than an acorn, gazed up at Adam Sawyer with hand-painted, soul-unsettling smile.

Glass chinked and tinkled, cheap chinaware salt-and-pepper sets ranged themselves on his doorsill like dutiful soldiers preparing for a final battle. Here was the moon and there was the sun, here a lover and his lass both with holes pierced right through the tops of their pretty little hollow heads, and yonder stood the saltiest of St. Georges ready to stab the peppery breath from the bosom of the green-glazed dragon. The yellow bunch of buttery crocus beside the granite slab nodded approval at each item plucked from the pack, but when the last came to the last, the flowers stood stiff, ignoring the spring breeze. And still Adam stared, spellbound by a gypsy harvest of the bric-a-brac and trifles of the world.

"Adam? Adam, what is it?"

The voice from inside the white clapboard farmhouse was enough to break the peddler's witchery. Adam blinked behind his black-rimmed glasses and tugged nervously at his gray-streaked moustache, holding onto a slip-away reality by the bristly hairs.

Preceded by her nine-months belly, Linda arced into the doorway. The peddler's smile creased his brown face so deeply his bright blue eyes were nearly lost to sight.

"Ah, gonna have a baby. That's super, man. My old lady, she's got two; one's mine." He tried to share a shrewd wink with Adam. "She says it's mine, anyhow. Who cares? Loving's not owning. I learned that when I ran away from home."

"Dear," said Adam—not to the peddler, of course not,

no. "Dear," he said, and turned his back on all the vaga-bond's spilled riches, his canny, knowing asides. He took Linda's hand and held it tightly, a grip grown tighter daily since first she'd told him her secret, secret now from none. "This kid's selling something—God knows what. I guess he's from that commune in the mountains old man Harrow told us about in town; you know, sixties leftovers."

Linda's laugh was part of the morning. "Don't let me interrupt, then. A good sales pitch needs momentum. But if you buy one of those tacky salt-and-pepper sets, I'm getting a divorce."

"Oh, all he's offered to sell me so far is some fairy oint-ment." Adam shrugged, trying to look comic and casual. For Linda's laugh he'd gladly put on a cap and bells, cut capers, play the parti-colored fool. "Fairy as in fey; elfin. Not meaning to cast any aspersions on his own preferences, you know. His . . . 'old lady' would be happy to swear to that, I'm sure."

"Fairy what?" said Linda, and they were full circle.

The squat glass jar the size and shape of a snuff tin caught a malicious twinkle of sunlight as the peddler held it up for her inspection.

"See, I make this myself. Use a recipe *she* taught under the mountain. Didn't know I was listening, the old cow, but hey! I didn't owe her anything. I didn't ask to be snatched from my cradle, now did I? Some pug-faced, goat-rumped changeling tucked in to take my place. No, see, you take some of this, you rub it on your eyelids, and there isn't a fairy glamour from here to Elfhame that you can't see through. Seely Court, Unseely, elves light, dark or dusky, nothing they can do but grin and bear it when you see them as they are. Or poke out both your eyes, but most of 'em have turned too mellow to bother with the big gestures anymore. I blame disco. Here, give it a try; you'll be sur-prised."

"Linda," said Adam huskily, giving his pregnant wife a

gently urgent push as he placed himself between her precious body and rogue madness. "Linda, get inside."

Linda shook him off like rain. "Oh, Adam, grow up. He's only a hippie, for pity's sake; a relic. He's not *dangerous*." She took the jar from the peddler's hand and unscrewed the painted metal lid. Raising the rosy gray paste to her nostrils, she breathed deep.

"Dangerous? Me?" The peddler laughed in Adam's face. "That's what comes of reading the papers instead of the scrolls. Look, I'm a changeling, I'll admit it. The Queen herself played switchies with me and one of her own brownie brats."

"The Queen?"

"Her Majesty Underhill, the Lady of Illusions, sweet Morgana, Mom to me." The peddler rocked back on his hams, twiddled with the treasures on the doorstep. "Beauty, beauty all around, that's what I was meant to see. But one midsummer's day while I toddled around Mama's palace, I found my way into her boudoir. Nurses and nannies in their satin gowns were gone, riding down the summer greenwood ways. No one about to see a tot stick one little fist into an open pot of this guck on *her* royal dressing table.

"Well, you know kids . . . or you will, soon enough. Smear stuff all over, that's the nature of the beast. Next thing I know, stuck my finger in my eye. That's when I *really* saw where I was, who I was with, who I was. Some nice wake-up for a three-year-old child, believe me! Oh, the Queen's okay—still flower-fair, though with the ointment on she lost all her sweet, maternal muzziness, showed me some age-old edges I'd rather not have seen—but the others—!"

He shivered. "Brown wrinkled faces squinched up like monkeys', and hard eyes full of dull red fire, like these." He held up a garnet node that sucked up sunlight and only gave back a meager, miserly glow. "Patchy thin black hair, scrawny gangling bodies, fingers like twisted willow twigs, ugh! All the sweet-faced nurses and nannies, all the tall, golden, gloriously shining knights who ringed the Queen on Maying, I saw all of them as they truly were, bent and wizened as an old, old lie. I never forgot, even when the ointment wore off. I cut out of there as soon as I was big enough to run." He grinned, a prince of the underworld released at last into his birthright of bright day.

"Very pretty," said Adam. His eyes fixed coldly on the happy peddler. "But we're not in Fairyland here. I doubt I'll see much of anything unusual in Brattleboro or White River Junction even if I smear a handful of that goop into both my eyes."

"Hey, man," said the peddler, his smile gone, his voice suddenly lower. "Hey, can I have a word with you? You know, privately?"

"Go on, boys," Linda said, waving them away. "But if you're selling dope, Adam won't buy any. He's so damn straight you can use him for a ruler. He's no fun anymore."

The peddler took an only semiwilling Adam around the corner of the white clapboard house. Linda sang on the front steps, and her song came floating faintly after them, but still the peddler spoke in whispers.

"Listen, I'm not here by chance. Your old lady's pregnant—"

"Observant of you."

"No fooling, man; I'm serious. You buy that ointment and go into White River, you might see more than you bargained for. Just because we rip some pages off a calendar, you think it changes anything? The Queen still has her brats, and they're still too ugly for Her Esthetic Majesty to bear looking at long. Human babies are more pleasing to her eye. She still rides, man, and rules, and brings the world 'round by the nose ring to give her her own selfish way. The Queen rides the winds of the world, and her minions ride after in her train, always watching for the chance to serve."

He gave the soft April sky a look full of coldest suspicion and dread. "When a woman has her baby, that's when they make the change, now as always. Only now that you folks think it's safe to quit believing in what you can't see, the Queen's having a field day! Changelings all over the map, man! Boston Brahmins and Valley Girls and the grinning chick who plays Snow White at Disney World, all changelings. Then there's the halfborn—"

"Look, if I give you two bucks, will you just go away?"

The peddler clutched Adam's fist, crushing the proffered two bucks in their double grip. "The halfborn are babies, born to true humans, like us, when we breed with changelings and don't know it. Remember your high school bio course? Mendel and all? The fairy strain's the dominant, the halfborn come out almost as ugly as their changeling dads or mommies. Changelings can breed with humans, but the halfborn are mules, sterile, cut off and thrown away from both worlds. You want your real kid snatched as soon as he's born? You want a changeling fathering your grandkids, your grandkids never able to have kids of their own?" He released Adam's hand and the crumpled bills fluttered down to the grass like dead luna moths.

"Linda!" Adam wheeled from the peddler and all his uncomfortable insanities. Marching briskly back to his front door, he took the jar of ashy rose paste from his wife's hands and thrust it at the peddler.

"Not interested."

"Adam, don't be silly." The jar was in Linda's hands again. She dug into a pocket of her maternity jeans and pressed a five on the peddler. "It's a very pretty story and this stuff feels like silk between my fingers. It smells divine, just the thing for my stomach. My Lamaze instructor said to use massage, and I *won't* submit to massage without a decent cream. Please come see us again and I'll buy another jar after the baby arrives, for stretch marks." She wafted back into the house under full sail.

Adam glared at the peddler, who was retying the rawhide braid that bound his forehead. The man stuffed the fiver away in his belt pouch and plucked out a pocketwad of moldery bills that made even a computer salesman of

Adam's caliber hate the sight of money. "Got change coming," he said, scraping a faded greenskin off the roll.

"Keep it." Adam slammed the door so hard that he was plucking shards of broken salt-and-pepper sets out of the crocus bed for a week.

Linda packed the ointment with her hospital things and when she first went into labor she instructed Adam to rub it over her stomach and back as the pains came and went. She smiled when she could, and sometimes when she knew another woman couldn't. She kept up a chat about old times, not so old, back in the city less than a year ago "—before you went country-crazy. What were you, jealous of all my friends?" Then he'd blush, because what she said held true. Who was Adam, what was he to dream he'd ever lay claim to Linda's beauty by exclusive right? When he was on the road, he envied the sly, sleek crowd of city Pans who piped her thoughts away from him. So, soon as she told him there was to be a baby, he'd pounced on the unborn excuse to drag her up into Vermont's comfortably domesticated wilds. Adam Sawyer, stubborn old dog staunchly guarding his too-pretty bit of tender flesh and bone from the wolfpack they left behind.

Linda labored on while Adam watched and danced attendance and didn't enjoy the game. At last his patience snapped. She'd played her nerve wars with him long enough, held off heading for the hospital until he slung her overnight case into the Volvo and claimed he was game to try the fireman's carry on her if she delayed their departure one contraction longer.

On their arrival the nurse-midwife and the doctor (he was there on feminist sufferance) both pronounced Linda nine *sahn*timeters dilated, almost ready to roll. Adam suited up, scrubbed down, and followed the crowd into the delivery room. It was impossible to tell the doctor from the anesthesiologist; the interns, midwives, and pediatricians from the med students, student nurses, and assistant this-and-thats of various Aesculapian stripes. Oh, an exaggeration, perhaps, in view of hairy forearms glimpsed here, breasts convexing surgical greens there. But gender was the only line of demarcation separating one flock of millers-about and hoverers-over from another.

And then Linda stopped.

That is, her labor stopped. The doctor sighed and pronounced it something he'd seen hundreds of times before. The nurse-midwife mumbled that he'd have attended the Virgin Mary and made the same half-bored, all-knowing comment. They waited, and when Linda's labor refused to recommence, they wheeled her out of Delivery and back into the labor room.

"What's my coach going to say?" she moaned, wreathing her stubborn belly with her arms.

"Who the hell cares?" Adam snapped, answering that. He was out of the scrub suit and gloves, in civvies again. Tension made him waspish. It was much hotter in the labor room than it had been in Delivery. Sweat was trickling inelegantly down his forehead, stinging his eyes.

"Maybe if you gave me some more massage—?"

He complied, but not graciously. As he dipped his fingers into the hippie-bought pot of ointment, he found its fragrance particularly irritating, affecting his nose the way a half-remembered tune afflicts the mind. He passed his greasy fingers across his forehead, wiping off sweat.

"Oh!" said Linda. She stared at her belly in happy surprise. "Adam, you'd better ring for the midwife."

"In a minute, in a minute." He was truculent as a honey-cheated bear. His eyes felt prickly, and his glasses kept slipping down the sweat-smeared bridge of his nose. He took them off and rubbed his eyes.

"How's everything coming along here?"

He hadn't heard her come in. Her, whoever she was. She was a fresh face, pretty, previously unknown, probably one of the masked mob from the delivery room, Adam reasoned. She threw back Linda's oversheet and made a swift

and skillful examination, as crisp in her manner as her prim
white uniform.

"Oh my," she said.

"I want to push," Linda panted.

"I should say you would. I'll get the doctor. We won't
have time to get you into the delivery room." She whisked
away and must have waved a magic wand outside the door,
for in a moment the little room was packed with people.
Adam was shoved this way and that, jostled, barked at. He
wasn't scrubbed, he couldn't stay. The pretty nurse was first
and firmest at overruling Linda's pleas, and Adam himself
was too wrung out to care. Still wiping the sweat from his
eyes, he was elbowed out of the room, into the corridor.
Inside he heard Linda's cries, and someone saying, "Yes, it
looks like—" The rest was muddled.

"Excuse me, could I get inside?" asked a female voice of
rubber-soled white-shoe Authority behind him. "Can I get
this Isolette through? We'll have to get the baby up to New-
born Special Care as soon as it's born."

Adam stepped aside, automatically obeying. "Yes, yes, of
course," he said, turning to let her pass. "Go right—"

No; wrong. Wrong to see a nurse with red, red eyes,
glowing like rough-cut garnets, in a mask of skin brown and
chestnut-wrinkled. Wrong to see a green scrub suit thrown
over a body that was mostly well-gnawed bones. The creature's knob-knuckled hands clenched themselves around
the cold metal handle of the wheeled Isolette cradle like an
owl's talons death-gripping a hazel branch.

The changeling child lay in the should-be-empty Isolette.
Should-be, because hadn't the nurse-thing said she'd come
for the baby? For Adam's baby? To wheel away Adam's
baby and leave—and leave—

The changeling skreeted and croaked with an infant
raven's throat, waving limbs like sticks of wood and strips
of leather.

Adam seized the plastic lip of the Isolette and tore it from
the elfin's grasp. He raced it, ran it down the corridors of the

hospital with the flame-eyed being rattling and gasping after. Hall to hall, corners done on a dare, and into a lucky elevator, doors slip-slamming shut in his pursuer's knotted face. Down and down, prayers at work to keep the elevator's plunge uninterrupted, and into the basement at last where with a final shove Adam sent the small chariot with its wailing cargo careening toward the stacked and tumbled bags of trash. It struck green plastic, toppled over sideways, and crashed to the floor.

It was empty when it hit. Not seeming-empty, but empty in truth. The flower-faced lady who stood between Adam and the upturned Isolette was lovely, even with that much rage rising hot from her slim and supple body. She cradled the ugly, misused infant to her mist-white breasts and suckled it with care. Her sea-born eyes summoned a storm of pelting ice and soulless cold, her hatred hurling it at Adam.

He caught the force of the Queen's anger full in the chest and dreamed his heart had stopped. Crystals of winter shattered over his eyes, starred his hair, rimmed his trembling moustache, stung him without mercy. He reeled back, slipped, staggered into a cinder-block wall, and waited to die.

But all she said was: "There are some of you shouldn't be spared!" Then she whipped around her and her uncomely babe a mantle woven from one of the winds she kept always bridled, and vanished.

Slowly Adam Sawyer made his way back to the maternity floor. He blessed the mad hippie peddler in his heart, blessed too the fairy ointment and all the doors it opened, blessed them both in spite of the aches and twinges he now suffered in aftermath of the Queen's displeasure. He rode up in the elevator with a woman whose ugliness came close to that of the false nurse and the changeling child. Casually he wondered if her fairy blood was full or halfborn, reveled in his purchased smugness, idly played with the thought of what she would look like if he'd wipe the rose-gray stuff of vision from his eyes. Not that he would. Not now.

Linda and the infant boy lay together. She had just finished giving him his first milky welcome to the world, and
now the little one slept. Adam stood there in silence, trea-
suring how purely human both of them looked, molding the
new-made face to his heart.

"He's got red hair," he said.

"Oh, so what, silly? My cousin Robert's got red hair. You
don't just get your looks out of thin air. And isn't your Aunt
Emma's hair reddish blond too?"

"She's only my aunt by marriage."

"Well." Linda shrugged and gazed at the boy. "I'm sure
he's got your eyes."

He left them to rest—there were people who must be
called and told. On his way to the public phones, he imagined that the smile of pride and love on his face couldn't
really be as wide as it felt, so just to make sure that it was,
he ducked into the men's room to let the mirror tell him he
really was *that* happy.

And what the mirror said was this: *Not your son, Adam;
never now your son. No matter what the woman your sometime
wife may say—"I'm sure he's got your eyes"—there is no truth to
her adulterous telling. Not your son at all.*

The baby didn't, couldn't, have his eyes; not Adam Sawyer's eyes nor any other share of his being. If Adam Sawyer
was the true name of the scraggle-thatched, darksome, halfborn sterile witch-brat creature now staring back at him out
of the merciless glass, staring and staring with tear-wet
garnet eyes.

The Pale Thin God

Mike Resnick

He stood quietly before us, the pale thin god who had invaded our land, and waited to hear the charges.

The first of us to speak was Mulungu, the god of the Yao people.

"There was a time, many eons ago, when I lived happily upon the earth with my animals. But then men appeared. They made fire and set the land ablaze. They found my animals and began killing them. They devised weapons and went to war with each other. I could not tolerate such behavior, so I had a spider spin a thread up to heaven, and I ascended it, never to return. And yet *you* have sacrificed yourself for these very same creatures."

Mulungu pointed a long forefinger at the pale thin god. "I accuse you of the crime of Love."

He sat down, and immediately Nyambe, the god of the Koko people, arose.

"I once lived among men," he said, "and there was no such thing as death in the world, because I had given them a magic tree. When men grew old and wrinkled, they went and lived under the tree for nine days, and it made them young again. But as the years went by, men began taking me for granted, and stopped worshiping me and making sacrifices to me, so I uprooted my tree and carried it up to heaven with me, and without its magic, men finally began to die.''

He stared balefully at the pale thin god. "And now you have taught men that they may triumph over death. I charge you with the crime of Life.''

Next Ogun, the god of the Yoruba people, stepped forward.

"When the gods lived on earth, they found their way barred by impenetrable thornbushes. I created a *panga* and cleared the way for them, and this *panga* I turned over to men, who use it not only for breaking trails but for the glory of war. And yet you, who claim to be a god, tell your worshipers to disdain weapons and never to raise a hand in anger. I accuse you of the crime of Peace.''

As Ogun sat down, Muluku, god of the Zambesi, rose to his feet.

"I made the earth,'' he said. "I dug two holes, and from one came a man, and from the other a woman. I gave them land and tools and seeds and clay pots, and told them to plant the seeds, to build a house, and to cook their food in the pots. But the man and the woman ate the raw seeds, broke the pots, and left the tools by the side of a trail. Therefore, I summoned two monkeys and made the same gifts to them. The two monkeys dug the earth, built a house, harvested their grain, and cooked it in their pots.'' He paused. "So I cut off the monkeys' tails and stuck them on the two men, decreeing that from that day forth they would be monkeys and the monkeys would be men.''

He pointed at the pale thin god. "And yet, far from punishing men, you forgive them their mistakes. I charge you with the crime of Compassion.''

En-kai, the god of the Maasai, spoke next.

"I created the first warrior, Le-eyo, and gave him a magic chant to recite over dead children that would bring them back to life and make them immortal. But Le-eyo did not utter the chant until his own son had died. I told him that it was too late, that the chant would no longer work, and that because of his selfishness, Death will always have power over men. He begged me to relent, but because I am a god and a god cannot be wrong, I did not do so.''

He paused for a moment, then stared coldly at the pale thin god. ''You would allow men to live again, even if only in heaven. I accuse you of the crime of Mercy.''

Finally Huveane, god of the Basuto people, arose.

''I, too, lived among men in eons past. But their pettiness offended me, and so I hammered some pegs into the sky and climbed up to heaven, where men would never see me again.'' He faced the pale thin god. ''And now, belatedly, you have come to our land, and you teach that men may ascend to heaven, that they may even sit at your right hand. I charge you with the crime of Hope.''

The six fearsome gods turned to me.

''We have spoken,'' they said. ''It is your turn now, Anubis. Of what crime do you charge him?''

''I do not make accusations, only judgments,'' I replied.

''And how do you judge him?'' they demanded.

''I will hear him speak, and then I will tell you,'' I said. I turned to the pale thin god. ''You have been accused of the crimes of Peace, Life, Mercy, Compassion, Love, and Hope. What have you to say in your defense?''

The pale thin god looked at us, his accusers.

''I have been accused of Peace,'' he said, never raising his voice, ''and yet more Holy Wars have been fought in my name than in the names of all other gods combined. The earth has turned red with the blood of those who died for my Peace.

''I have been accused of Life,'' he continued, ''yet in my name, the Spaniards have baptized Aztec infants and dashed out their brains against rocks so they might ascend to heaven without living to become warriors.

''I have been accused of Mercy, but the Inquisition was

held in my name, and the number of men who were tortured to death is beyond calculation.

"I have been accused of Compassion, yet not a single man who worships me has ever lived a life without pain, without fear, and without misery.

"I have been accused of Love, yet I have not ended suffering, or disease, or death, and he who leads the most blameless and saintly life will be visited by all of my grim horsemen just as surely as he who rejects me.

"Finally, I have been accused of Hope," he said, and now the stigmata on his hands and feet began to glow a brilliant red, "and yet since I have come to your land, I have brought famine to the north, genocide to the west, drought to the south, and disease to the east. And everywhere, where there was Hope, there is only poverty and ignorance and war and death.

"So it has been wherever I have gone, so shall it always be.

"Thus do I answer your charges."

They turned to me, the six great and terrible deities, to ask for my judgment. But I had already dropped to my knees before the greatest god of us all.

About the Authors

Robert Abel is the winner of the Flannery O'Connor Award for Short Fiction (1989) and is the author of three collections of stories and two novels, the most recent of which is *Ghost Traps* from the University of Georgia Press. He lives in western Massachusetts.

Eleanor Arnason has published four novels, all science fiction or fantasy, the most recent of which is *A Woman of the Iron People*. She is currently working on a trilogy set in the universe of "The Hound of Merin." A resident of Minneapolis, she is secretary-treasurer of the Twin Cities Local of the National Writers Union.

Steven K. Z. Brust is a Minnesota writer, author of ten novels, and father of four children, not necessarily in that order. A founding member of the Minneapolis Fantasy Writers Group, a.k.a. The Scribblies, he is also a drummer and songwriter for folk and rock bands like Cats Laughing and Morrigan. His latest novel is *The Phoenix Guards*.

Pamela Dean lives with her husband, David Dyer-Bennet, and a fluctuating number of cats in Minneapolis. A founding member of The Scribblies, she is the author of four published novels and a number of short stories. Her latest book is *Tam Lin*, part of Terri Windling's Fairy Tale Series.

Gardner Dozois is a Nebula and Hugo Award–winning author and editor of the *Isaac Asimov's Science Fiction Magazine*. He lives in Philadelphia with his wife, science fiction writer Susan Casper.

Esther M. Friesner holds a doctorate from Yale, which hasn't kept her from writing a dozen fantasy novels, most of them humorous: *Hooray for Hellywood* and *Gnome Man's Land* among them. Her short stories have appeared in all the major science fiction magazines. A member of the SCA, she lives in Connecticut with her husband and two children.

Frances Stokes Hoekstra is an assistant professor of French at Haverford College. She has been writing short fiction since 1988, and her work has been published in such literary magazines as *The Virginia Quarterly* and *The Southern Review*. She was awarded a fiction-writing grant from the Pennsylvania Council on the Arts for 1991.

Anna Kirwan-Vogel's first novel, *The Jewel of Life*, came out from Harcourt Brace Jovanovich in 1990. A published poet, she is on the board of directors of the Amherst Writers & Artists. She lives in Williamsburg, Massachusetts, with her musician-husband and three children.

Nancy Kress is the author of six books of fantasy and science fiction, including the forthcoming *Beggars in Spain*. A Nebula winner for the short story "Out of All Them Bright Stars," she writes a monthly fiction column for *Writer's Digest* magazine. She lives in Brockport, New York, with her husband and two sons.

Tanith Lee has published forty-nine books, including prize-winning novels and short story collections. Four of her radio scripts have been broadcast over the BBC, and she wrote two television scripts for the U.K. series *Blake's 7*. Her latest books include *Dark Dance*, *Heart Beast*, and *Louisa the Poisoner*. She lives in Kent, England.

Ursula K. Le Guin has won the Nebula, the Hugo, and the National Book Award for her fiction. Considered one of the world's finest writers of fantasy and science fiction, her elegant books include the four *Wizard of Earthsea* volumes, *The Left Hand of Darkness,* and several short story and poetry collections. Her essays and speeches have been collected in two volumes as well. Ms. Le Guin lives in Oregon.

Elise Matthesen currently works as a "dataherd" for Minnesota Public Radio, but has had a variety of "starving artist" jobs, including security guard, tarot reader, loading dock laborer, bookseller, storyteller, and folksinger. Her previous publications have been in the anthology *Bi Any Other Name* and in *Locus Magazine.* She lives in Minneapolis with her husband.

John Morressy is the author of twenty-three books, among them the five humorous Kedrigen fantasies, the Iron Angel trilogy, seven interrelated science fiction novels, three mainstream novels, and three books for young readers. His short fiction has appeared in *F&SF, Esquire, Omni,* and *Playboy.* He lives with his painter-wife in New Hampshire.

Lesléa Newman is the author of a dozen books, including *A Letter to Harvey Milk, Secrets, Heather Has Two Mommies,* and *In Every Laugh a Tear.* Her short story in *Xanadu* is part of a forthcoming short story collection, *Every Woman's Dream.* She lives in Northampton, Massachusetts.

Patrick Nielsen Hayden is a sometime writer and a full-time SF and fantasy editor for Tor Books. "Return" is his second published story, and came to him while writing cover copy for the paperback edition of Ellen Kushner's *Thomas the Rhymer.*

Mike Resnick is the award-winning author of well over a hundred novels, including *Santiago* and *Soothsayer.* Other works of his include anthologies, such as *Alternate Presidents* and *Alternate Kennedys,* story collections, and film scripts. He also owns and runs a major dog kennel with his wife, Carol, in Cincinnati, Ohio.

Pat Schneider's poetry, plays, and fiction have been widely published and produced. Her libretti have been recorded by the Louisville Symphony and performed in Carnegie Hall. Fourteen of her plays have been produced, nine published. There are more than three hundred recorded productions of her plays in this country and in Europe. Director of Amherst Writers & Artists, she lives in Amherst, Massachusetts, with her husband.

Will Shetterly, author of four published fantasy novels, is the copublisher with his wife, Emma Bull, of SteelDragon Press, a tiny publishing company specializing in fantasy and science fiction comic books, trade hardcovers, and collector's editions. He is also coeditor of the *Liavek* anthologies. His latest novel is *Elsewhere* from Harcourt Brace Jovanovich. He lives in Minneapolis.

William Stafford is one of the best-known poets in America. He is poetry consultant for the Library of Congress. His works have been published in *Atlantic, Harper's,* and *The New Yorker.* Married with three children, he lives in Oregon. His most recent books are *An Oregon Message* and *Passwords,* both volumes of poetry from HarperCollins.

Lisa Tuttle, born in Texas, was a journalist and television critic in Austin before moving to England and becoming a full-time writer. After ten years in London, she moved to the west coast of Scotland, where she lives with her husband and baby daughter. Author of many short stories and four novels (most recently *Lost Futures*), she has also written nonfiction and edited anthologies such as *Skin of the Soul.*

Donna J. Waidtlow homesteaded north of the Yukon River for thirteen years. She has a B.S. degree from the University of

Washington's School of Medicine and lives in the Seattle area. She is a member of the Avalanche Poets, and her poetry has been published in a number of literary journals.

Jane Yolen, author of over one hundred books, has won the World Fantasy Award, been nominated for the National Book Award and the Nebula, was president of the Science Fiction Writers of America for two years, and has been on the board of directors of the Society of Children's Book Writers since its inception. Her latest books include *Hark: A Christmas Sampler* and *Encounter,* as well as the novel *Briar Rose* for Tor. She lives with her professor-husband in Hatfield, Massachusetts.